Death's Lover

Death's Lover

Death's Lover

MARIE HALL

New York   Boston

Copyright © 2013 by Linda Hall
Excerpt from *Death's Redemption* copyright © 2013 by Linda Hall
Cover design by Elizabeth Phillips. Cover illustration by Craig White.
Cover copyright © 2013 by Hachette Book Group, Inc.

Forever Yours
Hachette Book Group
237 Park Avenue
New York, NY 10017
hachettebookgroup.com
twitter.com/foreverromance

Previously published as *The Witching Hour*

First Forever Yours ebook and print on demand edition: September 2013

Forever Yours is an imprint of Grand Central Publishing.
The Forever Yours name and logo are trademarks of Hachette Book Group, Inc.

The publisher is not responsible for websites (or their content) that are not owned by the publisher.

The Hachette Speakers Bureau provides a wide range of authors for speaking events. To find out more, go to www.hachettespeakersbureau.com or call (866) 376-6591.

ISBN: 978-1-4555-4986-3 (ebook edition)
ISBN: 978-1-4555-4988-7 (print on demand edition)

To my husband, who never stopped believing in me. To many fans for reading my books and always wanting to know when the next one is coming out. I write for you guys!

Acknowledgments

To my agent, Jessica Faust, for never quitting on this book; to the fantastic cover artist; and to Latoya Smith for taking a chance on a story about death and love.

Death's Lover

Chapter 1

Eve Philips gripped her husband's arm tighter as they walked across the sidewalk to the mall entrance. She hadn't felt good this morning; she'd been haunted by bad dreams all night long. Dreams of blood and violence and gore. She'd screamed herself awake, clinging to her husband with a vague unsettling feeling. But as dreams often do, the intensity of it faded until now all that was left was a lingering echo of it and an annoying headache.

It was almost Christmas, and she and her husband had a shopping date planned. She refused to wuss out now over some stupid dreams. Still, the unease of this morning lingered in the darkest corners of her mind. Usually she could just shake these things. Maybe it was just the old, burned coffee the java shack had served her this morning. Either way, she really wanted to stop stressing about it. There were too many other real things to worry about.

Like the fact that in three days her coven would be required to vote on the fate of a werewolf who'd been caught stabbing his human wife. No matter that his wife had tried to kill him first with the aid of a warlock's spell. Humans demanded the supernatural folk—or "supers," as they preferred to be called—governed themselves as swiftly and brutally as possible, especially when the crime involved one of their own. That was the life of a witch, especially one who chose to live in a city in as much turmoil as San Francisco. Still, there was no other place in the world she'd rather be.

By congressional act, California had granted the first and only place that the others could come out of hiding and live as they truly were. Werewolves no longer had to hide in tunnels, vampires could roam the streets freely at night, and witches could practice their craft without fear of retribution by the normals. That was ten years ago, and she'd never looked back.

Not to say that it was one big love fest. A snake could shed its skin several times in a lifetime, but that would never change its true essence. In the end a snake would always remain a snake. Just as a vampire could not help but feed, or a werewolf would go mad by light of the full moon.

Having so many volatile and sometimes dangerous groups in such close proximity practically begged for the violence to occur.

But she accepted it and moved on, because freedom was worth any price. Glancing around, she inhaled the sharp nip to the wind. It was a cloudless, gray day. The type that made her want to curl up in front of a roaring fire with a steaming cup of chamomile, cocooned against her husband's body.

She didn't notice the small rut in the road and stepped down hard. Muddy water splashed up her leg. A large black gob of goo landed square on her bloodred pumps.

"Damn it!"

Michael glanced down. One side of his mouth curled into a half-formed grin. She growled and picked up a dead leaf to scrape off the nasty mixture.

"I don't even want to know what that was." He laughed.

Eve stood and glared at her husband's smiling face. Turning her nose in the air, she dropped the leaf with disgust and walked away.

"Honey." He grabbed her hand and chuckled. "You gotta admit…it was pretty funny."

"Ha-ha. I'm just howling with laughter." She pointed a finger to her deadpan face. "This is me in hysterics."

Michael hugged her and slowly she smiled, never really that mad to begin with, but loving to be a little dramatic all the same.

"Why does that only ever happen to me?"

"Because you're just so cute, the goddess had to give you some sort of flaw."

She nailed him with a glare and then sighed with exasperation when he refused to look at her. Michael refused to be ruffled today.

The mall was appropriately decorated: a large Christmas tree sat guard to the entrance, festive lights hung swag from one light post to the next, and there was, of course, the melee of people shoving against her at a constant, repetitive pace with barely an apology to be gained. She sighed. To say she had a love-hate relationship with the holidays was putting it mildly.

But Michael had been acting secretive all day, alluding to some great gift she'd find under the tree come Yule. In truth, her husband's enthusiasm for life was contagious. She wouldn't miss the annual last-minute shopping for the world, though she'd never tell him that.

"Michael," she grumbled, "let's go home. It's freezing. My feet hurt, and…" She paused, trying to think of the next excuse to come up with.

He only smiled as expected. "Love you, shrew."

She rolled her eyes, trying desperately not to snort with laughter.

Then as if the weather felt some need to remind her just how cold it was—and that she had no freaking business being out in the first place—she was blasted with a sweep of frigid air up her trench coat.

She shivered. "Stupid weatherman. I should hex his ass. He said temperatures of sixty."

Michael's lips twitched. "When are you gonna learn that *were* don't know his ass from his head? The man's worthless. Call a toad a toad and a bad weatherman a bad weatherman. Period."

She nodded. "Hear, hear."

Ten minutes later Eve fingered a delicate gold-and-emerald butterfly brooch. "Baby, do you think Tamryn would like this?"

He glanced up from browsing at a case of black pearl necklaces she'd considered buying for her sister. "Sure. I guess."

She laughed. "'I guess'? The standard male answer for everything, right? Why do I even bother?" She caught the heavily made-up clerk's eye and nodded.

The blonde glided over in a sea of expensive perfume and sent a blatantly lustful smile in Michael's direction. Eve hid her laughter under a pursed lip and raised brow. "The butterfly," she prompted and handed the lady a fifty.

Michael grinned and encircled Eve's waist from behind, laying his head on her shoulder. A soft lock of his doe-brown hair brushed the side of her neck. She swept the hair aside and sighed.

"You just love it when that happens, don't you?"

"What?" he asked in a rush of innocence.

"'What?'" she mimicked. "You're too gorgeous for your own good."

Throaty laughter spilled from his lips as he swayed with her in time to the strains of "Jingle Bell Rock" floating through the overcrowded department store.

Eve snuggled deeper into his arms.

Michael nuzzled the side of her neck.

Her whole body tightened up in reaction to his touch. Even after five years of marriage he still had the power to make her heart flutter and her knees tremble.

"Michael," she whispered.

"Hmm?" He placed a gentle kiss on the nape of her neck.

Goose bumps skimmed along her forearms. "I'm ovulating."

He went still for a split second then nipped her earlobe. His large hand framed her stomach. "Let's go make babies, then."

Her lip twitched, and she wiggled her bottom against him. Michael growled low in his throat and pinned her arms to her side, holding her still. "Eve," he warned.

She turned and draped her arms over his neck. "What?"

He dragged her closer, a mischievous twinkle in his emerald-green eyes. "Imp. You're lucky I'm wearing a coat long enough…"

"Excuse me." A strained voice interrupted them.

She turned. The sales clerk held her purchase and change in one hand. Her narrowed eyes and curled lip were too much for Eve to ignore.

Taking the bag and without missing a beat, Eve leaned forward just enough to part her button-down shirt at the collar, causing her pentagram to swing free from between her breasts. "He ain't on the market, babe."

The clerk, obviously human, turned deathly white. No human liked to tangle with the dark arts. And though that wasn't what Eve did by any means, the blonde didn't know it, and Eve sure as heck wasn't going to correct her assumption. Judging by the reaction, the threat had done its job.

With a smile and a jaunty wave, she turned on her heel and marched off.

Michael held out his arm. "What in the world did you say to her, Eve?" She didn't miss the tinge of humor lacing his voice.

She just grinned. "What? And give you a bigger head than you've already got? I don't think so."

He chuckled and grabbed her hand in his, caressing her knuckle with the pad of his thumb. Laughter glittered in his eyes. Then he became serious and turned her face to look directly at him. "I love you."

The way he said it made her shiver. One of those freaky moments in time that made her wonder if there was some sort of sixth sense involved, then she thought of the dream again and the visions of death.

Her smile slipped for a millisecond. She always tried to be aware of the signs and the environment around her. What if she was being purposefully ignorant? Ignoring the obvious? What if that dream really was a warning?

Don't make more out of this than what it is. Everything's fine.

Pushing the neurotic fears to the back of her mind, she gave him a crooked smile. "I know, Mikey. And I thank the goddess every day for you."

* * *

Cian waited within shadow just outside the entrance to the mall; the mortals he'd been sent to harvest should appear soon. Keeping his back to the crowd, he stood in such a way so that he had a clear view of the door as pedestrians filed and in out of the busy shopping plaza.

Using his essence, he transformed himself into an ordinary guy, hardly worth a second glance. Through all the years of using this guise, he'd never once been remembered. Right now, he needed people to look past him, not see the peculiarities that branded him not quite human. Unfortunately he couldn't go fully invisible until the harvest time came upon him.

His hair turned a drab brown, short and barely reaching his collar, his eyes much the same color. The process happened so fast, no one even had time to react at all.

Staring at his gloved hand he waited for the next step of his transformation to take place. He didn't have to wait long. A shock, like a burst of flame, ran down his arm and into his hand, turning him from man to monster. Fire traveled his veins, making him grunt with a momentary flash of pain. He hissed and snatched off his left glove, making sure he was well within shadow. The day was so drab and gray that unless he did something obvious, like flash the crowd, no one would turn his way.

He clenched his hand, studying the bones of his fingers. For an outsider, to look at the transformation would seem surreal. Above the wrist he was man—flesh and blood. But when the change overcame him, and it was time to harvest souls, the hand turned to a design of the macabre. The flesh, muscle, and tendon literally faded from sight.

Human depictions always had the grim reapers wearing the traditional black cowl with a sickle in their skeletal grip. In truth, reapers were as normal as man. You could pass them on the street, commenting on their remarkable beauty, little knowing that beneath the white smile and ever-present gloves lurked the killer of legend.

A small, noisy crowd of humans walked toward him. Shoving his hand into his pocket, he leaned against the wall and waited; it wouldn't be much longer now.

After centuries of doing this job, he'd learned patience, the art of stealth, and the endless waiting game of death. For such a vital and intricate part of life, the actual moment of death could be unbelievably boring.

Several minutes later, an electrical rush of power surged through his body when a couple walked out. A man and a raven-haired witch. He felt her power ripple through the air like a powerful ocean current. The man though exhibited no energy, which meant he was fully mortal. The man grabbed the witch around the waist, pulling her close for a quick embrace.

Cian's pulse pounded when she smiled. It was a good smile, the kind that made him want to return it, to see her do it again just so he could have the enjoyment of gazing on that kind of radiant and rare pure joy.

The man hopped in front of her and grabbed her hands, toying with her fingers. Her laughter was a rich, lilting sound, deep and throaty, hot and sexy, and for the first time in his life, Cian wondered what it might be like to have a woman look at him that way. He envied mortals in some ways, specifically the way they could enjoy life, short as it was, and how they loved one another. He couldn't think of anyone who'd look so happy to see him.

Those thoughts were jerked from him as the final phase of his transformation washed through his body. A charge, like static energy, traveled through his pores, his blood, and in seconds he'd gone completely invisible. Only able to be seen by those straddling the line between life and death, he strolled purposefully toward the car garage.

Today's scenario would be no different than the thousands of others he'd seen through the years. He could see it in his mind, like an image on a television screen. A carload of teenagers barreling through the garage, the interior of the car heavily laced with the thick stench of cannabis. The driver was laughing, blaring the Ozzy tune "Crazy Train," unaware that soon he'd be indicted for two counts of vehicular homicide.

Cian often wondered at times like these why the humans couldn't feel it. The end of their lifeline, the disturbance in the air, death; for him it was like the blast of trumpets, loud and hard to ignore.

Turning his attention back to the couple, he waited. The man popped open the trunk of a green sedan, laid down his packages, and flashed the witch a smile. She stood by the hood of the car, her midnight curls blowing in the stiff wind.

The faint rumble of an approaching engine echoed eerily through the garage. The vibrations traveled through the soles of his feet. *Soon. It'll all be over soon.*

For a crazy second he wanted to scream at them. *Move. Get out of the way.* But he held his tongue. He wouldn't interfere, that was the single most important rule of the reaper. His skeletal hand twitched, and he yanked it out of his pocket. No mistakes.

The car made a sharp left around a concrete post in the garage and swerved headlong toward the couple with a loud, echoing cry of rubber.

For Cian the scene was agonizingly slow, each detail sharp and clear, as if it were taking minutes, though in truth it would be done within seven seconds.

When they finally noticed it was already too late.

The witch's golden eyes grew wide in her face. Blood rushed from her skin, leaving her a pasty white. Her hands covered her mouth as a scream of raw fear flew from her lips. "Michael!"

The smile on the man's face died. He turned—unable to run for cover, to hide from his fate. She ran forward, arms outstretched, and tried to pull the man toward her.

Metal exploded against flesh. The sickening crunch of bone and tearing muscle warred with the scream of tires braking. The man was dragged under the car. She was flung aside, her limbs at odd proportions.

Cian's heart clenched painfully when he saw her ravaged body lying so helpless on the ground. She looked like a morbid porcelain doll. Beautiful and broken.

Blood spattered everywhere. All over the windshield. Even on the neighboring vehicles in the next three slots. The overwhelming metallic stench was all around.

The car squealed to a halt, slamming against the side of the sedan. The shattering of glass echoed through the garage with an eerie finality. It was done; their bodies slowly dying, their souls waiting only for him to harvest and carry on to the appropriate afterlife.

The driver, a pimply-faced redhead emerged. "Oh no! No!" he sang the litany over and over. He ran a trembling hand through his hair and glanced up. A family in the next row over stared back in openmouthed shock.

"Get back in the car, Derek!" the girl in the passenger seat screamed.

The wind picked up flurries of snow, enclosing them in winter's peaceful embrace. An ironic scene, at odds with the gruesome sight of death before him.

The kid jumped back in his car and squealed off with one last *bump-bump* in his wake.

Cian closed the gap between himself and the victims. First the male. The man's face had been nearly sheared off. His forehead was cracked open and a constant stream of blood gushed from the wound. Kneeling, Cian extended his skeletal hand, ready to harvest the soul and carry it safely to the afterlife.

The man moaned and opened green eyes glittering with pain. He didn't question why Cian was kneeling over him; instead he parted ruptured lips and croaked, "Save my wife."

Cian glanced over at her prostrate form for a brief second and then shook his head with a sad, bitter twist to his lips. He'd seen many broken bodies in the past, never feeling more than quiet detachment. But seeing her now, hearing the wet gurgle of her breaths, it was like razor-sharp spikes driving through his heart.

He closed his eyes, chanting over and over in his mind: *This is the order to life. Without order there would be chaos. To prevent the chaos there must always be order.*

Taking a deep breath, he plowed on, finishing what he'd started. "Find your peace, human…" *For us both.* Then he gently caressed the man's exposed cheek.

The light of death filled the man's eyes, and a single tear slipped down his cheek. The mask of pain relaxed, and a soft blue mist exploded from the caved-in chest—the soul pulsed with energy and differing shades of blue.

A glowing portal of brilliant white opened before him. The

melodic song of a bubbling brook and rustling grass momentarily made Cian forget—forget the pain and loneliness.

The soul glided toward the light. It shimmered and glowed as it stepped through the portal. Then it was gone. The light went too, and with it the temporary peace Cian had sought his entire existence.

One left. The thought was a needle stabbing into his brain. He tried to remain clinical and study her not as a victim, but as a task and a duty to fulfill.

She wasn't in nearly as bad a shape as her husband had been. Both legs were broken at the hips. One foot was pointed north, the other south. Besides the obvious injuries, she also suffered a ruptured spleen and would soon die from internal bleeding.

Short, shallow breathing turned his gaze to her face. Thin and heart-shaped with full pink lips and almond-shaped eyes.

His hands trembled, something was causing him to hesitate, a strange feeling he had no name for. What was it? Curiosity maybe? Something about the witch tugged at his normally detached feelings about death and life. *Do it. You must. Take her from this misery.*

Her eyes snapped open. The lioness gaze ensnared him. Her bloody hand grabbed his fleshy one and his world turned upside down. Instantly images and thoughts came to him. The face of her husband, a sensation of overwhelming, heartrending love. The pain. The fear. The hope. Her hope exploded inside him like a seedling shooting through black earth.

His brows dipped, and his breathing spiked. He continued to share her emotions. He bit the inside of his lip, and the bitter taste of blood pooled on his tongue as he fought off the onslaught. He'd known upon first seeing her that she was a witch, had sensed her energy, but her powers were intense. He'd never come across a projecting empath as powerful as she was.

Cian took slow breaths and pushed his will against her own in an attempt to extricate himself from her furious assault. His will was like talons ripping and clawing at her insides; the back blast resonated through him. He reeled from it but couldn't block himself off. She whimpered, moans spilled from her lips, and still she fought him.

He could break her wrist, force her to let him go. Force her to end the emotional battering. So why wasn't he doing that?

Because he couldn't. Because for the first time in an eternity she was making him *feel*—not just her pain, but her desperation for life. Emotions he'd never felt before. It was all so confusing, and yet…he'd never felt more alive. All his life he'd walked around in a daze. Moving from one soul to another, not living, just existing. For the first time he wanted. He felt. Because of her, and he'd betrayed her in the worse possible way.

Her eyes, glazed with pain, held his own. Defying him to take her life. She wanted to live.

Another shot of emotions slammed him. They felt like churning waves of angry sea crashing against him, stripping the flesh from his bones. Her anger beat at him, clawed at his throat with desperation.

Right then he made a decision. In defiance of his queen, the ruler of the reapers, he let her live.

Chapter 2

Cian opened the portal between the here and there with a swipe of his hand and stepped through. No one witnessed the shimmering disturbance of air, the growing crowd still entranced by the grisly scene before them.

He crossed the threshold, and an immediate soothing heat engulfed him in an explosion of sifting colors. Reds melded into gold, greens into blues. The dizzying array of shifting lights blurred until suddenly it opened, revealing a shrouded gray and misty isle.

He stepped through and studied the familiar surroundings, inhaling the sharp tang of salt in the breeze and allowing the awareness of home to ease the worry from between his brows and the throb of pain from his heart.

Algae-tinted water crashed against rocks, and foam bubbled up, looking like a witch's frosty brew. The wind shrieked, its tone almost magical in quality. If one listened closely one could hear the voice of the land and its children speaking. Hence its name: Isle of Whispers.

But the locals knew the isle as something else. Alcatraz. The atoll had been home to fae long before any human had dared to step foot upon it. There'd always been a hint of danger settled within the foundation of earth and stone. A natural fallout of magick linked to the longtime association of faerie. In truth, the island itself was not home, but rather an entrance to the sithen. Alcatraz Island was only one of many openings to the fae kingdom.

Cian bowed his head against the whipping winds and walked toward a tree. An old oak, its limbs twisted by age and roots gnarled and curled out the ground, that was the life-sustaining mother of this sithen. The shrill scream of twin crows forced him to glance up.

She knows.

The knowledge did not come as a surprise.

The birds circled him twice then landed silently by his feet as they cocked their heads in unison, their hard glares boring into him. Cian clenched his jaw and waited for the summons.

Follow us.

He didn't hear the words so much as feel the push of their will against his mind. After what the witch had just put him through, the push felt more like a stab. He winced, still sensitive.

A golden quickening surrounded the crows, the crackles of light appeared as a sunburst—variegated colors of red and gold cut through the fog. The birds landed before the entrance and passed their feathered wings across the bark in unison. A loud creak, similar to the groaning of shifting earth, rumbled through the air, then, smooth as silk, the center of the tree separated.

The hollow tree encased a trove of glorious splendor—rolling emerald hills, meandering streams of liquid crystal, and craggy cliffs. Thick, billowing mists sheathed the surroundings.

This was truly a world within a world. To travel through the entirety of the fae world would take years, if not decades. But he knew where he was going: to the very center of the realm. The queen's castle rose through the mists as a spiraling steeple.

The crows cawed. Haunting, wispy calls echoed in return. The sylphs—winged beings resembling angels—flew overhead. None but immortals could ever see them. Their butterfly-like wings were a splash of glorious color against the gray of the sky.

The closer Cian drew to his queen's side, the more he felt her fury. It boiled inside him like a festering wound. He grimaced, tasting the blood from where he'd bitten his cheek earlier, and knew that bit of spilled scarlet would not be enough to assuage her thirst for revenge.

He went now to plead his case for the witch. The woman was still far from safe; he'd only granted her a temporary asylum. The queen could choose at any moment to send another reaper out there to finish what he hadn't. Whether the beating stripped all the flesh from his body or not, he meant to see her safe.

* * *

"Well, now, this has been a most interesting turn of events. Wouldn't you agree, Chaos?" Dagda—king of the earth elements and of the fae—asked.

The Morrigan—goddess of strife, war, and death—narrowed her eyes at him. "I despise when you call me by that name." The air quickened with the sharp nip of frost.

Oh yes, his queen was in a fury. He ignored her typical protest of his pet name for her with casual cool.

"You do revel at my misfortune, ugly bastard." Though her words were harsh, they were laced with a thread of humor.

Dagda chuckled. The thunderous boom of his voice filled their antechamber with resonance; it echoed off the high ceiling and caused gold dust to shower down upon them.

Despite the fact the fae god seemed merry, his voice held the power to kill if he chose. He'd done so on rare occasions. Though he found he didn't have the same taste for blood as his bonny Chaos did.

He covered her ivory hand with his dark one and proceeded to run his thumb along her knuckle. "Chaos, you old hag, calling your king a bastard. I take offense."

A swift smile played on her bloodred lips. Then the humor was gone, replaced by an immediate, unnatural calm.

"Frenzy, bring me my cat-o'-nine-tails and sharpen the blades on the ends until they gleam," The Morrigan said in a calm monotone.

He, however, was not deceived. Dagda had seen her like this many times; this mood never boded well. She was as the eye of a hurricane, merely an illusion of quiet, peaceful tranquility.

The stealthy figure of a reaper emerged from the shadows of the wall. Frenzy dipped low to his queen, his long crimson hair trailing along the stone floor like a sea of blood. Straightening, his silver eyes flashed with a hint of madness.

Normally Dagda would not interfere in The Morrigan's punishment of death. But he must find a way to temper her; far-reaching works had been set into motion and she was not to do anything with lasting consequences. An oracle to the chosen ones had warned him long ago this day would come.

Though it grieved him to do so, he must now assume the role of order to his queen's chaos.

"Chaos," he said.

Her eyes flashed with annoyance—their normal icy blue changing to the ruby red of her crows, Badb and Nemain.

Dagda drummed his fingers on his armrest. "What do you pro-
pose to do with Cian?"

Her nostrils flared, and the fire and shadow of her hair swirled as
she cocked her head. "Ten thousand lashes for his disobedience."

Dagda stroked his smooth chin. "And the mortal? What of her?"

"I'll send Frenzy. She will not escape her fate this time."

"I see."

She lifted a curved black brow, a knowing glint in her eyes.
"Dagda," she cautioned, "do not interfere."

His lips curved at the corner, but he didn't say another word.

Chapter 3

Cian entered the castle gates and immediately felt the sense that all was not well. It was like a rush of ice down his spine. He scanned the dimly lit corridor, noting how the inhabitants shuffled here and there, never glancing up and unnaturally quiet. An expectant hush filled the stone keep.

The only eyes that stared back at him came from the skeletal heads affixed to the walls as candelabras. Golden flames flickering inside empty mouths cast strange and undulating shadows down the hall.

The Morrigan kept tokens of all her conquests. The leering bones meant nothing to death. He knew all these bones by name and who'd they'd been in a former life—farmer or great hero, it didn't matter. Now, be they humble or famous, they were resigned to an eternity of being little more than decoration.

He took a deep breath, inhaling the delicious aromas of roasting meats and baking breads. Warriors sat at gnarled oak benches, heads bowed over their chipped bowls of stew. They whispered amongst themselves; hundreds of voices buzzed in his ears. He could only make out snatches of conversation.

"Live..."

"...death..."

"Foolish boy..."

He ground his jaw, knowing they spoke of him. Rumor traveled fast and The Morrigan's rage could be sensed like a living entity within every crevice of the castle. It was a choking sensation, stealing the breath and lying heavy on the lungs.

The gray, dank stone echoed with the sound of his footsteps. He turned a corner and then there was nothing. This portion of the castle was unnaturally empty. Cian glanced down the shifting maze of hallways and doorways, keen to pick up the sound or scent of something. But it was like walking through a mausoleum. Desolate and foreboding.

He glanced up, studying the flight of The Morrigan's crows. The red-and-black banners of the royal court affixed to wooden beams on the ceiling fluttered at the birds passing. The Morrigan rarely sent her crows, preferring instead to use other methods of contact. A clap of thunder, a whisper in the wind. She saved her crows only for the direst of circumstances.

Polished doors of silver grew from a mere speck in the distance to large arches the closer he drew to the royals' private chambers. The ground beneath his feet shifted, a vibration traveled up his soles as if from the pounding of several trampling feet.

Had she sent her guard? Why? She had to know he was coming of his own free will.

Then he saw them, twenty of her most experienced and lethal, marching to block off the entrance to her room. Their steps were unified and absurdly beautiful in their precision. The lead guard, dressed in a tunic of burnished bronze and buffed brown leather, halted the procession by lifting his fist into the air, and as one the group turned on their heels, all done in absolute silence.

They extended their spears and, like a coordinated ballet, slammed the ends onto the floor. The sound of metal slapping stone reverberated through the room like gunfire. Austere faces gazed at him.

The Morrigan's pretentious show of force and power nauseated him. It wasn't enough for her that she command the most lethal, and loyal, battalion in all of faedom, but she couldn't resist trying to prove her superiority even to death.

He stopped, eyeing them. Each had hair tied back at the nape in a severe queue. Their delicate features made them look weak, effeminate. But they were deadly thanks to the swords attached to their dun-colored scabbards. Resting within the hilt of each sword was a red stone. *Mereth en draugrim*: feast of the wolves.

One nick from the blade and the victim went instantly mad, beginning to crave such things as bloody meat, marrow from bones. It was a sickness that only overcame the sufferers when the moon grew pregnant with light. The truth of the weres was that they were the original creation of fae.

"Grim reaper," Cahal, the lead guard, intoned in a deep barrel-chested voice.

Cian's nostrils flared. Heat snapped down his spine, turned his blood to molten lava. A tightness centered in his chest, and the dread and hatred he'd harbored in his soul awoke from their slumber.

"Let me pass, Cahal. I only wish to speak with the queen," he said, his words edged in steel.

Cahal lifted a snow-white brow and shook his head, a glitter of antipathy gleaming in his ice-blue eyes.

"No."

In fury, Cian roared, knowing the queen would hear him and wanting her to. There would be no escaping the beating, and with that thought came freedom. For the first time he need not fear the repercussion; they would happen anyway.

"Morrigan!"

Cahal hooked his arm through Cian's. Using the guard's momentum against him, Cian turned on his heel and slammed his palm against Cahal's cheek. More guards jumped on Cian.

Fingers clawed into his flesh. Nails drew blood. But he didn't care. He swung his fists and yelled.

"Craven whore," he bellowed, praying the goddess would hear him. "Hiding behind your dogs. Meet me!"

There was no reason for the queen to do this. He'd come with no arguments; he'd known the punishment he'd receive. But he knew her perverse love of violence and blood all too well. The queen was a sadist through and through, and this was nothing more than a blatant show of power, of letting him know she was boss. He hated her now more than ever.

Bodies slammed into his back, bringing him to his knees under the weight and choking the air from his lungs. But the adrenaline was spiking and he no longer cared.

Cian writhed, the preternatural strength in his body refusing to fade out. This was a fury he'd suppressed for far too long. The indifference and hostility of the righteous fae toward his kind, the indignity of being called "dog" or, worse yet, not being called anything at all, had the festering hatred boiling over.

The sounds of snapping bones, quick grunts of breath, and the muffled noise of flesh striking flesh echoed down the hall.

He grabbed two heads and knocked them together. The dull sound was sickening as the bones crumpled against the other. A boot slammed into his face. It felt like his nose had been rammed through his skull.

Then more feet connected, busting in his teeth, his cheeks. He was on the ground now, facedown and being crushed under the pressure of a blanket of bodies. They slammed sword hilts into his face; the explosion of razor-sharp pain inside his brain was immediate and excruciating. He hissed, finally blacking out as one connected with his temple.

* * *

Badb and Nemain returned, gliding toward The Morrigan. They landed on either end of her throne and cawed.

She caressed the thick rope of leather in her hand. "Is Cian shackled in the chambers below?"

She'd heard all the words the fool had spat as he'd fought with her guards. He'd pay for the remarks with blood.

Nemain blinked her ruby-red eyes.

"Good." The Morrigan strode toward the hallway. Her fingers twitched with anticipation. Her obsidian gown tightened at the chest with the excited rise of her breathing.

"Be well, Chaos," Dagda called after her.

She turned and nodded toward her scheming consort. His eyes gleamed differing shades of gold and black. A smile cut his features, the white of his teeth in sharp contrast to the natural tan of his flesh.

The Morrigan turned on her heels and proceeded toward the rack room.

Dagda was keeping secrets. He never involved himself in her affairs. Now twice he'd done so.

Anger sizzled through her veins. Her nostrils flared. She cracked the whip against her thigh in agitation.

Only strategically placed torches lit the winding stairway of stone. Thin jets of light cut through the shadow at intermittent spaces. The gloomy, dank path had been designed with purpose. To create a sense of panic. Of fear. To increase the heart rate into a pounding melody of terror. There wasn't much that could scare an immortal centuries old. Nothing, that is, except the rotten stench of dried blood, the torn flesh of their kith, and knowing they'd soon be next. She bit her lip, her fury increasing with each step she took.

Finally, three flights down and in the darkest corridor of the castle, she arrived at the rack room. Two guards with crossed sickles stood before the door.

Her lips twitched at the sight of Cahal. One eye was beginning to swell with an overflow of blood. The white was now a shocking sea of busted blood vessels. She loved death. They were such a lethal predator.

Cahal's good eye was a startling blue in contrast. He remained aloof, but she could tell by the pounding of a vein in his neck that he was agitated by her cold perusal. A thrum of electrical pleasure hummed through her body, she vibrated with the beginnings of bloodlust and reached out a hand to caress the side of Cahal's face.

He shivered under her touch and leaned in just slightly. A perfect teardrop of blood slid from the corner of his eye onto her pinky finger. She held it up to her nose, inhaling the scent of autumn leaves. Excitement quickened her pulse and with a delicate flick of her tongue she lapped it up. The sweet taste filled her mouth.

"Cahal," she said with a husky tenor, "you are truly a prize to be savored."

He closed his eyes, his chest rising and falling with breathless wonder. The redolent musk of his pride filled the air with the thick scent of turning leaves and sweet apple cider.

A feral need for more blood ripped through her. "Leave me now," she growled, wanting to save the fire of her madness for Cian.

"My queen," they said in unison and not with a small amount of relief. As one they turned and marched off with exact precision.

She opened the door. Cian was shackled to the wall with his back toward her. A sliver of light fell across the sculpted beauty of his body. He shifted and the locks of his long hair swished across his shoulders. Alternating strands of polished sable and ivory gleamed with unholy light. The long, hard lines of his body flexed with his movement.

"What are you waiting for?" His voice was like fine whiskey. Smooth, hot, and raw.

She narrowed her eyes, excited by the rising fury rolling through his veins, and walked up to him with catlike movements. Already the taste of Cahal was making her crave death itself. She trailed the grip of her whip against his back, the itch flowing through her for the sight of his blood. "You know what you're here for, don't you?"

His body tensed, and the rigid cording of his back flexed as he turned his head to glare at her. The midnight blue of his eyes turned black with rage.

That was when she finally got a good look at his face. It was a bruised mess. His jaw was nearly twice its normal size. Blood already covered his chin and long gouges ran the length of both cheeks. She chortled, grabbing his chin in her hand and squeezed tight. He was a masterpiece of pain, but her guards had barely begun to scratch the surface of her blood thirst, she wanted to do so much more to him than this.

"Such tough words," she spat. "I'll enjoy making you beg for mercy."

"You'll have none from me," he said low and menacing. He narrowed his eyes and his face twisted into a frightful mask of arrogance and fury. The look was enough to quell many, but not her. Not the goddess of battle and strife. The Morrigan fed off rage; she lived for it. She inhaled the heady scent of his wrath and gave him a hungry smile.

"You've disappointed me, Cian."

His jaw hardened. "That was never my intent. She is meant to live. Do not harm the mortal."

She slapped him across the cheek. The power of the blow forced his head to crack against the wall. "How dare you make demands to me!"

He studied her like a predator ready for the kill—silent and with an undercurrent of lethal power.

In answer he spat by her foot. The sight of the crimson-streaked saliva had her barely suppressed bloodlust rising to the surface.

"Oh, my death. That was most unwise."

The Morrigan stepped back and snapped the whip through the air. Its shrill sound was like the crack of thunder. Cian never flinched. She threw her head back and laughed. "You were always my best. So heartless, so perfect."

Then she struck him. The metal tips at the end of the cat-o'-nine-tails tore into him. Thick crimson spilled down his back.

Cian's fists clenched; his body went stiff. Tremors traveled the length of his legs. The Morrigan licked the blood that settled against her lip—its sweet, metallic taste only made her want more.

His blood was the sweetest of all. It wasn't just scent, it was memory. The memory of every soul he'd taken was within each drop. She relived it all through him and couldn't contain the rushing need for more. He was death, life, and power, and she wanted it all.

She walked up to him and laid her hand against his lacerations. He hissed and hung his head, and then, leaning toward his ear, she whispered, "Now imagine how much more the rest will hurt. You'll never disobey me again, Cian. I vow it."

* * *

Dagda glanced up as the door to his chamber cracked open with a loud boom. The Morrigan stood in the entranceway. Blood and gore covered her from head to toe.

He stood and held out his hand. She walked toward him and dropped a gentle kiss against his cheek. "It is finished," she whispered.

He nodded. "Now?"

She eyed her clothing and sneered. "I'll clean up before sending Frenzy to finish what Cian could not."

Dagda blinked.

An explosion of magick took her breath. The aftershocks of so much power sped through her veins. She pulled out of his embrace and gazed at him. Her brows lowered. "Why have you sifted the strands of mortal time?"

"To make the fight fair."

She cocked her head. "How very, very interesting. Whatever are you hiding from me, consort?"

He raised a brow. His face remained impassive. "Why would you think I'd be hiding anything?"

"You won't win."

"Who said this was a contest?"

She shook her head. "I don't trust you."

He lifted her hand and kissed her knuckle. "Take your bath, Chaos. I have matters to attend to."

She eyed him and turned. "Whatever it is you have planned, Dagda...don't."

His lips curved as he walked from the room.

* * *

Cian lay crumpled on the floor as spots danced before his eyes. A rush of vertigo had the room moving in circles. The burst of energy that had ripped into his back from the witch at the club paled in comparison to the madness of the queen.

The door to the room opened, and a shadowy figure entered. Its movements were lithe, fragile. Like a delicate bloom on a stem. Not The Morrigan.

He blinked. A gentle voice drifted toward him, and a soft hand touched his face. "Cian. It is me."

"Wistafa," he croaked. Now recognizing the mass of riotous brown curls. "Leave before she catches you here."

She knelt and pulled his head into her lap, crooning softly. Instantly Cian became drowsy and closed his eyes. Wistafa was the great healer to the house of feathers of the royal court. Her scent of mint and sage wrapped him up in a comforting cocoon. Like a mother's warm embrace.

He took a deep breath, wanting to inhale more of the intoxicating aroma. Fire sizzled through his veins. He felt like the needles of a million scorpions had suddenly stabbed him, and every breath was agony. His eyes opened sharply.

"I've come to help," she whispered, her brown eyes twin pools of compassion. Her fingers massaged a circular pattern on his temples, distracting him for the pain. "Close your eyes and simply relax."

Cian gripped her wrist. "Why are you doing this? I'm a grim reaper. Death," he stated with emphasis. Even the fae had always treated him with contempt and spite. A dark smudge to the beauty they worshiped. Power play with death, fine. But show any mercy or compassion, goddess forbid.

She only smiled, a small curling at the corners of her mouth. "You are just a man. What you do is not who you are, Cian. I would have come had I not been commanded."

"Commanded? By whom?" he demanded. Who could care?

"Dagda."

He narrowed his eyes, instantly distrustful. What game were the gods playing at?

"He said that you were to be healed and sent to the mortal woman immediately."

Was this a trial? It didn't make sense. Why would Dagda want to help him?

"Your eyes, Cian. Close them now. Or I'll force them shut," she said authoritatively.

Normally her tone would incite Cian into a riot of anger, but her words possessed a lyrical, soothing quality that instantly calmed the beast within and stamped out the fury of resentment. She'd laid the full charm of her healing magick upon him. His response was immediate and instinctual.

He closed his eyes.

A warm heat spiraled from her fingertips throughout his body. It was a soothing balm healing the throb traveling his limbs. It felt like tiny fingers manipulating the ache in his joints, tendons, and muscle. The next breath he took was free of pain. He opened his eyes and saw he was healed. His flesh looked firm. Smooth. What would have taken him days on his own to mend had taken only seconds.

He stood up and patted himself to make certain it was real and not some illusion. There was no pain. There were no lacerations. He was whole.

Unaccustomed to kindness, he was unsure of what to say.

"Thank…you," he hissed, the words foreign on his tongue.

Wistafa shook her head. "No thanks required, reaper. Find the woman. Dagda will come to you in a couple of days. Go now."

She stood and turned to leave.

There were too many gaps. He hated being kept in the dark and knew something was amiss. If the god wanted him to go to the woman, why not come to Cian himself and demand it? The secrecy and subterfuge had him on edge, making him uneasy.

"Is that it? Is there no more? Does The Morrigan know of this?" He gritted his teeth in frustration.

She stopped but never turned. "If you don't leave now, all will be lost. Find the woman." Then she was gone, her soft scent the only clue that she'd ever been there.

He marched from the room, dressed himself using his essence, and opened a portal between the here and there with a swipe of his hand.

Curiosity, an emotion he'd buried long ago, rose to the forefront. What game were The Morrigan and Dagda playing, and why was he involved?

He stepped through the portal. The witch's lifeline beckoned. Already familiar with her spirit, he attuned himself to her. Perhaps it was as simple as finishing the task he'd been sent to accomplish in the first place. His gut clenched. Could he even do it? He'd tried once and failed.

He glanced at his hand. It was flesh, not skeletal, a small comfort that only compounded his confusion. What was going on? Dagda and The Morrigan always had an agenda, but usually they worked on the same side. Having Dagda act so secretive made Cian troubled.

The Morrigan had not stripped the flesh from his body because she planned to easily forgive in the next breath. Her anger and ability for revenge were legendary. Which meant everything Dagda was doing now was without The Morrigan's knowledge. A fact that was not lost on him. Cian, whether he'd wanted to or not, had now become Dagda's pawn. A game piece easily sacrificed for the greater good.

When he stepped through the portal, he expected to arrive back at the gruesome scene he'd left. Instead he found himself peering at his witch through a shop window with the words WITCH'S BREW stenciled across the front.

She looked healthy, full of vigor. Her hair was longer, hanging well past her lower back. A rosy flush encompassed her pale cheeks.

The sight caused his heart to twist painfully against his chest.

He frowned and shoved his hand through his hair. Who had

sifted time? The gods rarely manipulated mortal time. The instances were rare, few and far between.

All the scenarios he'd anticipated suddenly took a turn for the worse. Dagda's conspiracy was greater than he'd at first imagined, and a black chill rushed down his spine.

"What have they done?"

Chapter 4

"Argh! If I have to make another effing love charm I'm gonna tear my hair out." Eve eyed the dangling piece of clay with disdain.

Tamryn snorted. "Don't worry. In another hour we'll be sipping on Gorilla Farts and man scouting. Life can't get better than that."

Eve wrapped her hand around the charm and dragged it to her heart, almost as a protective shield. *Not again.* Her sisters were going to try and force the issue. She wasn't ready. Period. End of story. Not wanting to wax on again about a subject she'd rather see dead and buried, Eve switched topics.

"Why do humans insist on buying this charm? Money, protection, luck. Okay, those I can understand. But love? Don't they know that's not how love works? You can't force it on someone." She tried but couldn't keep the hurt from creeping into her voice.

Tamryn eyed her. Aware, Eve was sure, of her inner torment. For the moment, however, her sister didn't pursue the matter and shrugged her slim shoulders instead. "Why do you care? I'm always up-front about this particular charm. If they insist on buying it anyway it's their business.

"Besides"—Tamryn yanked on the dangling leather chain in Eve's hand—"we both know humans come to San Fran because this is horror central. Weres, vamps, and witches, living out in the open, unlike Podunk middle America, where some redneck jackasses still try to burn us at the stake." She shuddered. "You know better than anyone that it's us on display and not our wares. So no, I don't feel bad at all taking their money. Tit for tat, far as I'm concerned."

"Touché." Eve snapped her fingers with a grin.

She then turned her attention back to the table, hoping the message was clear. Go away. Leave her alone. But her sister didn't walk off. Eve's palms grew increasingly sweat slicked, as she knew her sister was still behind her boring holes into her back. She closed her eyes. *Please don't do this, Tamryn.*

"So..."

She groaned and turned, knowing no amount of ignoring her would get her to leave.

Tamryn trailed her finger along the spine of a grimoire. "You coming tonight, or what? It's time we reinstate our weekly get-together, don't you think? Drinks, chips, and gossip. Fun, huh?" Tamryn wiggled her brows, using a different tactic to entice Eve. Thing was, she wasn't ready to go back to the life she'd lived before Michael's death.

"No." She set her mouth in a thin line.

"Eve. C'mon."

"No. Okay." She pushed away from the workbench, scattering several charms in the process. "Why do you keep doing this to me?"

Tamryn huffed. "Because you've become a shell of your former self. Do you honestly believe for one minute that Michael would have wanted this?" She lifted a brow and laid a hand on her hip, her stance defiant.

"That is not fair!" Eve jumped up, glaring daggers at her sister. "You wouldn't understand. You wouldn't even know what I'm going through," she said, her voice breaking.

Tamryn's violet eyes narrowed into dangerous slits. "No, of course I wouldn't. It's not like I lost a brother-in-law. It's not like I went through the pain of Mom's death. Of course I wouldn't understand, Eve."

Eve winced and glanced away.

Tamryn blew out a heavy breath. "I'm sorry, I didn't mean that…"

Eve shook her head, holding out a restraining hand as the truth of the words sank deep into her heart. Her sister was right. Fact was, she knew she was being ridiculous, and it was hard to admit this—especially to herself—but what hurt most was the guilt. Guilt for surviving when Michael hadn't. Guilt for actually wanting to go out and have fun again.

Tamryn had never had anything but the best of intentions for her. Mentally, Eve knew hanging onto the past brought a lack of resolution. She'd loved Michael, and she had to believe that somewhere up there he knew and would understand that eventually she'd have to move on. Still, it was hard to think about making a fresh start.

Just the idea of starting over, of having to reenter the hit-and-miss world of dating, made her heart stutter. Women her age were usually nice and settled, with two-point-two kids, the white picket fence, and all that jazz. Here she was, thirty and contemplating a life of spinsterhood, not because she was too old but because she was in a comfort zone she feared changing. Deep down she knew Michael would have been furious with her for mourning him these past two years. But that was love, and she'd loved him hard.

She blew out a deep breath. He shouldn't have died so young, and that was the irony of the situation. Michael had seemed like the man of steel. So strong, virile, and full of life. To have seen his life snuffed out by such a senseless act—the thought still made her twitch with anger.

But she couldn't keep doing this. It had to stop sooner or later, she admitted to herself with reluctance.

With a sad smile she turned toward her sister and gave a weak nod. "You're right. I've been selfish. You and Cel were there for me when everyone else left." She pulled Tamryn into a quick hug. "I don't want to go to the club tonight, but I'll do it for you. Deal?"

Tamryn grinned and ran a hand through her unruly red curls. "Good. For a second there I thought I was gonna have to get all kung fu on your ass."

They laughed.

* * *

Later that night Eve studied her wardrobe dispassionately. She hadn't returned to Club X after Michael's death.

Breathe, Eve. She closed her eyes for a split second. *You can do this. You have to*, she repeated the mantra over and over.

Not only would she do this, but she'd go all out. She stripped off her clothes, showered, and then returned to her closet.

She grabbed a black chiffon skirt, one that hung snug at her hips and gently flared around her knees. She nibbled on her lip, studying her tops, finally deciding on a black-and-red off-the-shoulder corset.

Grabbing the first pair of red stilettos she found, she sat down on the edge of her bed and slipped them on.

Done, she studied her reflection in the mirror.

Her skin glowed from the scalding water and hard scrubbing she'd just subjected herself to. The deep gold of her eyes shimmered in the light. She hung her head.

"Breathe. Just breathe," she mumbled.

She growled, decided she'd done about all the primping she was willing to do and before heading out the door, grabbed a trench coat in case of cooler weather tonight, then went to fetch Tamryn and Celeste.

Stupid. Stupid. So freaking stupid.

* * *

Cian heard the shuffling of feet and high-pitched voices of females before he saw her. His dark witch. He'd followed her home from the shop, contemplating what to do, how to approach her, and then here she was. As if she'd stepped from his thoughts into reality. His gut churned with anxiety.

To her it would seem as if two years had passed, but for him to see her hale and whole after the horror of seeing her body twisted and broken took his breath. The glimpse of her through the shop window did not compare to this moment.

He was transfixed. She radiated an alluring mixture of power and sensuality. He sensed in her a great sadness that touched his heart, suddenly feeling a burning ache to hold her. Comfort her. He clenched his jaw, knowing what he felt was the effect of her magick flaring to life inside him.

She and her sisters walked down the sidewalk. The blonde and redhead wore smiles. His witch did not.

Her misery scorched him like a fiery brand. Cian remembered the sparkle in her golden eyes the first time he'd laid eyes on her.

She shouldn't feel this way. It's all my fault.

He followed at a discreet distance, silent as a thought. The sisters moved with purpose, threading a winding path through alleyways, around condemned buildings and stinking Dumpsters. The path was a familiar one to him.

He watched as different sets of eyes studied the women. The furtive glances and faint odor of male lust riding the winds told him of their intent.

But the women weren't weak, and the men knew it. They crackled with power, like a burst of electricity from a live wire. Their ramrod shoulders and straight backs gave off a clear message: *Screw with me at your own peril.*

One by one the sets of eyes left off, seeking easier prey.

Cian's lips quirked.

The ladies stopped at the entrance of the club and knocked.

A peephole slid open and a large brown eye peered out.

"Password," the gruff voice asked.

"Asylum."

The large, wrought-iron door opened on silent hinges. Pale wisps of blue smoke escaped the club to curl around their ankles, creating an illusion of ethereal beings floating slowly inside.

A tingle ran like quicksilver down Cian's spine. And he knew without turning that another reaper was around. The hunt was on. It was small comfort to know that while the sisters were inside Club X, no harm could come to them.

But how the hell am I supposed to keep them safe the rest of the time? Especially when The Morrigan is determined to have her?

After a few seconds passed, he knocked on the door, spoke the password, and continued his pursuit. The pulsating rhythms of Danzig vibrated through his body. The loud music keyed him up, pumped him full of adrenaline. Made him want.

Quickly he followed their scent up the stairwell, only slowing down when they were a few feet ahead. He stared at her backside. At the gentle sway of her hips and the wealth of black hair trailing down her back.

Of course you'd want what you could never have.

He clenched his hands into fists, climbing step after stone step.

Cian had expected the sisters to heard toward the coven floor—the place where all practicing witches, wizards, and warlocks who preferred to keep to themselves partied—but was stunned when they bypassed it. Instead they headed for the fourth-floor door. The mixed flock.

On this level only, the pack, clan, and coven put aside their differences and prejudices to party together.

Many centuries past, the fae would have been included as part of the revelry. Now no fae were allowed save the reapers. Death was an essential part of life and it could happen anywhere, at any time. Supernatural laws and rules did not apply to the reapers.

"Ah! My favorite sisters three."

The sisters turned at the sound of the melodious voice.

Cian glanced at the source.

"Lise," his witch cried and rushed into the proprietor's frail embrace.

Madam Lise's snow-white eyes roamed the witch's face with

unerring accuracy. She laid a liver-spotted hand against her heart. "Such sadness."

Cian shifted. Electric currents of Lise's power pulsed through him. The woman was immortality personified. In her voice he heard not just words but an ancient knowledge of the beginning and the end.

The mystery that was Lise teased his mind. She was more than the gods and goddesses. She was time, origin, everything. Somehow he knew when this world passed away and he was nothing, not even a memory, Lise would remain. She was the chosen one.

It was a cold-shiver-down-the-spine type of thought.

He was suddenly yanked from his reflections when he saw a white glow began to spread from between Lise's fingers. Like a spiraling helix, they shot through his witch's flesh. She radiated from the inside out. A dark-haired priestess caught within a silky, ivory web.

The ground trembled. Glass bottles behind the bar shook and rattled, not from the music, which had gone suddenly quiet, but from the living force springing from Lise's hand.

He expected to see stunned looks upon the faces of those dancing. But there were no looks of shock. No one had even bothered to stop dancing. He knew then that the music hadn't stopped, so much as Lise, himself, and the three sisters seemed to be within some capsule of time completely separate from the outside world.

Now aware of it, he felt the cocoon's embrace. It was warm, inviting. Meant for privacy more than anything. It rippled like the soft lapping of a stream against a bank.

His witch grunted. An obsidian winding curl of smoke escaped her parted lips. Then as if someone had cut an invisible string holding her up, she slumped to the ground.

He ran forward. Not thinking about what he meant to do, the

need to comfort overruling his desire for stealth. All he wanted was to touch her. Hold her and keep her safe.

The emotion was alarming and stopped him cold in his tracks. *What the hell is wrong with me?* He backed up, into the safety of shadow. Who would find comfort from death?

The sisters helped his witch up. Her golden eyes were wide with shock.

Lise gripped her shoulder. "I've healed the ache in your heart. The rest, my dear witch, will be up to you." She turned her unnatural gaze to Cian.

He took a sharp breath and heard the old woman's voice in his head. *Well met, death. Be ye welcome here.*

Cian gave a solemn nod. *Chosen.*

"Come, sisters three." Lise spread her arms wide. "I've saved you the best seats in the house."

With those words, the music that'd been blocked out because of the time capsule now filtered through once again, along with the sharp smells of bodies pressed close and alcohol-tainted breath. The scents were suddenly overpowering and cloying, seeming to stick to the roof of Cian's mouth, and he grimaced at the stench.

The women sat down in a corner booth next to the dance floor. All three heads joined together to form an odd circle of gold, black, and red. No doubt they were talking of the incident and what it had meant.

There was nothing to do now but wait. So Cian walked over to the bar and sat. He dropped his stealth, nothing more than essence he'd draped himself in. He wouldn't call it exactly going invisible, but unless someone looked in just the right spot they wouldn't see him.

"What'll you have?" The bartender was cleaning a glass with a dishrag, staring at him, and waiting patiently for his answer.

"Firewater," he said.

The bartender nodded, poured him a tumbler full of the green stuff, and slammed it down on the grainy wood. He hadn't actually expected the mortal realm to serve drinks created in the lands of magick.

His lips quirked as he brought the tumbler to his mouth and took a sip. It was just as he remembered it. Smoky, with a bitter hint of overripe cherries. It smoldered going down, making him feel like the flesh was being stripped off his throat.

"Reaper."

The rumbling voice, that always made him think of a volcano ready to explode, could belong to none other than Bezel, demon of the lower night abyss. Cian had known Bezel for many centuries now, and though his kind rarely made friendly with someone not of their own caste, Bezel and he had developed a warped sort of bond through the years.

Cian turned and stared into glowing lavender eyes. "Bezel." He frowned. "What are you doing in the mortal realm?"

The blond, trucker-cap-wearing demon raised a brow. A lascivious smirk was on his face as he hooked his thumb over his shoulder to the retreating figure of a man. "Been bound."

Cian stared at the pale, freckle-faced sorcerer cutting a path through bodies toward the bathroom.

"Someone finally know your true name, demon?" Cian cocked his head. "Took me three centuries to learn it. Not the easiest name to find."

Bezel shrugged. "That overinflated bag of dog waste thinks he does. But he don't and he won't." A deep Kentucky twang twisted the demon's words.

"You plan on telling him any time soon? Or are you going to let him discover that the way your last bindsmen have?"

The demon raised a brow, a smug look on his face. "What do you think? Pass up a chance for a little blood sport later? No way. You know the drill, Cian. I lull them into a false sense of security. Then bam!" He slammed his fist down on the bar. "When they need me most I turn on them instead. Ha..." Bezel shook his head. "Nothing better, 'cept for maybe *wratzling* a greased-up pig. Now that's fun right there."

"There" came out sounding more like "thur."

"A greased-up pig?" Cian chuckled. When the demon set his mind to a character, person, place, or thing, he played the role better than an Oscar nominee. "Playing the country boy this time, I see?"

Bezel took a swig off the Corona bottle in his hand and burped. "Yeah. Been pretty fun. But I'm 'bout through with this one. He's getting boring, thinks a little too highly of himself. Bastard. Thinking maybe I'll twist his head clean off, or maybe fillet him down both sides." He nodded, a pleased expression on his face. "What do you think?"

Cian shook his head, an I-don't-wanna-go-there look on his face. "Little too gruesome for me, demon. How about I just take care of the mess afterward?"

Bezel gave a toothy grin.

Cian took another sip of the firewater, his gaze searching out his witch. She was still sitting in the booth, watching as her sisters gyrated on the dance floor.

It was as if time had been suspended. The thrum of music faded to an insignificant noise in the background. His only focus was on the dark witch. Watching her as she sucked her bottom lip between her teeth and played with the silver bangles on her wrist.

He was aware of several men staring in her direction with something other than just mere curiosity. There was hunger, raw and wild, glittering in their eyes. Hers was an exotic beauty rarely seen. He seethed with jealousy, wanting to break several necks for even daring to let their gaze linger for too long. He chugged the last of the fiery brew and scrubbed a tired hand down his face. He shouldn't be jealous; he shouldn't be anything. The witch did not belong to him, but something about the woman twisted him up on the inside and made him think stupid, crazy thoughts. Thoughts like: *Mine. Mine. Mine.* What the hell was happening to him?

Bezel snapped his fingers, breaking Cian from his trance. The demon looked from Cian to his witch and back again. His lips curled into a slow smile.

"The death of a man is a woman." His lavender eyes glowed like amethyst flames in the darkness.

Cian nodded and turned around, facing the bar once again. She was a topic he wasn't willing to discuss, especially not with the demon. "So," he said, switching subjects, "any of your bindsmen ever allowed to see your true form? I can't imagine that anyone would bind you if they did."

"Bastard." Bezel snorted, a smirk curling his lips. "But no"—he swallowed the last dregs in his bottle—"don't want any of them ever learning too much about me. Knowledge is power, and I ain't in a sharin' mood." He shrugged. "Simpler to just become what they want. Makes it easier to control them later on."

Cian's brows drew together. "Then why disguise yourself as a corn-fed country boy?"

Bezel gave him a deadpan stare.

Then it clicked. "Ah. Of course." He chuckled.

That moment to the next was a blur as rough hands yanked on Cian's shoulder, twisting him around. Fangs dripping with saliva and the rage-twisted face of a were greeted him. "We don't tolerate fae around these parts."

Cian shouldered the hands off. "You have two seconds to get out of my face."

The were growled, drawing attention from the group surrounding the bar. "Or what?" His spit landed on the side of Cian's face. Brown eyes turned black with the beginnings of going feral.

Cian stood, his nose mere inches from the werepanther. The tension was as taut as a bowstring ready to snap.

Hair sprouted from the were's body, bones cracked and snapped, beginning to reform. The panther pressed a heavy paw against Cian's throat, its claws tearing slowly through his flesh.

Cian narrowed his eyes, his muscles tensing with the need to rip into the panther. But years had taught him patience. Anger made you sloppy, and he was waiting for the panther to screw up.

The half man, half cat screamed as only a panther could. The were prepared to strike.

Cian didn't give him a chance. He struck first, grabbing the paw and crushing down. The sickening sound of tendon and bone breaking reverberated around them. The were screamed in agony and shifted back to human, falling to the ground in a writhing ball.

Lise's gaze was on him, heavy and assessing. Pressing in, making him feel claustrophobic. He turned to look at her. She glanced from him to the fallen were and back again.

She snapped her fingers and the rolling body of the were disappeared.

"Nothing to see here. Dance," Lise ordered to the immobile throng still held spellbound by the threat of violence lingering in the air. Her words were a compulsion to obey. At once they all dispersed and returned to what they were doing.

Bezel chortled. "Hell, man! Now that's why I like you. Always guaranteed to see some action when you're around. I promise if you ever bind me I'd probably let you live." He slapped Cian on the back.

His heart thudded painfully against his chest knowing how close he'd come in one night to oblivion, first from The Morrigan and then from Lise. Thankfully she'd been aware it'd been the were who'd begun the fight. With Lise, there were never any bodies to recover, a mystery he'd always wondered about. What happened to the souls she made disappear? Did they simply cease to exist or were they sent to some sort of purgatory even death couldn't reach?

"Dirty fae." Bezel's sorcerer appeared out of nowhere, wearing a mightier-than-thou sneer.

Cian turned to look at the slender frame of Bezel's bindsman. Any empathy Cian had once held for the sorcerer's ultimate fate melted.

"Come now, demon. I'll not cavort with the likes of him." He stamped off, heading toward the exit. "I'll have to speak with Lise about this."

Bezel stared at the retreating figure of his bindsmen. "On second thought, Cian, you'll probably be cleaning up my mess sooner than later."

Cian glanced at the exit as the sorcerer stepped through. But something else caught his eye.

His raven-haired witch.

Her brows were lowered, her lips parted, and she was projecting an intense feeling of confusion.

Not good.

Chapter 5

Where have I seen him before? There was something oddly familiar about the man at the bar.

Eve studied him, perplexed as to why she couldn't seem to rip her gaze away.

His hair was long. Longer than most men wore it, trailing to just below his shoulder blades. The soft blue lights illuminated the black-and-white strands, making them stand out in a bold relief of ebony and ice. It looked natural if only because he wore the look so well, which intrigued her more. What man had hair like that? Not normal.

The man was a chiseled beauty. He went way beyond handsome. Sculpted cheekbones. Square-cut jaw. Long, strong nose tapering into a full, firm mouth.

Just looking at him made her feel as if she'd bitten into decadence, and her body definitely noticed as hot shivers coursed down her spine. Her breathing increased by a notch.

Like two magnets being drawn together, he finally looked her way. Mesmerizing eyes the color of sea frost held her enthralled.

Those eyes.

A thread of a memory tried to worm its way out.

"Gorgeous, isn't he?" Celeste grabbed her elbow.

Startled, Eve jumped. "What? Oh…him?"

Her sister's full red lips curved. "Mmmhmm."

She could lie, but the drool on her face was a dead giveaway. "Yes." Her stomach clenched.

He wasn't just gorgeous. He'd fully crossed over into the hot category.

"He's gotta be vamp. Too pretty." Celeste smacked her lips. "Just my type. Too bad he's looking at you like you're dinner. I wouldn't mind a nibble before bed. Yum."

Eve grinned. "You're pathetic, Cel. There *is* such a thing as knowing too much."

"Pft." Celeste rolled her eyes. "Please, you're my sister. You've heard worse."

"Heard the panther he pounded call him a fae," Eve said low. She knew all about them, but had never seen one for herself. Fae were said to be a dangerous seduction, leaving many a human to mourn lovers lost to their deaths.

But beneath the mythic beauty of a fae also lay a deadly history. Eve hadn't been around during the Great Wars, but she'd lost several ancestors to the treachery of the faerie.

No one wise cavorted with them. Damn shame too. The tantalizing daydream of sleeping with the enemy never sounded more appealing. So long as it was tall, dark, and handsome over there.

Celeste narrowed her moss-green eyes. "No way," she said with conviction. "He's missing the ears. Definitely vamp. Besides"—she shrugged—"you know fae aren't permitted in Club X. Lise would have kicked him out long ago."

"True." Eve smiled, her thoughts again veering toward the gutter. Suddenly he was even more appealing.

He was still staring at her with that same intensity, devouring her. A hot shiver traveled down her spine. The man was erotic turned flesh.

His looks made her think of a pirate, legs spread wide on the bow of his ship, hands resting casually on his hips. That long hair would be whipping behind him, white shirt exposed, tanned flesh peeking out, like one of those heroes on the covers of a cheesy romance novel.

Eve rolled her eyes at the image, and if it weren't for the fact that he was so darn sexy, she'd have turned and walked away.

She imagined those full lips nuzzling her throat, maybe even the sharp scrape of fangs against her flesh. Liquid heat crashed between her thighs.

Down, girl!

"Hey, babe." Celeste's calm voice cast a spell, dragging Eve kicking and screaming back from her carnal thoughts. "You're spitting energy like a firework. Turn down those projections, please. I would rather not know how sex-deprived my little sister is right now. Thanks." She rubbed a hand down her arm. "Jeez, Lise worked a number on you."

The fine hairs on Eve's arms stood on edge. "Ugh. Sorry." She turned her back on the man. "I don't know what Lise did to me. I feel like a big ball of horny right now. Get me out of here before I embarrass myself."

"Too late." Celeste grinned and flipped her golden braid over her shoulder. "And good luck trying to get Tamryn away from that bear."

Eve followed Cel's pointing finger to see Tamryn with her arms wrapped around a big hulk of a were, laughing. He was a nice, dark ebony. A werebear. Just Tamryn's type. She always did go a little nutso over them. Something to do with the myth being true. Eve hadn't wanted to ask more.

"Well," she sighed. "Maybe we can stay a little longer."

* * *

"Eve. Celeste, this is Harry," Tamryn said, making quick introductions.

Eve stuck out her hand. "Hey."

His grip was firm, the skin rough but pleasant. He grinned, revealing a straight row of white teeth.

"Hey, witchy woman."

Her lips quirked and she shot Tamryn a look. *Witchy woman?* Only through sheer will did she refrain from rolling her eyes. Like she hadn't heard that one before.

Tamryn seemed oblivious, a goofy grin on her face.

"Right." Eve dropped his hand, not altogether happy with the way the bear kept pinching Tamryn's ass. Her sister had terrible taste in men. "Well, let's go, please. I'm tired."

It was well past midnight, the time when all the baddies went bump in the night. Sorry, but she wasn't really in the mood to become someone's light snack.

She thought of frost-blue eyes and smirked. Well, for the right baddie she just might.

Eve walked quickly through the club, down the stairs, and out the entryway. As soon as she stepped foot outside, she took a deep breath. The city smelled of salt, fish, and danger. It quivered below the surface, like a pot of water two seconds before boiling. San Francisco always seemed on the brink of erupting into violence. And she loved it.

This was home. Truth was, she felt more at peace living alongside the so-called evil. Maybe because she was one of them. Solidarity in numbers. It was comforting. Peaceful, even.

Her sisters and Harry finally caught up. Eve snuggled deeper into the black leather trench coat. It was just this side of nippy tonight, but that tended to happen living so close to the bay. Regardless that it was nearly springtime.

They walked.

Minutes later, Harry growled low in his throat, alerting her a split second before her natural instincts kicked in that something was really wrong. She stopped walking. An unmistakable prickle of danger danced across her flesh.

The sisters huddled close. They linked hands and waited to see if the threat would pass and leave them be, or insist in drawing them into a battle. Fear thundered in her ears as she listened to the sounds of night. The soft lap of water against rocks, the buzz of flickering streetlamps. She closed her eyes, searching, stretching, her senses.

A soft bump. The distinctive crunch of bones. The sound slithered down her spine and coiled around her heart.

She opened her eyes. Whatever *it* was, was in the alley.

"Tamryn," she hissed. "What the hell is out there?"

Tamryn's violet eyes were wide. "I can't place its aura."

Things were going from bad to worse. Tamryn was a rock. Her

powers never backfired. She'd always been depended upon to get a read on a person's aura and tell the sisters what it was and how to prepare. Run, stay, or hide. It was creepy not knowing what lay up ahead.

She licked her lips, the uneasy feeling that they were walking into a trap making her breathless.

Celeste groaned. "Great time for your powers to fizz out on us. What do we do now?"

Harry was in the halfway stage between bear and man. His muzzle was there, but the incisors weren't. He was still able to talk. "There's no other escape. We have to cut through the alleyway. Just follow me. We're four to its one. We should be fine."

Then he dropped to his knees and switched to bear. Black, thick hairs tore through his skin. His feet and hands transformed into large, heavy paws. Lethal-looking claws ripped through the toes. He was frightening in were form.

Eve liked him a little bit better for it. But just a little.

Harry lumbered forward and they followed.

Each step she took sounded like thunder to her ears. She tried to hold her breath. She didn't want the thing to notice them at all.

This wasn't some vamp or were out for food. This thing could only be an ancient if it'd been able to block Tamryn's mental push, and from the frantic sounds of slurping, it was enjoying itself way too much.

Her gaze shifted around the slithering shadow of the alleyway. The sounds were getting louder. They were close.

A blur of red standing beside a Dumpster caught her eye. Its silhouette was man. It didn't move. Her skin crawled, like the feeling of having a thousand maggots roll across her body.

Eve bit her lip, thinking it might be the ancient something. But the slurping was still going on a little farther up.

She clenched Cel's hand so hard she bunched the fingers. Her sister hissed and glanced at her.

Eve pointed at the Dumpster, but the man was gone.

Icy fear rammed through her skull.

Then suddenly the night exploded with sound.

Harry was standing on his hind legs, swiping with a massive paw at a hunched figure.

The figure roared and with a taloned hand ripped into Harry's stomach. The bear snarled and rammed its head into the creature's shoulder.

It stumbled back, but didn't fall. The thick stench of blood filled the night like a beacon. Soon it would attract every vamp and were to the area like a shark's feeding frenzy. They needed to end this now.

The sisters formed a circle and began to chant. A red haze seeped from the silver talismans hanging around their necks. The large center stone of Eve's necklace, a ruby, began to glow with heat and shots of red flame. It was the manifestation of their power. It grew bigger, wider, transforming into the image of a burning phoenix. Orange flames snapped and popped from the body of the bird. Its great golden beak rose into the air, and it let out a piercing scream of warning.

But the fighting between Harry and the creature was far from over. The creature grabbed Harry around the middle and threw him against a brick wall. The side of the building shuddered and cracked. Dust and stone flew through the air.

To throw a half-ton bear through the air like it weighed no more than a feather brought fear, sharp and twisting, to Eve's gut. What was this thing?

She didn't have to wait long for an answer. The creature unfurled from its crouching stance and faced them, half in and half out of shadow. A streetlamp illuminated its features.

"Oh my god!" Tamryn breathed.

A chill black silence enveloped them.

Demon. It was a demon. They couldn't contain it. Not without its true name.

It advanced. Each step deliberate. Slow. Toying with them. Lavender eyes, set in a farm-boy face, glowed with malice.

Her heart slammed against her ribs and yet she couldn't rip her gaze away, like watching a train headed straight at you. Knowing you had no chance to escape the death that awaited on impact.

As one, the sisters hurled their phoenix into the advancing form of the demon. The demon hissed and spit, swiping at the burning fire as the phoenix gouged into his flesh with its dagger-like beak.

The battle was intense and the sisters trembled, trying to contain their energy as the demon ripped and clawed at their bird.

Sweat beaded on Eve's brow, her body ached as she pushed her will at the creature. Black tracks of ooze slid down the demon's sun-kissed face, but it wasn't enough. With one mighty swipe, the demon cowed the phoenix and twisted its head off, shattering the illusion and knocking the sisters to the ground, spent and shivering.

Small stones and rubble bit into Eve's cheek. The chill from the asphalt seeped into her pores. Her jaw clattered as the numbing cold of ice traveled through her veins, freezing her from the inside out. They'd used too much magick; she had none left to defend herself.

Blearily she looked for her sisters, fear hammering in her heart for their safety.

Then her eyes widened as the silhouette of the man she'd seen standing by the Dumpster appeared by the demon's elbow. He was whispering words she couldn't decipher.

The demon grinned and then his gaze zeroed in on her. That's when she knew…

She'd been marked for death.

Chapter 6

Cian watched as one by one the sisters left the club, followed closely by a large were.

He rolled his neck from side to side and waited. Last thing he wanted was to have the bear catch wind of his scent.

The women wouldn't know he was friend and not foe. Never a good idea to startle three witches and a bear. Rubbing his skull, he nursed his drink. He should have gone up to her when they'd made eye contact; he should have introduced himself, said hi at least. All of this, what he was doing, following her around like some lovesick stalker, it just wasn't him. He didn't act this way, ever. But he didn't know how to do *this*. In all the years he'd walked as death, he'd never felt a need to know someone. He had no skill when it came to approaching the opposite sex, to simply talk. He clenched his jaw, he should have at least tried, but every time he contemplated doing it, his pulse would race and his tongue would feel ten times too thick in his mouth and he'd lose every word in his head.

Reaping a soul didn't require him to learn how to interact with others. So now he just felt like an ass sitting in a bar thinking about a woman he desperately wanted to meet and not having one damn clue how to do it.

He glanced at the clock wall. The club was still packed to capacity at one in the morning.

Five minutes passed before he felt it safe to follow. Scrubbing a tired hand down his face, he stood, ready to call it a night himself. First he needed to make certain that his witch made it home safely. Tomorrow he'd come up with the impossible plan to keep her safe from The Morrigan's clutches. And maybe figure out some way to initiate contact without letting her know who he really was.

He didn't stand a chance in hell of coming up with one, but he was working hard at being more positive.

Positive. He snorted. *The Morrigan will roast my head over a spit-fire while Dagda chomps on my bones. How's that for positive?*

With a growl he covered himself in stealth and moved quickly through the club.

Death.

He stopped and turned.

Lise stood toe to toe behind him. She'd moved so quickly she hadn't even blurred.

Lise.

She smiled. *You should hurry.* Gray wisps of hair curled around her delicate face, giving credence to the illusion of frailty.

He frowned. What did she mean?

And then she was gone. Not even a trace of her remained. Cian shoved blunt fingers through his hair and refocused on his witch's lifeline.

He wasn't sure when he'd started thinking of the dark witch as his, but somehow it seemed right.

Suddenly there was a ripping sensation of panic gnawing at his brain. She was in trouble. He felt it. In his heart. His soul. Her fear hammered at him.

Running wouldn't get him to her in time. He opened the portal between the here and there with a swipe of his hand.

Immediately he was engulfed by color. The shifting lights a dizzying blur as he attuned himself to her spirit.

Fire rammed through his body, down his skull, and into his hand, turning it skeletal.

Not now. Please.

He moved quicker than he'd ever dared before. He fell out of the portal to his knees, landing in a putrid, brackish puddle of water.

Vertigo slammed through him. The world shifted out of focus. Dark fear, sick and twisting, filled his nostrils, his head. A carnivore devouring his soul, driving out all sanity, all reason, until only a mad desperation remained.

She needed him.

Now!

That thought gave him impetus enough to stand and fight off the overwhelming sensations. What he saw made his insides clench.

Bezel was crouched before her fallen body. Her sisters were thrown aside, their bodies contorted into unnatural positions. They didn't look broken, just unconscious. The were was slumped half in a Dumpster, a stunned look on his face.

The prickle of another reaper shot down his spine. He turned to see Frenzy in shadow.

Stupid, Cian. You failed her. You should have sensed the trap.

He clenched his jaw as the dark haze of fury blanketed his mind. He ran, slamming his shoulder into Bezel's, throwing the demon to the concrete.

Bezel hissed, his lavender eyes swirling with needles of red. The demon was mad with the taste of blood. One drop was all it took to bring out their baser instincts. Cian stood in front of her prone body, his arms outstretched, his legs bent into a fighting stance. "Bezel," he growled, "she's mine."

The demon jumped up, his normally gregarious face split into one of insanity. He licked his incisors. "Cian, move aside. I'll kill you if I must." His voice was hollow and gravelly, like the rumbles of an earthquake.

Cian glanced at Frenzy, and that's when he noticed the silvery thread of illusion netted across the alleyway. Frenzy had cast a chimera and incited Bezel into the fury.

Cian couldn't see what illusion he'd used, but knowing that a demon responded to blood the way Bezel was doing now, he knew that was the likely culprit.

"Frenzy, quit the chimera," Cian barked at the silent figure.

Frenzy shook his head, his silver eyes sparking with amber flame. "I'm sorry, Cian. I cannot."

His hands clenched, there was no other choice but to battle the demon and fight off the illusion through pain.

"Move, Cian!" Bezel howled.

When Cian didn't move, Bezel pounced on him. The demon was in a rage, ripping and clawing at his face.

He hissed as a talon tore through his cheek. Warm blood oozed from the wound into his mouth.

Cian grabbed Bezel around his scrawny farm-boy neck and

squeezed. Appearances were deceptive, though. The scrawny neck was as tough as steel, refusing to give way under his grip.

Bezel wrapped his legs around Cian's waist, constricting like a python's deadly squeeze.

"Wake the hell up, Bezel," Cian repeated over and over, trying to snap the demon out of the chimera.

The demon snarled and slammed a fist into Cian's chest, taking the breath from his lungs. He dropped to his knees, bringing Bezel down with him, aware enough to roll them away from her body.

This had to end now. It was incredibly hard to overcome a reaper, but he felt too close to it for comfort.

With one last shot of adrenaline, Cian snatched Bezel's arms and yanked them behind the demon's back, pulling them up higher and higher.

Bezel struggled to free himself, but to no avail; he was trapped. Cian planted a knee into the demon's lower back for leverage. Bezel howled with rage, kicking at his balls.

Cian hated to do this, but there would be no other way to stop the demon when he was fully entranced. With a swift upward stroke, he snapped both arms at the wrist.

"Bloody hell!" Bezel cried, bucking Cian off his back and crawling away on his forearms. Instantly, the silvery net of illusion faded. The chimera destroyed by Bezel's pain.

Dragging air into his lungs, Cian hung his head, spent. His body felt like it'd been thrown into a trash compactor. Everything hurt. But he couldn't rest, not now. He stood on shaky legs and made his way to her. Using his essence, he created leather gloves and slipped them on—he couldn't risk the chance of accidentally grazing her with his skeletal hand.

Then he picked her up and cradled her slight body to his chest. He trembled, and not from her next-to-nothing weight. She was so soft. Her scent wrapped around his body like a gentle embrace.

Cian glanced at Frenzy.

Frenzy sighed. "You know I'll have to come back."

He nodded. "Please, no more this week, Frenzy. Make this fair and give me a fighting chance."

Frenzy didn't move or say a word.

"Swear it," he growled when Frenzy failed to respond.

The reaper gave a slow nod. "For the kinship we share, I give you my word. But you know the queen is not bound to this oath. I'll do what I can." Then he swiped his hand, opening the portal between the here and there and stepped through, vanishing.

"Cian, you dirty bastard." Bezel chuckled. A dark-green mist sheathed the demon. The snap and crack of bones reforming sounded. "You knew how to stop me." He shook his head. "You're either incredibly stupid or just plain screwed in the head."

Cian licked the corner of his mouth, tasting the drops of pooling blood, the spreading ache of his wounds a constant throb. "Both."

The demon snorted and hooked his thumb over his shoulder. "Mortally wounded my bindsman. He's in the Dumpster, I'm sure praying for your services right now."

"I'm sure."

"Anyhow"—Bezel frowned and shoved a fist through his close-cropped hair—"sorry 'bout this. Lost my head. All that blood, then she showed up. Couldn't stop myself."

Cian shook his head. "She's safe, that's all that matters."

"Yeah." The demon shook his head and walked off, hands shoved deep into his pockets, appearing yet again as nothing more than a harmless frat boy on his way home from a late-night binge.

Cian couldn't contain a sigh of relief; she was safe for now, at least from Frenzy. The Morrigan could still choose to send another. He fervently hoped that Dagda could somehow get her to agree to the terms. The fae god had sent him back to his dark witch after all. Surely he had some vested interest in protecting her as well.

For now, he'd bought some time, and that was all that mattered.

But it was not enough. Not nearly enough.

* * *

Eve groaned. *Did I die?*

Pain flared through her head like a nova about to burst.

Probably not. I hurt like hell.

All she could remember was demonic purple eyes, the taste of sulfur on her tongue, and finally, darkness.

She shivered, feeling cold. But this wasn't a normal chill. This was a marrow-deep, soul-sucking abyss.

Eve wanted to scream, rage, and cry all at once. Tears welled in her throat. A hollow, mind-numbing void consumed her.

Sharp bursts of pain came lightning quick and stole her breath. It was like an ice pick ramming through her brain.

She hissed through her teeth. Panic and fear for her sisters hammered at her heart. Were they okay? But she couldn't open her mouth to speak when every breath hurt so badly.

Eve whimpered, on the verge of hysterics.

"Shh. You're okay. Demon bespelled you. Rest. You are safe."

The voice wrapped her in a pool of silk. Warm fingers ran gently across her forehead. The touch comforted, anchored her to the present and away from the hellish nightmare of a stalking demon. The needle-hot pain slowly subsided down to a low throb.

She relaxed into the warmth, the touch. The last of the lingering ache faded away like mist over rolling waters. Finally able to take a breath without the flare of pain dulling her senses, Eve opened her eyes.

Frost-blue and gold eyes collided, along with a wicked sense of déjà vu, though she wasn't given much time to think about that odd prickle.

Instead she was sucking in a breath when the reality of who held her finally seeped through her sluggish mind. His gaze was a soft caress that seemed filled with hunger. The kind that promised danger and lust and dark nights.

A hot shiver ran down her spine and filled her with liquid heat. The quick glimpse of him at the bar had not done the man justice. Not a blemish to mar the sculpted beauty of his face. He seemed made of marble, every feature chiseled and clearly defined.

For a split second, she wondered whether the body under the clothes was just as carved, and a warm curl of desire tied her gut in knots. His breath tickling her neck made her aware of other things. The rise and fall of his chest. Her arms wrapped around his thick neck. She was filled with a sudden need to run her fingers through his hair and see if it felt as silky as it looked.

The stranger gently sat her down but she didn't back up or move away. For some reason the thought of putting distance between them never crossed her mind.

"Are you okay?" he asked, grazing a finger down the side of her neck.

Goose bumps trailed a fiery path across her flesh. She winced when his fingers ran over two hard bumps. "What is that?" she asked, a bit breathless and dizzy.

"Demon's kiss. Befuddles the mind. Makes it easier to dominate."

"Eve." Tamryn's voice broke her trance. Eve jumped and turned, nearly bowling her sister over in the process.

"What?" she snapped with embarrassment.

Tamryn narrowed violet eyes, her gaze sharp and assessing. Celeste crept up behind Tamryn, groaning as she rubbed her left temple.

Both sisters were scratched and banged up. Tamryn wore a nasty gash over one eye, while Celeste had a long vertical cut up one cheek. Otherwise, they looked to have fared the fight in one piece.

"You okay?" both sisters asked at once.

She nodded, knowing by the glint in their eyes that she'd been projecting again.

For once can I just lust in private?

Celeste gave her a small smile, then turned her attention to the stranger with a raised brow.

"Oh." Eve turned toward the man, his blue eyes threatening to hold her captive again. "This is…"

"Cian," he said, his gaze never leaving her face.

Her cheeks burned. The man was intense. Oh, but who cared. He was totally hot.

Lame, Eve. So lame.

"Cian," she repeated slowly, tasting the vowels.

Harry grunted in the background as he fell out of the Dumpster to the unyielding pavement below.

Tamryn rushed to the were's side.

Celeste, the most curious of the three, held out her hand in welcome first. "Well, thanks for the rescue. That demon went totally ape. No way we could have handled that without your timely rescue."

Cian nodded. "Glad I was around to help." He bit his bottom lip and glanced back at Eve.

She wanted to squirm under his hot gaze. Carnal thoughts knocked at her door.

Tamryn shuffled up, her shoulder braced under Harry's arm. Harry leaned against her heavily, looking slightly worse for wear with his cracked lips and swollen eyes. That was going to be one hell of a mug tomorrow.

They each glanced at each other, an uncomfortable tension growing between them.

Finally Harry blurted out, "I'm going home."

"Wait," Tamryn said and turned to Eve. "You gonna be okay if…"

"Yeah." She nodded, knowing her sister felt a need to tend to the sickly. Though if you asked her, Harry was really milking it with that ridiculous woebegone expression on his face. Pathetic. Men. Catch a little cold and it was like doomsday; their world was thrown into a tailspin.

"Go. Go." She shooed Tamryn and Harry off. "Just be safe and call me when you get there. K?"

Tamryn nodded and walked off, murmuring soft words of encouragement.

"Oh brother," Celeste said in an aside. "That bear's begging to get a poor-baby lay. Well, I hope Tamryn's smarter than that. He's not gonna stick around after tonight, if you ask me."

Eve nodded, not really paying much attention to her sister. She couldn't stop herself from repeatedly glancing at Cian. It was more than just the good looks. There was something about the quiet, unpretentious stranger that beckoned her. Somehow he seemed so familiar. Yet she knew his face was not one she'd ever have forgotten. What was it? The nagging thought teased at the back of her mind.

And yet the memory just wasn't there. Infuriating. She wasn't going to be able to go to bed until she put the mystery of the man out her mind. She sighed. Nothing for it; she was in for a long night.

Cian was quiet, watching the alleyway warily. With a gentle grip he held her elbow and steered her and Celeste in the opposite direction.

"I'll walk you both back. Death still walks amongst us."

Chapter 7

H ow dare he commit to that oath?" The Morrigan growled her disgust into hers and Dagda's chambers.

Dagda hooked his thumbs together, quiet and contemplative. The Morrigan stalked through the room. Her black gown trailed behind her agitated march like shadow.

She whirled on Dagda, pointing her finger directly at his chest. "How dare he?"

He shrugged. "I couldn't say."

She flared her nostrils, the ivory of her skin mottled with anger, her eyes a glowing red. Dagda inhaled her rage with each breath he took. It stretched inside him, powerful and malignant, spreading its poison throughout his body. He was immune to her sorcery, but the mortals had never been. This was how his queen incited her wars.

She looked like a warrior priestess, her multihued hair crackling around her head as a charmed cobra. "I'll obliterate Frenzy for this."

He took a deep breath. These were icy waters and he needed to tread lightly. "And what would that accomplish, Chaos?"

"Why do you care?" she snapped. "Is that any concern of yours?"

He cocked his head, feigning disinterest.

She narrowed her eyes, stalking toward him, slowly, methodically. "Why do you continue to involve yourself in these matters? What aren't you telling me?"

"Nothing that concerns you, dear queen." His tone was velvet edged in steel.

A wicked grin curved her lips. "So, we are once again at an impasse, fighting on the opposite side, it would seem."

He inclined his head.

The Morrigan licked her lips, now only mere inches from his grasp. Every nerve in his body was aware of her, the energy thrumming through her veins, the fire of fury in her eyes.

"A wager?" Her black brow cocked in challenge. "I get to the human first, she dies, as do Cian and Frenzy."

Dagda grabbed her wrist, yanking her into his lap. She was stiff, but only for a minute. Then she relaxed and began to rub her nose down his neck.

"What makes you assume this is about the mortal woman?"

She bit his left earlobe. Gentle at first, then hard enough to get his attention and make him wince.

"Don't play the fool, Dagda."

Shifting, he moved her directly over his cock. Her eyes widened and she wiggled her bottom on him, making him groan in response.

"Fine," he said, voice husky and full of desire. "I win and they live. Those are the terms."

"What about the week Frenzy committed to?" Her warm breath, spiked with mint, tickled his nose.

Digging his fingers into her waist, he strained against the desire to rip off her clothes and have her now.

"We let them have it and begin in earnest six days hence."

She nipped the corner of his mouth. He tittered on the brink of an explosive violence.

"Maybe. Then again, maybe not."

"Six days. Minimum."

She inhaled. "Three."

"Chaos," he growled, "that is not acceptable."

She sucked on his bottom lip. "Five. But that is all I'm willing to pledge."

Clenching his jaw, he knew bargaining for more would be futile. When his queen set her mind to something, she was as unshakeable as stone. "So be it. It is sealed. I bind you to your oath."

The air quickened with a hot rush of fire. Wind howled through the room, knocking books from shelves and glass containers from desks. Gradually the gale died and an unnatural lull filled the chamber. The pact had been sealed. To break it now meant eternal damnation.

She smiled, a delighted glint in her royal-blue eyes. She looked happy, ready to gloat. That didn't bode well. The queen hid a secret. He could almost see the cogs in her head spinning. She'd already formulated her method of attack. The Celts called her the goddess of war and strife for a reason: rarely could anyone outmaneuver The Morrigan in strategy.

He frowned, only guessing at what she might be thinking. Knowing his queen, it would be something ingenious and devious. It was now up to him to figure out a way to thwart her. For now, his thoughts were of other things. With an animalistic growl he claimed her lips for his own.

**

The Morrigan sat up, clutching the sheet to her breasts and watching the slow rise and fall of her king's chest. She slipped on her robe and tiptoed out of the room. With silent steps she walked down to the rack room, Frenzy's flogged and bloody body still hanging from the chains.

She smiled, admiring her handiwork, and walked up to him. His breathing came out in short, shallow gasps.

"Listen to me," she leaned in and whispered in his ear.

He turned bloodshot eyes to her. Even after all this, fear did not glitter in their depths.

"I'm releasing you. Find the witch"—she cocked her head—"don't take her soul." She paused, leaving the rest unsaid. By the question in his eyes, she knew he caught her meaning. Not taking one's soul had nothing to do with not harming. There was a difference. She lifted a brow and nodded, then continued, "Follow her. Gain her trust if you can, and when these five days are up, kill her."

"I vowed a week," he said through clenched teeth.

She grasped his chin, pulling his face toward hers. "Five days," she hissed, "that is all. Follow her, then kill her. Is that clear?"

He ground his jaw and yanked away. "I'll do as you say, my queen." The words lacked warmth. No matter. What did she care whether death groveled at her feet, so long as they were loyal. And Frenzy was *very* loyal.

The Morrigan narrowed her eyes. "See that you do. I'm offering you penance, Frenzy. Don't make me regret it."

His nostrils flared. He reminded her of a caged panther: incredible power and deadly grace.

"I want no contact except for the day before her death. Come to me at the witching hour. I'll make sure I'm alone."

He nodded.

"Good." She tipped her chin and ran her hands down his back, doing something she rarely did. Heal.

A black mist flowed from her palms into him, sealing the lacerations and stitching the flesh together. She was not of the great healer bloodline, but what she had was good enough. Within hours he'd be whole, for now, this would do. She reached up and released his bonds.

He rubbed his wrists. Hair like a sea of fire crackled around his head.

"Here." She shoved a pewter amulet against his chest.

He trapped her hand between his, yanked the chain from her cold fingers, and looked at it, then at her.

She pulled her hand back and growled, "So that Cian does not detect you. If you are to be around his mortal, your mark will be all over her. Cian cannot detect the subterfuge. Keep it on at all times. You'll remain cloaked by the charm within."

Silver eyes narrowed, a dangerous gleam of madness burned in their depths. Grinding his jaw, he slipped it over his head. Muted blue light flared from out the amulet, covering him. He shone palest blue and then the light faded, swallowed into his flesh.

Frenzy was now undetectable to any fae. They could look at him but all they'd sense was the mark of mortality. Warm satisfaction seeped through her veins. Everything was going according to plan. There was no way she'd fail.

Who'd suspect the treachery she was about to put into motion?

She smiled.

"And how am I to get close to her?" He yanked on the amulet, gruff voice full of displeasure.

She patted his cheek, a mocking smile tilting one corner of her mouth. Impatience built inside her chest. The heaviness of budding anger settled in her gut. "Have you forgotten all your skills, Frenzy? Perhaps I was wrong in keeping you in my court so long." He fingers trailed up the ridged scars of his bare back. "I could always find another if you don't feel up to it." With a deft flick of her wrist she sank one of her nails into his flesh, not deep, but enough to draw blood.

He growled low in his throat and pulled out of her grasp. She laughed and licked the stain of blood off her nail.

Silver eyes swirled. Frenzy was so unpredictable, so animalistic, on the verge of insane. With none of Cian's weakness toward mortals, he was the perfect scout.

"Wait out the night. You'll know what to do on the morn. And for your sake, do not fail me again." Then she turned and fled back to her chambers and the warm body of her consort.

* * *

Eve's heart was in her throat. Fire scorched her lungs as she ran barefoot through a wild thicket of trees. She gasped as sweat poured freely down her forehead.

The footsteps were gaining on her, crashing through the trees, swishing aside the blades of grass. Stones bit into her feet. She felt the sticky wetness and knew she bled, but she couldn't stop. She had to keep running.

She pushed herself harder, her arms pumping, her muscles screaming in protest.

It was so dark, the sliver of moon the only light around for miles. The footsteps were close.

An icy chill swept down her spine. She glanced behind her shoulder, ignoring the stinging pain of tree branches slapping against her cheeks.

A dark silhouette followed, a barrel shape ripping through the woods with purpose.

A paralyzing fear gnawed at her brain. *Keep running. Don't stop.*

She twisted around trees, jumped over fallen branches. She slipped on a pile of dead leaves, her bloody feet making it slippery and wet.

She scrabbled for purchase, her nails clawing at the dirt until she stood upright.

Breath on her neck.

Oh goddess.

Fingers grazing her back.

She tried to run away. Hard hands clamped onto her waist, pulling her down. Eve screamed through her teeth, her ankle twisting out from under her as she fell hard and wrapped her arms around her head.

Her heart was like the toll of bells, pounding in her throat, her head. A whispering wind riffled through the woods. Crickets chirped. Owls screeched and wolves howled.

Nothing happened. The breathing was still heavy, lungs grasping for air, but nothing was happening. Curiosity was a burning thing. Who was this? She had to see. Cautiously, she dropped her arms and opened her eyes.

"You," she whispered, her fear turning to shock.

Solemn blue eyes studied her. Cian knelt before her.

"I'm sorry. So sorry," he said, tracing her jaw with his knuckle. Then he leaned in and kissed her.

Eve shot up, pushing the covers off her legs. Her breathing came in short, sharp gasps. Her bedroom was bathed in shadow, the only light coming off the red lava lamp sitting on her dresser.

She blinked, trying to clear her head of the dream. Her mouth was dry, stale. She got up and wrapped herself in a bathrobe, rubbing her temple and releasing a shaky breath.

Shot full of adrenaline, her veins thrummed. That had felt so real. She touched her cheek, not feeling a physical sting but remembering the sharp slaps with a clarity that astonished.

She looked out the window, at the safety of the city, miles away from any forested area, and wondered what the dream had meant.

It was dark outside, the moon a thin crescent dangling in the fog-banked sky like a silver pendant. She leaned her head against the cool glass and closed her eyes.

Why had Cian been following her? Chasing her? Why had she felt such fear of death and then only comfort?

Dreams were real for her. Not a prophecy of what would happen, but a way for the subconscious to show her something she wouldn't normally see.

She sighed. Maybe a nice cup of chamomile would help settle her nerves. She opened her eyes, ready to head to the kitchen, when a darting shadow on the sidewalk caught her attention.

Narrowing her eyes, she held still, waiting to see the figure move again, her nerves taut. But after a minute of standing still, her legs began to shake. She shook her head, her hands trembling as she glided away from the window.

Chapter 8

Frenzy stepped through the gnarled oak separating realms and into the perfect darkness of Alcatraz Island at night. The sky, obscured by low-lying fog, glowed a silver-grayish color. Dreamlike. Striking.

He narrowed his eyes, studying the land. Rotted out, abandoned buildings dotted the landscape like gravestones. Mortal-crafted stone rusted by decades of salt water crashing against it. Weeds shoved their sturdy stems through long cracks in building foundations.

Anger twisted a hole in his gut. Humans poisoned the land—turned all that was beautiful into a wasteland of disease and decay. Concerned only with war and what they could own. The fae liked to believe themselves superior. But strip them of magick and beauty and they were all the same. He despised every one of them.

With a snarl he swiped his hand, opened the portal, and stepped through. It took nothing to find Cian. All he had to do was attune himself to his brethren and that shared bond between them. A shimmering trail of ebony fire tugged at his chest like an invisible bond.

The dazzling colors of the portal rolled into one with dizzying speed. Surrounded by lava-like brilliance, lights sped past his eyes faster and faster. His heart rate picked up in cadence, threatening to rip a hole through his chest.

And then…he was there.

Frenzy punched his hand through the opening and jumped out, reappearing a few feet from where he knew Cian sat crouched in shadow watching the witch he'd become obsessed with.

Frenzy touched the amulet The Morrigan had given him. A part of him hoped it would work, keep him undetectable to Cian. But another part, the more reckless side, prayed to be found. To be drawn into a fight. Right now all he wanted was something solid to take his frustrations out on.

The rotten stench of rancid restaurant oil permeated the breeze. Frenzy grimaced, curling his upper lip and exposing his canines. Mortal land: it was a nemesis he'd hoped never to meet again. Tonight with the demon had been more than enough and yet here he was again.

It had been seven centuries since The Morrigan had granted him absolution from death reaper duties and allowed him to serve as personal retinue in her court. Not that it was any fun. Being slave to the queen's whims was a leeching feeling of misery.

And yet it kept him away from the insanity of death's duties. He could still remember the utter, soul-sucking blackness of being death.

He'd take his royal crone over this any day. Rolling his shoulders back, he walked down the crooked sidewalk. The heavy footfalls of his booted feet echoing down alleyways, alerting mortals to his presence.

Most just curled up into their newspaper burrows, too drunk on Listerine to care. A few glanced up from their positions around barrel fires. Dirt-laden faces full of sorrow and years' worth of hard living etched into their brows.

He kept walking until he spotted a liquid drop of golden light. The buzz of flickering streetlamps was a discordant cadence to the rhythms of the night.

Two stories up, in an old Victorian-style home, stood a silhouette of a woman. Curvy, shapely. The witch.

Fine hairs on the back of his neck stood on edge. Frenzy whipped around, scenting death only seconds before he caught a flash of Cian's multihued hair. Cian might not be able to sense him, but there was nothing wrong with his eyes, and Frenzy hadn't thought to use essence to cloak himself. Using it now might alert Cian. So he jumped behind a row of stacked moving boxes.

Cian stood within a pale circle of light, his upturned face and steadfast gaze proof of what he saw.

The silhouette behind the window stiffened and Cian slithered back into shadow. His face twisted into a mask of hunger, pain, and need.

Hours passed. A slow, steady drizzle filled the predawn hours. Frenzy shifted on the balls of his feet. Obviously the queen's charm worked; Cian was in no hurry to leave. Muscles of his legs cramped and screamed out in protest for him to move, to walk. But he was patient. Cian wouldn't stick around too much longer. He wouldn't want to be caught by her.

Already warm rays of sunshine began to crest the horizon, draping the world in a Salvador Dalí painting of orange and pink.

A heavy sigh and shuffling steps and Cian was gone.

"Fucking death," he growled and squeezed out from behind his hiding spot, rolling his neck from side to side with loud, satisfying pops. Blood rushed to his numb limbs.

"Now what?" he drawled, studying the home in detail.

A three-story Victorian, hardly fortified. Easy access. Top two windows open, gingham curtains fluttering. Windows probably led into the kitchen or living room.

Although… He narrowed his eyes and walked across the street, stopping on the first step of the stoop. He'd seen her profile last night on the second floor. At the time he'd assumed she'd been in her bedroom. The layout of the home was strange. Maybe it was more of a loft or apartment-style home, the three floors completely separate from one another, which meant there had to be neighbors.

He walked up the last steps and placed his hand against the red door. Dew on the golden brass knocker seeped into his palm. Taking a deep breath, he reached out with his senses and immediately detected the signs of several mortals inside. First one gentle flutter of a beating pulse pressed against his skull, then another. The second was heavier, labored. Unnatural. Sick but not close to death, only the beginnings of heart disease laying waste to a once-robust body.

Frenzy was ready to pull his hand back when a third heartbeat came to him with crashing force, filling his mouth with the taste of adrenaline. The beats were getting slower and slower still, becoming little more than a pathetic attempt at pushing blood through clogged veins and arteries.

Fire shot down his arm and into his hand. He smiled, pulled

back, and snatched the glove off. Skeletal fingers appeared bold against the weak rays stretching across the city. Inside the apartment complex someone lay dying. The scent of testosterone and cigarettes filled his head. The man had lived a hard life, and now he was reaping the rewards of his fast lifestyle.

He curled his fist. The Morrigan had told him the truth: a way inside would indeed be found this morning.

The streets were empty, beds still full of sleeping bodies. None would see him, and there were no other grim reapers about. It was time for him to do what reapers did best. Frenzy swiped his hand, following the weak hammer of a pulse, and landed in a dimly lit bedroom. A crack through the blinds showed the dancing dust motes floating through the air.

In the bed lay an older man, hair a crisp snow white, skin as dark as ebony. Full lips parted on a silent gasp. Next to him lay several cats. Some with their paws on his chest, others meowing and some waving long tails through the air.

Frenzy walked forward. Large chocolate eyes rolled toward him, anguished desperation glittering in their depths. He sat on the edge of the bed, grabbing one of the man's hands into his own. "Be well, stranger. Your time is nigh; I come to see you on."

Two fat tears rolled down the corners of both eyes simultaneously. The old body jerked. Oxygen-deprived lungs deflated and burning with the brittle need of a moment's relief.

Painful, empty gasps. Like a fish out of water, struggling for breath, for reprieve. But there would be none. With one last gulp the old man closed his eyes and went limp.

It took a moment for the soul to realize it had nothing to hold on to, no body to contain it. And then slowly a blue curl of winding smoke filtered through pores and openings, pulsating and waiting for him reach in and claim it.

Frenzy reached into the chest, his insubstantial hand phasing through, and grasped on to the viscous soul. A glowing portal of white opened up before them. But before he'd release it to the spirit world, he had one last task. If he was to be this man, he must know this man intimately.

Closing his eyes, he allowed the memories to wash through him—a life full of music, joy, highs, and lows. And then there it was. What he really sought.

The witch was Eve Philips. She'd been married to Michael Philips, and they'd been his neighbors for the past ten years. Curtis Lovelace had no family, no children, no one to grieve him or miss him. He was the perfect mark. Frenzy could assume his identity, get in close to Eve, who knew Curtis well.

"Thank you, Curtis." He then stood and walked the soul toward the portal and its final destination.

The white of eternity swallowed the soul and faded to darkness, leaving him with a body and several curious cats.

He sat on the edge of the bed. One cat, a fat orange tabby, jumped onto his lap and began rubbing its head against his cheek.

Soft purrs of delight rolled from out the muzzle. "Samhain." The name rolled off his tongue in a thick burr.

The cat yowled as if in recognition and curled into a ball.

The gentle patter of footsteps broke him from his petting trance. Above him Eve stirred, beside him a dead body lay cooling in the morning breeze.

Nobody could know Curtis had died. Not yet. With a flick of his wrist he engulfed the husk in flames. Hot enough to burn bone, teeth, anything and everything. Cool enough that the blanket wouldn't singe, that no smoke would be detected. The inferno pitch of heat so hot that in seconds the body was reduced to a smoldering pile of ashes.

He lifted the window and called to the wind to take it. A rushing breeze funneled through the room, picked up the black soot and dragged it out in an undulating wave.

Cream sheets, tangled and twisted—pushed back to the footboard—showed not a speck of dirt, blood, or fire. There was nothing save him, the cats, and an apartment full of dead memories.

There was still much work to be done.

Chapter 9

Eve shoved on a pair of latex gloves then bent over the apothecary table and ground the wolfsbane in the mortar at a furious pace. She hated grinding the stuff. If it weren't for the fact that it was a great herb for keeping out weres, she wouldn't touch it. Even the slightest touch would cause uncontrollable itching, which was why she should have been concentrating on the task with single-minded diligence. She *should* have been. But she wasn't.

For reasons that were beginning to blur, she hadn't been able to stop thinking about Cian. After that dream, and the scare of a moving shadow at the window, sleep had eluded her. Her thoughts kept pinging back and forth between why Cian had chased her the way he had and to those sinful lips that had touched hers. If only in her dream.

A golden puff of powdered wolfsbane flew from the end of her pestle, coming dangerously close to her nose.

She growled and squirmed on her seat.

Focus, Eve. Focus.

Frost eyes. Firm lips. Long hair. Chiseled body. *Oh yeah, baby.* Not working.

She stood and dropped the pestle with a dull thunk onto the table and walked to the minifridge, pulling off her gloves. She opened the refrigerator and squatted, staring at a row of water bottles. She could really go for a screwdriver. A little vodka, little OJ. Breakfast of champs.

She reached for the water with a growl.

Gonna have to talk to Celeste about keeping this fridge well stocked.

Taking a deep swig, she settled against the glass wall separating the front of Witch's Brew from the back. She hated the thing, but the normals liked to come into the shop and watch the magick being made. She was sure to assume the more clichéd version of a witch while at work. Lights, fog, hocus-pocus. And if she was in a really accommodating mood, she'd plop on a black pointy velvet hat.

It all smacked of the ridiculous to her, like she was some freak on display. However, since the tourists ate it up, the display room stayed.

Eve closed her eyes, clutching the bottle to her chest praying the chill would seep into her flesh and bank the fire the vamp had started. Those sinful blue eyes, the color of a wind tossed sea, was all she could see anymore. When she closed her eyes, when she opened them. Dreaming. Awake. They were there. That hot gaze that saw more than just the outer shell.

If eyes were truly the window to a soul, his was a deep, fathomless mystery. One that she was more than willing to explore.

I'll probably never see him again.

Her hand shook at the realization that she cared. A drop of water splashed onto her shirt. It had been a long time since she'd cared about anyone.

Was that what the dream had meant? After Michael, all she'd ever felt was fear, and then he'd come along. Cian. She couldn't explain it, but just by being near him she felt safe.

Michael. What am I doing?

"Ugh! Pathetic. I hate him."

She jumped, startled by her sister's grumble. Tamryn came striding in. Her red lips a razor-thin line of disgust.

"What?"

Her sister ran fingers through her unruly red curls. "Harry. That's who. Son of a monkey's whore. Can you believe it, Eve? I actually felt sorry for the bastard."

Eve frowned, feeling totally lost. "Wait, wait. Back up. What happened last night, Tam?"

Tamryn's violet eyes narrowed. She picked up a stoppered vial of wolfsbane and scraped at the black seal with a long red nail. "He kicked me out. Said I was too much trouble. Not worth the lay. Of course, he says this after I brewed him the healing potion. Self-righteous, officious..."

Eve tried her hardest not to laugh at her younger sister, but as her descriptions of Harry became more colorful, she couldn't contain the grin. A minute later her sister was still on a roll.

"...unholy mating of a bear and horse's ass..."

That was it. Tears started rolling down her cheek. "Tamryn, stop," she choked out. "You're gonna make me—"

Tamryn snorted, a proud gleam in her eyes. "You know, I feel better now. Glad to get that off my chest."

Eve rolled her eyes, hugging her sore stomach. "Why does it

shock you? You've always had a predilection for prettily wrapped empty packages."

Tamryn threw up her hand and sighed emphatically. "Don't I know it." Then all got quiet. The back of Eve's neck tingled as her sister's eyes morphed from playful bantering to calculating calm. It was a narrowing of the eyes, a lowering of the lids.

She knew that look. She hated that look. Nosy Tamryn was on the prowl.

"So..."

Yup. She knew it.

"What, Tam?" she asked and turned her back to her sister, gazing through the glass at the normals and supers browsing through the store.

She could always tell a normal from a super. The supers headed straight to the real magick, the potent stuff that might seem benign and unassuming to the naked eye. Herbs, clay talismans, candles. While the normals headed straight, and without exception, to the more flashy items. Cauldrons, crystal balls, wands. But they'd just look at it, with awe shining in their eyes, or pick up a wand and wave it wildly about.

Foolish how they treated such powerful magick like toys. Ah, but that was normals for you. Still, she wouldn't complain. They made her wallet fat. Goddess bless them.

"You gonna tell me about that sexy man last night? You've only been broadcasting all day. Horny, sad. Horny, sad."

Her lips twitched at the accurate description. "Tam, I don't want to talk about it."

"Listen." Tamryn laid a hand on Eve's shoulder. "I know you're afraid of what you're feeling right now but, it's a natural part of the healing process."

Eve turned and studied her sister. She wore a serene expression, her eyes no longer lit with the light of fury but with compassion and understanding. Tamryn had always empathized with Eve better than Celeste could. Which might explain why the two were bonded tighter than twins.

She snorted with self-derision. "I'll probably never see him again, so all the what-ifs in the world don't matter."

Tamryn gave a small, sad smile. "That's true. Look on the bright side. At least you're feeling again, Eve. That's something, right?"

"I don't know if that's a good thing. Get back with me in about two months and I'll let you know then."

Her sister laughed and gave her a quick hug. "As for me," she said, slipping the wolfsbane vial into her jeans pocket, "I got a little revenge on the mind."

Eve shook her head. "You're terrible."

"Mwuah-ha-ha." Tamryn threw her head back in a perfect imitation of Bela Lugosi. "I know."

The chime above the shop jingled as another customer entered. Eve glanced, then felt her heart slam against her chest. Every nerve ending in her body sprang to life, and her brain cells went blank.

"Well, speak of the devil."

* * *

Cian stood just inside the store, eyes roving, looking for her. He'd been standing outside the shop all day, taking two steps forward and one step back. He shouldn't be here.

All he'd thought about last night was that scent. Her perfume of patchouli and vanilla. The intoxicating combination of woodsy spice and sweetness as uniquely her as the eyes shot through with liquid gold.

He'd seen her through the window last night staring at him. He'd tasted her fear and moved deeper into shadow. He hadn't meant to scare her. Only was watching to see that Frenzy had kept his word and that at the very least he could ensure her a good night's rest.

It hadn't worked. The rest of the night he'd sensed her pacing, her thoughts, and yet the feeling of intense confusion and doubt had settled on him, making him ache to go to her. He'd stayed away but the need to comfort her, reassure himself that she was all right, had finally made him enter this store.

Cian clenched his fists, glancing from one face to another, the gut-twisting fear eating a hole in his sanity.

He couldn't believe he'd done this. He'd sworn last night it wouldn't happen. Couldn't happen. Yet he'd broken his oath.

He'd come. Not to defend her, or even harvest her soul. If only it were so uncomplicated. No, he'd come to *see* her, pure and simple.

Standing halfway in the door, doubt and panic crowded his mind. Death cowed by a mere slip of a woman. Laughable, if it weren't for the anxiety stealing the breath from his lungs.

He turned to leave. Maybe this was for the best.

"Cian. Right?"

He flinched and reluctantly turned, dropping his hand from the door. A redhead stood before him, a knowing gleam in her wide violet eyes.

"Did you come for anything specific?" She spread her arm, indicating the shelves of otherworldly goods.

His heart pounded in his ears, threatening to drown out the mystical harmony of chanting Gregorian monks playing softly through the shop.

Cian narrowed his eyes. The sister was playing naïve, which suited him fine, because right now he was drawing a blank trying to come up with even a petty excuse. It dawned on him then how half-cocked this idea had been. He'd come completely unprepared.

"I, ah…" He licked his upper teeth, a nervous habit he'd acquired in the past century.

"You know, vamp, we've got some of the red stuff in the coolers back there if that's what you're looking for. It's kind of a hush-hush thing—FDA hasn't approved it yet, but, hell…" She shrugged, her brow arched in a wicked curve. "…if you're hungry, you're hungry. And I'd rather you rip into the red baggies than my sensitive neck."

Vamp? Had she just called him a vamp?

He opened his mouth to correct her, when he caught the unmistakable scent.

"Tamryn, stop hassling him."

That voice, all sultry and sexy. He wondered what it would sound like in the morning.

"Hello, Cian. How are you?"

Tamryn laughed and sidled off, throwing a "Good luck, Eve" over her shoulder.

For the first time he learned her true name. *Eve*, he thought. *Like the dawn.*

Eve smiled—her cheeks flushed a pearly pink. "Don't mind my sister. She can't help herself."

He grinned. The monstrous knot in his stomach began to unwind. "I, ah…" He scratched the back of his head. "…was just in the neighborhood and decided to stop in and check out the shop. I had no idea you worked here."

"Oh really?" Her teasing gold eyes sparkled with disbelief.

The realization of how dumb that excuse was hit him like a boulder in the chest.

She gave a good-natured shrug, exposing the pale flesh of her shoulder as she did it. The soft pink-and-white top seemed to glow against her skin. The black mass of hair spilling down her back only added to the ethereal vision before him. She was heart-achingly beautiful.

"Oddly coincidental in a city this size"—she smiled—"but I'm willing to give you the benefit of the doubt."

Her fingers idly toyed with the ruby stone of her silver neckpiece. No doubt the conduit to her power. Beneath the ruby-and-silver necklace she wore another chain with a pendant: a small pentagram lay at the juncture between her breasts. He couldn't help but stare a little longer than was necessary.

She cleared her throat. He glanced at her face. A knowing gleam twinkled in her eyes. Realizing he'd been caught, he only shrugged and gave a crooked grin. What was he to do? Deny it? Not likely. She had nice round breasts that he could easily imagine filling a man's hands—*his* hands—to satisfaction.

Blood rushed through his veins and down to his shaft, stirring the length of him and making him all too aware of how feminine Eve was and how neglected he'd been for the past century.

"So"—she cocked her head—"want the grand tour?" She took a step closer. Her nearness agitated him, made him want to reach out and grab her, trail his finger down her neck like he'd done last night and watch the shiver course through her body.

Her rich smell surrounded him and he inhaled deeply, nodding as he did so.

Twenty minutes later the tour was winding down. Eve took him to the final row of paranormal paraphernalia.

She pointed at a nondescript white cooler sitting in the corner. "That is, of course, what Tamryn was teasing you about."

Eve lifted up the lid and pulled out a plastic bag filled with a thick red fluid. No doubt it had to be blood. She handed one to him with a smile. "On the house."

Cian blinked. What was he supposed to do with blood? His mouth twitched, his brain debating truth or lie and the consequences of deception, but she spoke up first.

"It's type O. Universal donor. It's the cheap stuff, I know. But Celeste would kill me if I gave you anything more exotic. Little more pricey, if you get my drift." She winked.

He nodded, deciding that he wouldn't see her again after tonight, so the lie was harmless. He pocketed the packet, careful not to show his disgust at the thought of what he was supposed to do with it.

"Well…" She shrugged and looked around. An uncomfortable silence filled the gap between them. His mind had shut down the moment he'd spotted her. It seemed that Eve wasn't overly anxious to move on herself. She seemed desperate to find something to say; her roving gaze attested to that.

Then she lighted on a shelf a few feet away. "Oh yeah, I forgot." She marched over to the shelf, which was filled with cases full of highly polished stakes. Her steps were quick and excited, and he could feel the relief running off her in waves. "And these are our vamp stakes."

She laughed and he decided he liked it. A lot. It was a rich, gravelly burr. Highly sensual—he shifted on the balls of his feet, anything to get the blood circulating properly instead of just centering on his growing erection—and highly erotic. A low throb built and twisted his insides in knots. By the goddess, he'd never wanted anything more.

One night. One night to pretend he was just a man wanting to be held. Nothing more. Nothing less.

"Celeste thought it would be a great laugh to place the blood and the stakes so close together. I'm sure the vamps wouldn't agree, but…" Her lips twisted, her raven's-wing brow raised into a high peak.

"Little ironic," he drawled.

"I think that was the point. But we're in neutral territory. In order to build a shop in this part of town you have to be willing to place biases aside and cater to all. We do, Celeste just enjoys the spectacle."

He grinned. She had a nice smile.

Hearing her say the word "bias," he immediately wondered if it was a business practice on her part, or if she was one of the rare few able to forgive and forget. The words blurted from his mouth before he'd thought them through.

"What about the fae?" Just a tiny flicker, a quick flash in her golden eyes, but it was enough. "I didn't see any items here for them," he continued, disheartened.

"What could we possibly have that they'd want? They've got everything. They're the magickal, mystical, beautiful ones."

Her contempt rolled over his body like sharp barbs. Only through sheer will was he able to keep his face composed.

"No." She shook her head, her black hair swinging behind her like the sharp blade of a pendulum. "We have nothing for them here."

He gave a small nod, falling quiet. He wasn't the stereotypical fae, but somehow he sensed that really wouldn't make much difference to her. The history of the reaper was a convoluted thing, not a path he wanted to travel down at the moment, but still her confession pierced his heart.

He should say good-bye, walk away, and never return. Cian felt himself falling quickly into something for which he had no name. A strange emotion that made him restless, crazy, and consumed by thoughts of her.

Save your heart, death.

If he didn't turn away now, he'd lose himself completely. She made him feel again, and something other than quiet detachment, loathing, or self-hatred. He found himself doing things for her he'd never wanted to do before. All to please her.

The baggie in his pocket was a heavy reminder of that.

If she ever found out who he worked for, the atrocities he'd committed during the Great War—not to mention what he'd done to her husband—Eve would never forgive him. The thought alone made his stomach churn with anxiety. He couldn't handle that.

Walk away.

Eve touched his sleeve, her brows bunched, a concerned gleam in her eyes. "You okay?"

Heat shot down his spine. The time to leave had passed a long time ago. It was already too late.

Chapter 10

Eve, go home." Celeste came up behind her and smiled, her gaze flickering toward Cian. "You shift's over. What are you doing here?" The last question was directed to Cian.

"Jeez, Cel, queen of blunt." Eve bristled, not sure why she'd gotten aggravated at her sister. She turned to Cian with an apologetic smile. "What my sister meant to say was hi. Right?" She turned, narrowing her eyes at Celeste.

Her sister gave a quick nod, throwing her thick blond braid over her shoulder. "Just moody, sorry. Last customer was killing me. Some faux vamp looking for the perfect claw ring. Totally sent me on a wild-goose chase. I mean wild, like I'm digging through twenty cases, even had to grab some from the back room, and then when we found it, well…" Celeste rolled her moss green eyes, a perfect look of disgust on her face. "Wouldn't you know the little wench was *just looking*. Ugh! I need an effing ciggy."

Eve lifted her brows, sure that Cian couldn't care less. Poor man, having to be subjected to her sister's tirade. "Well, I'm sorry to hear that, Cel."

"Yeah, me too, especially since I decided to quit cold turkey last week. Dammit." Celeste turned, muttering to herself as she walked off.

Eve bit her lip, not even wanting to turn around and see the glitter of shock in his eyes. Celeste was so different outside of the shop, carefree, spirited, but get the chick in the shop and she became one raging ball of estrogen.

"I'm sorry that you had to hear that—" she said as she turned.

"Don't apologize. Your sister did nothing wrong. Sometimes it's nice to have an ear willing to listen."

Her brows twitched, a soft smile playing at the corner of her lips. "That was nice. Thanks."

He shrugged, glancing at the shelves behind her head. "Thanks for the"—he patted his pocket—"blood."

She wrinkled her nose with a smile. "That was really hard for you to say, huh?"

He cocked his head, a tight grin on his face.

Why did that strike her as utterly adorable? He was so awkward. Shy even. This huge hunk of man, who just last night rescued her from a demon hell-bent on destruction. The disparity was so odd, she wanted to laugh, but she sensed that it cost him everything he had to even say that little bit. It made her warm up to him all the more.

"You're welcome, Cian." And because she couldn't help it, she brushed her fingers over his shirt again. His gaze flicked to her face.

She didn't want this to end. It was so easy being around him, but more than that, he made her feel something she hadn't felt since Michael. Cian made her feel alive and hot and, if she was honest with herself, excited. Excited at the potential, the possibility of something slightly reckless. Being around him was like standing close to a live wire; she resonated with shocks and tremors of full-on, in-your-face lust. And while that was exciting, there was also the very real feeling that maybe there was more than just that. Maybe he'd be someone she could share things with, go to the movies with, and just hang out with. Someone other than her sisters.

There were no dreams of a romantic involvement, and the hot sex fantasy playing in her head was only lust. Not the spiritual connection she craved with a life partner. But being around him made her want to at least try to stop being the self-imposed nun she'd been for the past two years.

"Listen, are you doing anything tonight?"

He blinked. She couldn't refrain from smiling.

"I have nothing planned."

"Good. Well, I know it's dark out, but I'm not really ready to go home yet. I'd love the company, so long as you promise not to bite."

He grinned, showing off his white teeth, the canines on prominent display. A delicious shiver ran through her. Those were some nice-looking fangs. Not too long, not too short.

Jeez, since when did I become a fang lover? Goddess help me.

Everything about this man was perfect. It would have made her sick except that he was looking at her with an answering heat in his eyes.

Friend, Eve. Friend. That's all you want right now. Keep telling yourself that; you'll believe it eventually.

She broke the electric silence first. "Okay, well, I'm gonna go grab my sweater and clock out. Give me about two minutes. In the meantime, why don't you go ahead and eat, I know you must be starving after just rising and all."

* * *

Cian waited until Eve was out of view, then he turned and headed outside, finding the nearest Dumpster and tossed the baggie into it. He didn't want to hurt feelings, but there were limits to what he was willing to do, and *that* was one of them.

He leaned against the brick exterior of the shop and crossed his arms, waiting for Eve. He should have told her no. But he was sick to death of all the should-haves. For once he'd decided to go with his heart. He only hoped he didn't regret it come week's end.

A flash of red. He narrowed his eyes and twirled, his senses heightened, the prickle of another reaper traveling down his spine.

"Frenzy," he hissed. The red could belong to no other. There was silence and yet the shadows breathed. He ground his jaw, his pulse kicking into hyperdrive. Footsteps pounding the pavement, he stalked to another Dumpster, tucked deeper in the alleyway. His eyes roved the darkness. The awareness of the presence grew steadily stronger.

The bell above the shop jingled as Eve walked out.

He turned, torn between finding Frenzy and going to her. It was his hand that decided for him. He glanced down and the fingers were flesh. Whatever the hell Frenzy had in mind, it wasn't death, not so long as his hand remained normal. With one last glare into the darkness, he turned back.

The confusion written on her brows gave way to excitement as she finally noticed him walk up. She smiled. "There you are."

"Aye." He held his arm out to her, and after a moment's hesitation she shrugged and slipped her arm in his.

Inside he trembled with rage. *Breathe. Breathe or she'll know something's wrong.* He couldn't help but cast a quick glance behind his shoulder. Nothing. She never noticed.

"'Aye,' hmm? That's very archaic."

He ground his jaw; he hadn't meant to slip into the old speech. He'd broken himself of the habit centuries ago, a telltale that had become too dangerous to use. Still, his mind was consumed. The betraying pulse of death was gone, but the memory lingered on. He rubbed his jaw, stretching out with his senses, listening for something. Except for the rustle of rodents and heavy shuffle of normals, he heard nothing to indicate danger.

She raised a brow. The smile on her face slipping, waiting for his response, a nuance, some validation that he'd heard her. He took a slow, deep breath and tried to pretend that everything was okay. That she wasn't marked by death.

The truth was that everything wasn't okay. Was it? Just like the fae he despised, he looked her in the eyes and, without missing a beat, forced a smile. Cruel deceit.

She sighed, and calm replaced the tension. "I like it." She flashed him her famous crooked grin. "Sounds very chivalrous. So were you Irish before the big change?"

Whichever reaper he'd sensed was now long gone, and yet the cold reminder of her plight settled heavy on his mind. Fact was he wasn't just a man. He was here to protect. Period.

"Yes," he said, almost as an afterthought.

She shrugged her shoulders, winding her knitted wrap tighter around herself. "I've always wanted to go there. Can you imagine the old magick permeating those hills?" She glanced at him under the cover of her lashes and chuckled. "Well, I suppose you could, couldn't you?"

"I probably could, Eve."

She snorted and rolled her eyes. "Not my brightest moment. I swear you'd think I was blonde sometimes."

A passing pedestrian jogged past, accidentally bumping into Eve and forcing her tight to his side. He noticed that she didn't bother to move, even after the jogger had disappeared from sight. He didn't know why, but that pleased him. The feel of her thigh grazing his and her scent mingling with the salty air of the bay had heat traveling straight to his loins. Lights dotted the sidewalk as late evening soon gave way to the dusky painting of night.

He looked at all the faces. Studying them. Committing them to memory. The walk, though pleasant, was a façade. A pretense of normalcy on his part. And he was used to pretense. It was like breathing, eating, or sleeping to him. To survive at the courts you had to be good at faking it. Until recently, he'd always been. Until her.

The busy streets of San Francisco boomed with life. Hawkers, their silver carts of goods standing at spaced intervals on the path, sold everything from Wharf souvenirs to steaming piles of crab and chilled oysters on the half shell. A city of mixed cultures and ethnic diversity. Seemed appropriate for his dark witch. Somehow she belonged, and he understood why the supers chose to call San Francisco home.

After awhile he relaxed. Not into a false sense of security, but at least enough to enjoy what time he had with her. Nothing attacked them. For now.

Carpe diem.

They took their time walking. Neither in any hurry nor with any real sense of where to go, only content to enjoy the company the other had to give.

A crisp wind slid in from the bay and settled over the city like a wet cloak, turning the slightly balmy day into a cool spring night.

Eve smiled and glanced up at him, her cheeks filled with a red glow. "How old are you, Cian?"

"Been wondering about that for a while now, haven't you?" he teased. Funny how easily he was able to do that with her. Comfortably.

She twisted her lips. "Guilty as charged. It's a thing for me. Being mortal myself, I sometimes feel a little envious of you immortals who got to see all these times and places I can only read about."

The reminder of her mortality was like a tight band around his chest. He lifted his eyebrows and shrugged. "I'm several centuries old and my exuberance for life has diminished. It's never-ending and ceaseless, one day rolling into the next with no end in sight. In truth, I envy the mortal who can live life to the fullest; only they can understand the true depth of what it means to live. I just carry on."

She slapped him playfully on the shoulder. "C'mon. Don't be so glum about it. Honestly. What a wonderful gift you've been given. To see the rise and fall of civilizations. The changing of time and people from one era to the next. You know, I would have given anything to be around during the Victorian era. Those corsets are a sinful fetish of mine."

He chuckled. Her enthusiasm filled him, touched the ache in his soul and made him remember moments from his past he'd have forgotten otherwise. "That was a prudish era. You'd have suffocated. Women were little more than chattel to the men."

"Well, not all. Take Lillie Langtry, for instance. An actress, a business owner, and let's not forget the self-confessed mistress to a future king. It couldn't have been all that bad."

He nodded. "She was indeed the exception."

"Ha!" She wagged her finger under his nose. "I gotcha! Should have probably let you know that I'm a research enthusiast. You know, much of the gothic movement takes its manner of dress and speech from the Victorian era. It's a hobby." She shrugged like it was no big thing.

In truth, he was impressed. Eve wasn't just a pretty face, she was engaging, and he found himself drawn to her like a moth to flame—a dangerous and deadly fascination because the moth was always consumed by the light.

She shook her head. "I'm such an awful romantic. I guess I wouldn't replace the convenience of a hospital for the fact that women died during something as simple as childbirth. I only want a glimpse. Is that too much to ask?"

"Anything you want to know, I'll be happy to answer."

"Good." She peeked at him. "Were you around during the great Roman Empire?"

"Mmhmm." Memories. The acropolis. Roman soldiers. Sweat. Tears. Blood. The coliseum. Caged fighters and beasts.

She stuck out her tongue in a mock drooling fashion. "Excuse me while the history geek in me geeks out over that bit of information. Seriously. That's amazing. To think I have my own personal history book at my disposal."

He shook his head with a smirk. "Geek, huh? I don't think I've ever seen one as appealing as you. I should hang out at the library more often." More teasing. This was unlike him. Different. But he liked it.

She snorted good-naturedly and hummed with her exuberance. It settled over him like a soothing balm.

"So you're pretty old, there, vamp," she said, hedging.

"So I've been told."

She chuckled. "You're exasperating, man. Worse than a female."

His lips twitched, but he didn't answer.

A rap beat grew in volume the nearer they came to the center square of Fisherman's Wharf. A man, painted entirely in silver, stood immobile, his limbs held rigid in an odd posture, his eyes unblinking. At least until a tourist decided to walk up and take a picture next to him, then he'd reach out to yank the hat off their heads and slip their purse straps from their shoulders.

They stopped to watch for a moment before they continued on.

"So," Cian asked, "how did you sleep last night?"

She shot her gaze to him, her eyes a little wide, panicky. He tasted the faint tremors of it on his tongue.

"Awful. How'd you know?"

He indicated her neck. The mark of Bezel long gone, her flesh was a smooth, creamy porcelain. "The demon's kiss. Its effect lasts for twenty-four hours. Though I hear it brings terrible nightmares afterward. I was wondering if you were okay."

She let out a deep breath, shaking her head, a weak grin on her face. "I'm sorry. That was so weird that you'd know to ask that question. Yes, I had awful dreams last night. I didn't sleep much afterward."

"I'm sorry to hear that. You should sleep fine tonight."

"Good to know."

The closer they drew to Pier 39, the more the overpowering stench of wet sea lion filled the air. Their honking and chatter could be heard long before they were spotted lazing about on the floating wood.

The sea lions came and went as they passed the pier without a backward glance. It seemed Eve had a purpose to the meandering, which was fine by Cian. Until she started taking him on twists and turns farther away from the tourist traps and deeper into the heart and soul of the city itself.

"Where are we going?"

"I've rescheduled this appointment about ten million times, always finding one reason or another why I couldn't make it. But tonight I have company, and I feel brave. So I'm going to meet my friend and you're coming with me."

He nodded, waiting for her to explain where exactly *it* was, but it seemed that was all she'd say on the matter.

The busy section of San Francisco—filled to bursting with humans—thinned out the deeper they moved down the alleyways. Soon they were in Chinatown and cutting a winding path through tall, slanting apartment buildings.

Sirens wailed, cats screeched and hissed. A steady drip of water became a pounding, incessant noise in the background. Cian's nerves were taut, his eyes roving the dark shadows. He could feel the supers like a second skin; their individual powers washed over him and made him keenly aware of the dangers the night held. The reaper he'd sensed earlier came immediately to mind.

Again he grew anxious for her, his gaze roving through shadow, searching.

Then he caught scent of were and thoughts of other reapers fled. Many weres, and all of different variety: wolves, panthers, bears, falcons. He stopped. It was one thing to make her happy, but he refused to walk them headlong into danger. "Eve, where are we going?"

"Don't worry. It's someplace safe." She tugged on his arm.

He ground his jaw, looked around, but when she tugged again he reluctantly continued. Then he felt something, a metaphysical sensation of hands scraping at a delicate neck. Fangs ripping through a jugular. A feeding.

"Get back," he whispered, grabbing her and shoving her behind him.

A rustle of leather and exhalation of sharp breaths had every nerve in his body zinging to life. The metallic stench of blood traveled through the air like mist.

He tensed, crouching on the balls of his feet. Rainwater dripped. A steady irritation. She felt his unease. It coiled around him, gripped him in a tight fist.

"Cian, wha—" Her panic clawed at his flesh. She was remembering last night. Bezel stalking her. Harry slumped over the Dumpster.

"Shh." He placed a finger against his lips.

The bump of a beating heart echoed like gunfire in his head. A pounding thump against his chest.

Boom boom.

Boom boom.

The caustic odor of hot blood wafted under his nose. He pulled his upper lip back in a reflexive motion, filling his lungs with more of the scent.

Heart was slowing down. The beats less pronounced, growing weak and fragile. Life being expunged.

"Feeding vampire," he whispered. The sounds were coming from up ahead, a few yards away. He narrowed his eyes, searching the dank surroundings. "We're going back. I'm not walking you into danger."

They needed to leave now, before she witnessed the truth of what he really was. He grabbed her elbow, but it was already too late.

Sparks of fire raced down his right arm and into his hand. He hissed and dropped her arm, shoving his hand into his coat pocket. Electrical vibrations pulsed through his skin. He curled his fist and within seconds felt nothing but bone touching bone. With a thought, he used his essence to create gloves and covered his hand in them. Never again would he come around Eve without the protection of real leather gloves.

"Hell," he barked. Sweat stained his brows.

"Cian? What's wrong?"

"Vamp sucked the mortal clean."

A flash of black flitted past the corner of his vision.

"Bastard," he snapped, drawing the vamp out from the shadows. "You killed it."

The lithe figure of a vampire stepped away from the wall and into a shaft of moonlight. It was female. Purple hair, the color of royalty, curled down around slim shoulders. Eyes so blue they looked black stared back at him without remorse. A scarlet trail stained the corner of her mouth to her chin. She rubbed the back of her hand against her lips.

Eve sucked in a breath. Recognition. Disgust.

He pushed her emotions away.

"Who the hell cares? Homeless trash." She sneered, exposing two long and pointed canines. "Nobody'll miss him. I did the world a favor by getting rid of that thieving beggar."

How could the others forget so soon? How could they afford to be so careless where mortal life was concerned? A twisting, churning anger consumed him.

"Have you forgotten the Great War? The fragile peace between our kind and theirs? Are you ready for the consequences of what you've done?"

Eve rubbed a hand down the small of his back. He leaned into the soothing comfort of her touch.

"Consequences." She scoffed and between one blink and another stood toe-to-toe with him. Power flowed from her body. A dangerous energy radiated in the space between them.

His gaze never wavered from hers.

"This is a new day, ancient. This is my land. We rule the streets and set the laws. Not humans."

He shook his head. "That type of ignorant thinking will be the downfall of us all. Predators are solitary creatures. Humans have always, and will always band together. That is why they are dangerous, that is why you cannot," he stressed through clenched teeth, "afford to disregard them. Be wary, vamp. This world is not as safe as you'd believe."

The vampire flicked her cold gaze to Eve. Bloodred lips tipped at the corners in a sickle-shaped smile. She reached out a hand toward his witch. "We meet again, dark one."

Anger rammed through his skull, choking him. Eve was projecting. Like concertina wire wrapping its thorny barbs around his heart. His gaze flicked toward the vamp. Her eyes were wide, nostrils flaring surely tasting Eve's wrath.

"Don't you dare touch me, Indigo. Too high on blood to remember the truce? Is that it? You know the rules of this land. The laws the government set. We are never to harm our human hosts. If you don't give a damn about the Great War, then maybe you'd better start thinking about where you're gonna live next year if the government decides we're a failed experiment," Eve raged.

A hateful glare burned in Indigo's dark-blue eyes. "You think we've forgotten what your kind did to us? The lives your people stole and tried to subvert to your own will? Someday, Eve, you'll be under my thumb!"

Eve snarled and took a step forward. The amulet around her neck began to glow its purest red. "If you knew your history, then you'd know those were our *ancestors*. Not us." She pounded a finger against her own chest in emphasis. "The witches have done nothing but try and make peace. And I'm getting damn tired of being grouped within that circle of murderers and deceivers. That was them, not me."

Indigo smirked, the flaming amethyst of her hair swinging back and forth with her shaking head. "Their blood runs through your veins. If I had my way, I'd kill you all."

Every muscle in his body coiled, ready to spring into action should Eve need him. It took everything he had not to reach out and rip the vampire's head off her shoulders. This was Eve's fight, though. He'd honor that.

Eve straightened her back and held her arm out straight, fingers pointed at Indigo's chest. "Try it."

The world around them narrowed down to a pinprick of absolute silence. Air shimmered and vibrated with a killing strain. One second passed.

Two.

Three.

Five.

With a hiss, Indigo transformed into a tower of black mist then disappeared from sight.

Cian clenched his jaw, his nostrils flaring. Adrenaline still pumped through his veins, and he looked at Eve through new eyes. Pride burned a hole through his chest and settled deep into his heart.

Eve dropped her hand. Her body hummed. He walked up to her, grasping her shoulders and giving them a gentle squeeze. She swayed slightly toward him and he closed his eyes in relief.

If he hadn't been here, Eve would have bumped into the feeding vampire alone. She'd seemed more than capable of taking care of herself…this time. Still, look how wrong it went with the demon. She was strong, but not strong enough to handle every element of the supernatural.

How the hell was he supposed to keep her safe? This world was in anarchy. Creatures of the night vying for a spot, turf, a place to call their own, while normals dictated all they could and couldn't have. It was a recipe for disaster.

"You okay?" he asked.

She stood still but slowly nodded and then turned, her small hand bunched into the fabric of his shirt. "Thank you."

"I did nothing."

"No, you did. You were there." Her gaze shifted back and forth over his face. "Your presence made me strong."

He nodded, reaching out a finger to caress the side of her cheek. Her lashes fluttered. "How did you know her?"

"We own the only shop that caters to the comforts of the others."

"She's trouble," he murmured, staring at the vacant spot Indigo had inhabited. "Naïve. And foolish."

Eve pulled her bottom lip between her teeth and gave an odd jerk of her head. Her emotions spoke louder than words. Indigo was reckless. Dangerous. And she was worried.

"We need to find the body, Eve," he said and tracked the scent of fresh blood. The mist-like particles filtered through his nose, drew him to the body.

She followed, close on his heels. They hadn't walked far before they spotted him. Lying deep in shadow and in the middle of a puddle of water was the slumped form. A knitted cap, full of holes, sat askew on his head. A vacant, glass-like gaze stared into the nothingness.

He frowned. Something wasn't right about this scene. He walked up to the body and knelt in front of the man, rolling him over and looking for the pulsating blue mist of a soul needing harvest.

"Is he dead?" Eve asked, a slight tremor to her voice.

He placed his hand on the man's chest. The body was dead. Brain synapses no longer shooting off, heart not beating, blood flow nonexistent, but the soul refused to leave. It wasn't this man's time to go. He'd be taken to a hospital, hooked up to life support machines, and made to live out the rest of his days in a vegetative state.

There was nothing he could do for him. His hand had turned skeletal because the body was dead, but if the soul refused to leave, he couldn't force it.

Shaking his head, he stood. "We have to go."

"But that man…" She pointed. "We can't just leave him here."

"Eve, neither you nor I can be caught near this body. Cops will come asking questions; they'll want to tack the blame on us."

She huffed. "They have to be smarter than that. C'mon, you can't think they'd pin this on us. We'll tell them the truth…"

"And what? Look at me, look at you. We're different. The human has fang marks on his neck. You honestly think they wouldn't try to lay the blame on us? Humans are looking for a reason to overthrow the government's ruling on the supers. Voices are getting loud. They don't want us here. This would be a good PR move for them."

"Not all humans are like that. Some are fair, good, just." Her lips thinned; she was thinking about her husband. Cian sighed.

"Eve, that is the minority. Supers have become a spectacle, something different and hot right now. When we become old news, that's when it becomes dangerous. That's when the humans no longer see us as oddities or quirks but something evil and deadly that needs exterminating. What that vampire did tonight, that's going to add fuel to the fire."

"You don't know this."

The scent of unwashed humans permeated the breeze. Tramps were coming out of the woodwork, looking for clothes, food, shelter. Soon they'd stumble across him and Eve. Last thing he wanted to do was add to the casualty of tonight by defending Eve against the riot of humans finding a fallen brother.

"Yes, I do. Life is an ever-revolving thing. That's why empires come and go, because people refuse to learn from past mistakes. This is how the Great War started and unless humans and supers wake up, this is how another Great War will begin. Now come." He grabbed her by the arm and led them quickly away from the scene.

She was angry. It felt like boiling oil poured over his flesh, melting it off. He winced, hating to be the cause of her anger, but after years of dealing with mortals, seeing history unfold before his eyes, he knew things never really changed. War was inevitable. Not today, maybe not even fifty years from now, but soon.

After five minutes of silence, she sighed and glanced at him. Her churning anger slid away, replaced by a fluttering shame. "I'm sorry," she whispered.

He grabbed her hand, thankful his had returned to normal the moment they'd left the body behind. Trying to always keep her from witnessing his transformations was getting exhausting. "Don't be. You only wanted to help. Who could blame you for that?"

"Life in the big city, gotta love it."

"Yeah," he said in a monotone with a small shake of his head.

"Look." She stopped and placed her hand against his chest, halting him. "I don't want that to ruin our night. We're almost there...and I just want to have a relaxing time. We can't change what happened. So let's move on. Deal?" She held out her hand.

Grudgingly he nodded and shook it. Her smile grew even wider, encompassing all of her face, crinkling her eyes and wrinkling her nose. The warmth radiating from her to him banished the last of his doubt and anger.

"Good." She turned and walked on.

Minutes later, dim red lights of a flashing neon sign caught his eye. REQUIEM'S TATTOO. He frowned. "This?"

She bit her lip, nodding. "I'm so addicted, it's not even funny."

She had tattoos? He couldn't help but scour her body for clues. He'd never suspected. She looked free of any markings. "Where?"

Her finger traced a winding line down her back and around her rib cage. "It's not finished yet, but it's pretty big. It's my animal familiar."

He was definitely curious.

"An ivory-billed woodpecker. Very, very rare and beautiful. It's white and black, with this bright-red crest on top. I dunno"—she shrugged, her cheeks bright pink with excitement—"that poor bird. It's almost extinct, but it keeps fighting, trying to hang on. That's sorta become my mantra these days." Her lips twisted into a self-conscious smile.

"Why a bird?"

"I've always had a bond with them. I love birds. You're gonna think I'm really weird, but it's almost as if I understand them." She glanced at him from the corner of her eye and laughed. "I'm gonna run you off with all this weird talk. C'mon, let's go inside."

He was quiet, but thinking. Instantly one of the six houses of the fae kingdom came to mind. The house of feathers. Any fae belonging to that house had a special affinity to birds. Bird whisperers, they were called. He studied Eve.

It seemed the second he'd start to figure her out, she threw him for another curve. There were layers to the witch, intriguing glimpses into the real Eve, and the more he learned, the more he wanted to know.

He followed her into the tattoo parlor and as he walked through the door he felt a warm pulsation travel the length of his body. He stopped, frowning, and studied the building. A small blue glow covered the shop's exterior, the light so dull it was out of the spectrum of human range. The magick was benign but powerful as it rippled and moved like a rolling wave over the place.

Eve glanced behind her shoulder and followed his gaze. "It's a warding spell set up by me. Mingan was having trouble keeping the humans safe from the supers. Finally he decided he needed them not to come at all, and in exchange for my tat I set up the spell. A true blood can enter; if a human comes across the building, they'll walk through the door and instantly forget the past hour of their life. They'll turn around and walk away."

To hear her speak of her work in such an offhanded manner made him respect her all the more. This was no simple spell. It had probably taken hours and years' worth of knowledge to have set up something so sophisticated. He held the door open for her, following her inside.

"It's impressive."

She laughed. "Thanks for saying so."

The entire shop was bathed in a soft red light, casting everything in a surreal quality. He frowned.

"Weres see better in red for some reason; they do their best work in this lighting," she said, as if reading his mind.

A receptionist, head bent over a table, tongue sticking out the corner of his mouth as he drew a design on a sheet of paper, finally noticed them. His brown eyes widened a fraction of an inch. He stood and ran a hand over his medium-length, orange-red hair.

"Eve," he said with a big smile and walked around the reception desk. "Damn, it's good to see you again."

"Noah," she replied, walking into his quick embrace. He placed a kiss on either cheek.

"So what have you been up to? Mingan's been getting cranky, wanting to finish up that tat of yours. He calls it his masterpiece."

She laughed. "He would. No, I've been busy with work and…" She stole a glance at Cian's face. "…other things. Noah"—she stepped away from him—"this is Cian. Cian, Noah."

"Hey, man," Noah said, extending his hand.

Cian clasped it, taking a moment to do a quick study of the man. He smelled garlic, peppers, and meat. Not the sick, sweet scent of raw meat, but cooked steak, and tons of it. The brown eyes were large. The pupils dilated into catlike slits. His grip was firm, the handshake done without hesitation. Noah was not frightened of Cian, merely curious. He was a confident weretiger most likely.

Matter of fact, the entire shop smelled of were. The odor was undeniable. It was the scent of fallen leaves, upturned earth, and animal pheromones. It lingered everywhere, invaded his senses, and told him much of the inhabitants. While many of them were new to the world of shapeshifting, a few were ancients and old enough to remember the Great Wars. Immediately Cian was on guard.

Yet Noah projected no feelings of hostility or guardedness, which tamed Cian's natural instinct to protect his turf. Namely, Eve.

He clipped his head toward Noah.

"Now that you're done taking my measure," Noah said, never breaking eye contact, "let's head back to Mingan. I'm sure he'll be happy to see you again, Eve."

* * *

"Eve." Mingan stood from his Indian-style sitting position on a brightly colored Turkish rug. "It's about time, witch," he grumbled.

She laughed. "Glad to see you missed me too, old wolf."

"Bah." He swatted his hand through the air, but there was a teasing sparkle in his liquid bronze eyes.

He looked so familiar, as did this room, this place, that she experienced a temporary pang. None of it had changed, from the Asian-inspired murals along the walls to the soothing scent of lilac incense. His eyes turned soft with remorse. Obviously she'd been transmitting again, not a surprise since she had such a flimsy hold on that power these days.

Bloody bane of my existence.

He gripped her shoulder and nodded, then turned around and walked to his workbench. He indicated the cot with a jerk of his thumb. "Lie down and take off your shirt. We'll begin as soon as I'm ready." The small swatch of a gray pelt tied into his salt-and-pepper braid flitted as he moved about, preparing his station.

He brought out a silver pan filled with blue and white baggies of sterile needles. He picked one out, set it down, and then proceeded to pour the ink colors he'd need into small, thimble-sized containers. Red, gold, black, and white. All this by heart. Yes, he'd remembered her tattoo very well.

Eve wrapped her arms around herself even as she sensed the soothing presence of Cian behind her. She closed her eyes and shivered. Goose bumps burned a fiery trail across her back seconds before his large hands gripped her arms. They stood so close together, the friction of their two bodies popped and cracked with currents of static.

He leaned in, his warm breath tickling her ear. "Are you okay?"

She took comfort where she could and leaned into him slightly. His concern for her was thoughtful, banishing the insidious thoughts creeping in. "I'm fine. Just memories. Old memories."

She turned. His blue eyes never swerved from her face, the intensity of his gaze made her feel like she was about to melt into one big puddle of tingling goo. By the goddess, she could get used to that look. It made her all twitchy and excited, made her feel alive again.

"I have to get undressed," she whispered.

His face remained impassive, but his fingers jerked ever so slightly. A heaviness centered between her thighs, her nipples tightened, and her body flared to life. If she didn't move away soon, she was liable to purr like an excited kitten. Hard as it was, she took a step back and out of his arms.

Her fingers were clumsy as she undid the buttons to her gray sweater. She pushed the sleeves down and let the garment flutter to the ground. His eyes were hot, hard, and heavy. Instantly her senses became extraheightened, aware of everything. From the abrasive texture of her blue jeans to the soft velvet of her top.

The pupils of his eyes dilated, highlighting the already-vibrant iris into an even more intense shade of sparkling blue. In that moment he looked surreal and otherworldly, and she decided she liked it very much. What had she been missing all this time? She'd never made a conscious choice to stick with humans. But that's all she'd ever dated.

Then again, she'd never met someone like Cian before.

Mingan continued to shuffle around, but his sounds were like white noise in the background. There was this odd sensation filling her, like it was just her and the vamp. Nothing else. There was something so erotic about this scene that it made her feel a little lightheaded and daring.

Biting her lower lip, she inched her top up and over her head. Slowly. Deliberately. Her fingers grazed bare skin as she dropped the shirt to the ground. There was nothing normal about the excitement flowing through her veins. The knowledge that she was a woman and he was a man. It was primal. Elemental. Natural.

Clothing for her was not a necessity. She'd never been shy when it came to nudity. She'd partially disrobed in front of Mingan many times, never feeling a hint of arousal, but with Cian standing so close, his eyes so riveted, she felt wanton and heady.

In her mind she questioned why she'd brought a perfect stranger with her to the tattoo shop where she was required to go topless. Shouldn't this feel so wrong?

The beat of her heart fluttered against her chest. It sure didn't feel wrong. Far as Cian was concerned, being with him felt natural. Like sex. The more you did it, the more you wanted to do it.

And why was she thinking about sex when she'd already decided they would only be friends? But then, there were all sorts of friends, weren't there? Friends to drink tequila with, friends to watch old sappy movies with, and friends with benefits.

With a slow curling of her lips, she reached her hands behind her back and undid the clasp of her bra, allowing the straps to slide down both shoulders.

The amulet lying between her breasts tingled with the rush of power flowing through her veins. It whipped around her, through her. He had to be feeling her need.

His face was unreadable, the rise and fall of his chest steady, and yet she felt the crackle of his desire snap around her like live wire.

The cool air grazing her skin was sweet torture. She was hot and cold, fire and ice, all at once. Her nipples beaded up, tightening into tiny, painful buds.

Her lips twitched when he finally dropped his gaze from her face to her breasts. Yep. He was a man after all.

She couldn't resist glancing down at the very visible bulge in his pants. A sense of female empowerment filled her. Nobody else but her had made him rise to half-mast, unless, of course, he had a thing for ancient-looking male shifters. Then again, she was pretty sure it was her and not Mingan that'd given him that delicious-looking hard-on. A warm glow flowed through her.

Eve covered her breasts with one arm and expertly slipped her bra off with the other.

Bolts of desire whipped through her veins as his gaze pierced her body, traveling a languorous trail. Starting at her breasts, then shifting to her navel, and finally to the tip of a bird feather beginning at the edge of her ribs.

He took a step forward and her lashes fluttered. Hot liquid crashed between her thighs, soaking the crotch of her barely there thong.

"You know I hate to break up a striptease. And while I'll admit that was pretty hot, I'm not getting any younger. Sit your butt down. Let's get this thing over with," Mingan grumbled.

So okay, maybe she'd gone a little too far. But who could blame her? The vamp was so freaking hot. 'Nuff said.

"Man, I tell you what, Min, I feel the love today."

A rumbling chuckle fell from his lips. "Hey. I'm on my best behavior for you."

"Well, heaven help the customer you actually don't like."

Cian cleared his throat and shifted around. With a snort in his direction, she walked over to the leather cot and lay down on her belly, stretching her arms over her head.

Cian wasn't the only one feeling the effects of lust. She was so wet she couldn't stand it. Thankfully a woman wasn't so obvious in her desire. One of the many blessings that let her know the female form was superior.

Of course, if you asked men…well, everyone knew what men thought. Gotta love 'em.

She huffed a strand of hair out of her face, seriously rethinking this lust thing; maybe it wasn't such a bad idea to give into temptation after all. Two consenting adults giving into their bodily needs, nothing wrong with that. Nothing at all.

The small room filled with the sound of a low, continuous buzz, and she found relief in the pain of the needle piercing her skin.

* * *

Cian felt like a volcano ready to explode. His cock was full, thick, and unspent. When Eve had dropped the bra and he'd caught a peek of coral-colored nipples, he'd nearly lost it.

She'd been a vision with the black hair cascading down her slender frame, her golden eyes wide and luminous, and her pale, perfect skin glistening in the faint red light.

He clenched his hands by his sides. Visiting her had been his worst idea yet. Tattoos had no right to look so beautiful. He was marked, not by ink, but by race. All fae bore a marking telling which house they belonged to. For some it was a feather, for others, a crescent moon. For him it was a skull. Huge, and covering his entire back. Death. The mark of the pariah.

He loathed his mark and considered it a sign of servitude. But Eve seemed to delight in hers. A soft smile graced her lips. He rubbed his chest and turned his back to her, needing a distraction, something to take his mind off the woman lying facedown with the paleness of her back exposed.

The walls were covered with white laminated sheets of colored and black-and-white designs. But these weren't the classic, run-of-the-mill variety. They had flair and a signature style. He walked closer and peered down.

There was a boldness to them. Sharp color contrasts and shading. Mingan was an accomplished artist. His illustrations were precise, linear, and clean. Chinese dragons, their bodies twisted in on themselves, their red-and-gold markings bright against the black of their scales. Koi fish. Tigers prowling through woods and ripping from out the page with regal snarls on their orange-striped faces and their pointed incisors gleaming.

"Noah posed for that one." Mingan's gravel pitched voice cut through Cian's study.

He turned. "You captured the essence of the animal. It's very good."

The tattooist never looked up as he ran the needle gun over Eve's pink flesh repeatedly, wiping up the excess ink with the tip of his gloved finger. "I've had practice."

Eve turned her face toward Cian. The flow of her energy—a wash of relaxation—wound through him.

"Never seen you 'round these parts before. Cian, was it?"

He nodded, took a seat on a brown swivel chair sitting next to the cot, and focused on the lines being applied to Eve's back.

"I'm a native. Just never been to Requiem."

Mingan looked up and licked his teeth, doing exactly to him as he'd done to Noah moments ago. Taking his measure as a man, as a monster.

His nostrils flared, no doubt tasting his scent. Trying to figure out what Cian was. And he knew by the gleam in the old man's eyes that he wasn't fooled into thinking Cian was a vampire.

This was an ancient. It was in his face. He bore the knowledge of history past. The tanned leather of his flesh crinkled with age. There was wisdom written upon his brow.

"That so," he said with a bored tone and returned to working on Eve. Cian knew the truth of who he really was hadn't been revealed. There'd been a question burning in those bronze eyes, but Mingan had kept the curiosity to himself. His lazy, tranquil posture indicated he thought Cian no threat for the moment.

But there was also a barrier erected. To an outsider, the old man's hunched shoulders and bent head might be taken as a sign of concentration only on the task at hand. When in truth it couldn't be more opposite. Tension, like thick dredges of sludge, filtered through the narrow room, making it feel smaller. More cramped, confined. If Mingan could growl right now, he would. He didn't trust Cian.

Fine. He hadn't come to make friends.

"Do you have a tattoo, Cian?" Eve asked. Her eyes were wide and acutely aware of the strain in the room.

He shifted on his seat, clearing his throat. The question caught him off guard. He answered honestly. "One."

"You'll have to show me someday."

He gave a noncommittal shrug.

She closed her eyes and turned her head, giving him free rein to inspect her closer.

The flesh Mingan was inking had long, tight whorls. Scars from her accident, no doubt. And yet the skin was smooth. He wanted to know, but wouldn't ask. She'd never told him about the accident and to reveal he knew that would also expose him. Not a good idea.

Her design glistened with color. The drawing of the woodpecker was elaborate and detailed. Its body was alternating shades of white, black, and gray. On its head was a scarlet crest and its eyes were a deep-hued gold. Not just a gold pigment, but gold. It glittered as the light struck it at odd angles with each up-and-down motion of her breaths.

The bird began at her left shoulder blade and wrapped around, down her ribs. He'd never seen anything so lifelike. It didn't just look like a painting on skin, but almost as if the bird were ready to take flight. Its proud beak lifted high in the air, its wings spread.

He'd always assumed he'd hate any marking on the body. In some ways he loathed the fae and all their trappings. The marks on their body revolting to him, and yet, looking at this proud bird resting on Eve's back, he thought she was beautiful.

Chapter 11

Eve and Cian strolled down the pier, the crowd long since gone, and a purplish thread coloring the sky. Shops began to open, pulling up the steel gates they'd closed and locked the night before. Sea lions were silent save for the whistling of their breaths as they slept. There was a soft lapping of water against the rocks, it was soothing, the setting as if from a dream.

The sharp, intoxicating scent of saltwater taffy was redolent in the air. Eve inhaled, savoring its richness and wishing she could pop a chewy piece into her mouth right now. Goddess, she had a serious sweet tooth. Not a figure-friendly pastime, that was for sure.

It was strange how fast time had flown by. Mingan had seemed possessed, not stopping to talk for the rest of the night. After a while the initial pain had died down to a dull throb and she had lost herself in the needle and Cian. He hadn't talked either, just watched with such a fascination that she'd swear he'd never seen a tattoo being done before.

It had felt weird to have those intense eyes studying her like she was a rare specimen, but in a way that was oddly endearing.

She gazed at Cian from the corner of her eye. He was leaning over the wooden railing, his eyes shifting around, looking at everything and anything. As if he was searching for someone, or something. She frowned and peeked behind her shoulder.

With the exception of a few lazy seagulls winging through the air, they were pretty much alone on this stretch of pier. A rarity that wouldn't last.

Was she that boring that he kept looking at everything but her? She cleared her throat and said, "Thanks for coming along. I had fun."

Finally his gaze rested on her face. The intensity so sharp she felt numb and rooted to the spot. Yet he still radiated a thread of anxiousness, as if he wasn't comfortable being outside. And then he smiled, making her forget.

"Me too. Does it hurt?" He grazed her clothed back with his finger. Dull pain bloomed at the contact.

She grinned, masochistic enough to not want him to stop. With the pain came the excitement of his touch.

"A little, but it was worth it. It's finally done, and I'm happy."

Again he looked away, his gaze flicking to that spot where water met sky. An orange hue crested the horizon. The sun was about to come up.

Disheartened, she twisted her lips. Probably why he kept glancing away. She was selfish enough that she didn't want him to leave, not yet. "I guess you have to go, huh?" she asked.

"Soon. But…how about breakfast?" He turned to look over his shoulder at a saltwater taffy store. "There. You pulse with pleasure every time you glance at it."

"That obvious, huh?" She narrowed her eyes and cocked her head. "I thought fangs couldn't tolerate food."

He coughed into his fist, a clearing-of-the-throat sort of thing. Then he gave her a weak grin and said, "Not for me, only you."

"Won't that make you a little queasy to see me eating?"

"I can't see why."

"Well, put it that way. I'd swear you're reading my mind, Cian. I love taffy."

He shrugged. "I figured you might."

* * *

Eve gripped her brown paper sack in her fist, sucking on a peanut-butter-and-jelly-flavored taffy. The slightly salty, sweet treat gummed up the roof of her mouth. She wanted to groan, it was so delicious. Cian had even helped her pick out a few. He'd looked at the Neapolitan-flavored taffy with such longing it almost made her feel guilty for buying it.

Almost.

"So," she said after swallowing the last bit of taffy, "I guess you should be heading back soon."

He twisted his lips and looked toward the ever-brightening horizon. They were about fifteen minutes away from full sunrise. Not really a problem for vamps, since they could travel at the speed of light. But she had to admit that, in a very small corner of her heart, she'd enjoyed his company more than she'd thought possible. So much, in fact, that she was going to have to make it through this workday on about three hours of sleep.

Not that she had any regrets.

"It would seem so."

"I'm sorry. I didn't mean to keep you out so long. Well, maybe just a little…" She shrugged when he laughed. "…but when Mingan is in his trance, there's no rushing him."

He grabbed her wildly swinging hand, his thumb grazing her knuckles. Fire sizzled through her pores.

"I had a good time tonight."

Her heart jumped into her throat, and she couldn't do more than nod.

"Come on, Eve." He still held her hand and dragged her behind him. "I'll walk you home."

"Maybe I'll lead, since you don't know where I live."

His lips twitched. "Sure."

She led him away from the business district and deeper into the brickwork jungle of homes, toward a three-story Victorian. The outside was a rich ivory. Ivy clung to the siding, its green fingers sliding up toward the triangle-shaped roof. People often described her place as a gingerbread house, which was a fitting description. Horizontally narrow and vertically long, with the customary chimney on top.

"Well, this is me."

They stopped and she stepped up on the stoop, facing him. "Big house."

"Yeah. I wish I could say I own the entire thing, but it's been renovated into three separate floors. I live in the middle." She hooked a finger behind her shoulder. Refractive light from a teardrop crystal hung in the window.

He nodded.

"So…" She bit her bottom lip, hoping he'd say something to break the gathering uncertainty. The silence became strained and more uncomfortable as time wore on. A golden wash crested the sky; the warm rays of sun were beginning to descend over the San Francisco Bay.

What was supposed to happen now? Shouldn't they say goodbye and move on? It'd been so long since she'd dated. She wasn't sure what she was supposed to do anymore. Where minutes before she'd felt alive and sexy, bewitching, now she was beginning to feel more and more unsure, like a young girl who'd just glimpsed her first flash of naked flesh.

And speaking of naked flesh…

She peeked at him. A five-o'clock shadow framed the rugged contours of his face. The startling blue of his eyes looked down the street. His shirt molded to the curves of his lean, muscular chest. Memories of him holding her against his body filled her with aching clarity. The slide of muscle against her breast as he'd inhaled, his sharp scent of leather filling her nose.

Her nipples beaded up, pushing against her bra almost painfully. She was hot and achy, her flesh tingling with expectant hope that he'd lean over and kiss her, tongue her, right here in public for all to see.

This was bad. But good. But oh so bad.

She couldn't help it; she glanced at his cock and wondered what it would look like. Would it be long and veiny, thick, and smooth? A wet tide of desire slammed between her thighs and she squeezed them together. Her heart fluttered a rapid tattoo in her chest.

A small groan spilled from her lips and when he turned his gaze to her, they were wild. The pupils dilated.

Hot pulses of energy flowed from her veins. She knew she was projecting but didn't give a hot damn. Goddess, she had to be the easiest lay in the world; no man had to wonder where she stood with them. And she wanted Cian now. But she wouldn't ask. She still had some pride left.

His eyes bespelled her. She was drowning in them and at the same time wondering whether vamps really could hypnotize with just a look. "I had a great time. I, ah, have work tomorrow, well, today…" She smiled. "…but later, of course. After I wake up. But if you want to come up for a drink, I've got a nice blush I've been saving…"

I'm babbling. The worst part was, the more nervous she got, the worse it became.

"Oh god, of course you don't drink wine. Blood, right? Duh. And I don't want you nibbling on me." She gave a nervous start. "I mean…"

She rubbed her neck, her face heating scarlet.

He glanced at her feet, his lips twitching. She wanted to groan. The most humiliated she'd ever been, bar none.

Then he stiffened, his gaze shooting past her shoulder. It was creepy, watching his eyes narrow, his nostrils flare, and his pupils dilate.

An eerie feeling, like cold fingers running along the back of her neck, made her turn. Elms waved gnarly branches in the wind. A dog yowled, keeping up a steady stream of high-pitched barks. A normal San Francisco day.

She could see by the look on his face something wasn't normal. Another feeding vamp maybe, a were feasting on some bones? What?

"You okay?"

His gaze rolled to her, and he smiled though she knew it was forced. The light didn't reach his eyes. He rubbed his hand down her arm. "I'm fine. But I've really got to go."

He grabbed her hand and dropped a scorching kiss on her knuckle. It was long and hard with smooth, firm lips. The heat from his mouth transferred to her flesh, raising goose bumps and her temperature.

"Of course you do," she hissed and leaned closer. An inch stood between her burying her nose in his hair and rubbing herself against him like some horny cat.

Move that kiss farther north or south, she thought wickedly, *and I'd be one happy woman.*

"See you around, Eve," he said, then turned and walked away.

It wasn't until he was out of sight that it hit her. He'd never asked for another date. She'd practically thrown herself at him—*okay, who am I kidding? I did throw myself at him, practically begged for some monkey lovin', and he walked away.* She was lubed and ready for the pounding of her life.

Eve groaned. She had an itch that needed to be scratched and nobody to do it for her. Frustrated, she growled. "What were you thinking?"

She thunked her head against the door, lifted up, and thunked again. Except this time her head didn't contact with wood but air. Losing her balance she took a step forward and tripped over the last step. She was falling, and fast. The polished wood floor loomed before her like a specter out of a nightmare.

Throwing her arms out she braced for the fall, a muffled yelp trapped in her mouth, her heart in her throat and a death grip on her bag of taffy.

Thin, surprisingly strong arms grabbed her.

"What the…"

"I got ya. Didn't know you were standing outside there, Eve. Woulda been more careful opening the door."

Nervously she patted her hair down and waited for the jackhammer stutter of her heart to subside. Dark chocolate eyes stared into her own, a spark of something burning in their liquid depths.

Her smile slipped with the nervous flutter of wings in her stomach. He looked the same, but the eyes. The eyes, something about them felt wrong. Unconsciously, she took a step back.

An agitated meow echoed in the brightly lit stairwell, breaking her from her trance.

"Mr. Lovelace, oh jeez…" She rubbed a hand across her brow. "You scared me. I was leaning against the door and—"

The bold ebony of his skin crinkled with laugh lines as he adjusted his tweed jacket, brushing out the wrinkles.

The uncertainty that had squeezed her heart to the point of pain vanished. This was Curtis. Just Curtis.

Tired. That's what it was. Still, the taste of weird still settled on her tongue.

"You know what"—she swiped her hand through the air and gave a shaky laugh—"never mind. It doesn't matter. Thanks for the rescue."

Last thing she needed to do was tell her neighbor how much of a donkey's butt she'd made of herself.

His smooth, easy grin made her smile in spite of herself.

"Happy to do it when they look as pretty as you."

"Oh man. Nice. That was smooth, really smooth. Bet you say that to all the ladies. Tell you what, if I were thirty years older…" she said, falling immediately into the easy banter they'd always shared.

"Pft." He waved his hand. "No way. If I were thirty years younger, you'd never stand a chance. Pretty charming in my day."

She cocked a brow. "Is that so?"

"Mmm. Yes, ma'am. All I had to do was play a few licks on my Gibson." He demonstrated for her, his nimble fingers playing the air guitar. His pink tongue was sticking out the corner of his mouth, head bopping to music only he could hear. "Oh, I swear. I was a player. Had dolls lining up around the corner to hear ol' Curtis play the strings."

She laughed. "I bet you did. Wouldn't hurt that you're a witch, probably enchanted them with a little love charm, eh? Admit it."

Eve walked to the silver mailbox affixed to the wall and checked her mail. Nothing but bills. She rolled her eyes, shoved the envelopes underneath her arm, and returned to her conversation.

"Well. Gotta use our goddess-given talents. Whatever they might be." He winked and played with his white goatee, then his eyes took on a faraway look. The memory, whatever it was, must be nice, because a slow, soft smile crept over his features.

The honesty on his face made her feel a little voyeuristic, like she was glimpsing something private. She shifted on the balls of her feet, wondering if she should walk away and leave him to his thoughts.

Meow.

A tabby cat slid between her legs, rubbing the length of its body along hers with a contented sigh.

"New cat?"

"Sure is." Curtis bent over and picked up the feline. "This is Samhain. Orange color makes me think of the season."

"Hello, Samhain." She scratched the furry head between its ears.

The cat closed his eyes and purred. For some reason the reaction made her think of Cian. Thinking of him brought on a new rush of fire through her limbs.

She cleared her throat. Goddess, she really needed to get control over herself.

"So this makes what, cat number seven?"

He nodded. "One can never have enough cats."

She yawned, walking toward the base of the stairwell and planting her foot on the bottom step. Exhaustion was finally beginning to claim her and blurred the edge of her vision.

"Spoken like a true witch."

He smiled and tipped his cap to her. "Well, g'day, Eve. I'm taking Samhain to the park."

"Yes, you too, Mr. Lovelace."

"After ten years, I think you can call me Curtis now."

She paused. Why was he looking at her like that? Studying her? Not like prey. Not the way fangs would a victim but the way someone did when they were really interested in everything you had to say. Like she was really that fascinating. "Curtis, then."

He nodded, tipped his hat to her, and left.

"Weird. Goddess, my life is so weird," she muttered with a small shake of her head and walked up the stairs. No sooner was she sticking her key into the lock than she heard the phone ringing.

"I'm coming," she yelled, like that was going to do any good. "I'm coming, don't hang up. Don't hang up." Maybe it was Cian. Oh goddess, maybe she hadn't made such a mess of things. Of course she hadn't given him her number, but she was listed in the white pages. There was hope. Right?

Her stomach twisted in on itself and flopped down to her knees.

She rushed into her living room, throwing the door closed and running to pick up the phone on its fourth ring.

"Hello," she said in a breathless whisper.

"Ohmygod, she's just getting home, Cel!" Tamryn squealed into her ear.

She winced and pulled the phone away until the shriek died down. To say that her heart dropped would be an understatement. It flat-lined. Okay, she should have expected this, but jeez, it didn't make it any less of a letdown.

"Oh, hey, Tam." She plopped onto the couch, covering her eyes with her hand and sighed. With disgust, she tossed the bag of taffy to the ground.

"Oh, hey. Please, try not to sound so excited."

"Tamryn, if this is the inquisition, I'm not in the mood." She kicked off her shoes and grabbed the cashmere blanket draped over her couch.

"You're just getting home and you expect me not to be curious."

She closed her eyes. "Sure, you can be curious."

A nagging, throbbing pain started at her sinuses and traveled up her skull. She frowned, rubbing the bridge of her nose. It wasn't so much painful as annoying.

She took deep breaths, counting backward from ten until the headache slowly subsided then vanished all together, leaving just as fast as it'd come.

She rubbed her forehead, exhaustion creeping in. Headaches tended to be a thing for her. Especially when she got overly stressed or tired, and right now, she was both.

A sudden rush of sleepiness filled her limbs. She couldn't keep her eyes open for anything. They felt like weights, repeatedly slamming shut.

Fuzz was growing in her head.

Tongue was feeling heavy. Just the thought of having to form a coherent sentence seemed too much right now.

"Eve." Her sister stressed her name. "I hear you falling asleep on me."

"Mmhmm."

"Fine. But you're telling me later."

"Yesh," she slurred and hung up the phone.

Chapter 12

Cian doubled around the sidewalk, running behind the homes. Searching, his heart pounded a furious tempo. Damn it. He'd seen him. There'd been a flash of red and a bright flare of silver, lurking around the bushes of her home. Frenzy.

Cian increased his speed, pumping his arms and legs, almost flying in his haste to get there. He could use the portal, but that might attract attention. As slow as this was, it was his only option. Finally he reached her house and walked around the backyard, searching through bushes. Not even out of breath from his exertions.

"Get your ass out here," he seethed.

He smelled death. Felt his brother to the depths of his bones. His ears rang in recognition. "Frenzy, you bastard…"

And then there he was, standing before him, as nonchalant as could be. His hair glowed a vibrant red in the first rays of sunlight; mercurial eyes staring back at him.

Something inside Cian snapped to even think of Eve in danger. He took a step forward with fists clenched tight. One wrong word, one wrong move, and he'd defend what was his to his dying breath.

"What the bloody hell are ye doing here?" he hissed, glaring at the man with open hatred.

A heartbeat within the house snagged his attention. It was the slow, gentle hum of one in sleep. A soft shimmer of happiness. A rushing warmth of joy. Eve.

His lashes fluttered. Even in sleep, she gave him peace, kept the madness at bay.

"I'm a casual observer, Cian. As are you." A corner of Frenzy's mouth tipped and his gaze rolled over Cian's face. "Maybe a little *more* than you. Accent's creeping out, old man. Thought you had more self-control than that."

Cian ignored the sarcasm. "Why are you here? You swore me a week."

Frenzy cocked his head. "Swore, yes, which the queen quickly stripped me of. Five days, Cian. That's all she's willing to pledge."

His jaw clenched. Not enough time. He glanced up at the second story, almost as if he could peer through the wood into her room and at her. He sighed and shoved his fingers through his hair. "So in five days you'll kill her? Is that it?"

Frenzy crossed his arms, his black shirt rustling with the movement. He wore black on black. Black shirt. Black jeans, with bright-red hair, silver eyes. The man was the freaking embodiment of the stereotypical fae. Perilous. Fatal. But with that sharp, lethal grace that had women wetting themselves.

Jealousy flared. It was bright, hard, and heavy, choking the air from his lungs. He'd never been a jealous man, but he didn't want this bastard around her.

"She's got five days. Leave her the hell alone."

The reaper lifted a brow, canines in prominent display. Fangs weren't the exclusive domain of weres and vamps; faerie had them too.

"Jealous. Ohhh," Frenzy breathed, "so unlike you."

He raised a fist, ready to tear into him.

Lifting his hands in a mock show of peace, Frenzy took a step forward. The air grew charged with the promise of danger. Cian shook as adrenaline coursed through him, but he refrained. Barely.

Two behemoths: both were powerful and each of them knew it. But neither of them was willing to back down.

"Don't worry, Cian." Frenzy walked around him and said to his back, "She can't see me."

Cian twirled, but Frenzy was already gone.

* * *

Frenzy walked to the bedroom mirror in Curtis's home and grabbed the silver amulet off the nightstand. He grinned, slipping the cold metal back on. It settled against him with a soft blue glow.

His plan had worked almost better than he'd hoped. Cian was now on his toes, alert and aware of Frenzy, ready for anything he might pull.

"Dumb bastard. It won't be Frenzy harming Eve." He watched as his skin turned mahogany rich, his eyes a dull brown. Curtis stared back at him.

Cian thought he had it figured out. He was on guard for Frenzy's deception. It made the rest so easy. *Too* easy.

While Cian was watching him, he wouldn't be watching Curtis. Now it was just a matter of slipping in and making her trust him.

He'd tasted her fear this morning, for a brief moment she'd sensed something amiss. Still, all he'd had to do was smile and talk about their past and she'd relaxed.

Too easy.

A meow snagged his attention. Samhain sat on the couch, licking a paw and staring at him. Cian stalked toward the cat. He'd taken the other six to shelters. What the hell was he supposed to do with so many cats? He didn't have time to sit and feed them—but not this one.

He swallowed and sat, pulling the tabby onto his lap. Dark, dangerous memories flooded him.

Hurt. Pain. Desperation. Blood.

No, he hadn't been able to give this one away. It reminded him too much of her. Adrianna.

He swatted the memories away, nostrils flaring as the old anger, old pain, seeped into his veins. It felt like a dagger piercing his heart, bleeding him dry. Samhain stared back at him with slanting green eyes, bright with intelligence and curiosity.

He touched the soft velvet of its fur and stopped thinking. Shut off the thoughts, the memories, and relaxed into the soothing melody of the cat's vibrating purrs of approval, the soft, steady bumps of Eve's beating heart a lullaby to his ears.

Chapter 13

I had a feeling you might show today," Lise said without turning. She was seated at the empty bar of Club X, reading a newspaper, a half-eaten bagel in front of her.

"You know me too well," Cian drawled. The anger of earlier still lingered in his blood. He sighed and glanced around the club squinty eyed. It was strange how a vibrant, pulsing room at night could look so foreign and sterile in the morning.

Red stools sat empty and in a row, pushed tight against the bar. The DJ's booth now silent. A blue velvet curtain covered the stage. Instead of seeing rows of martini glasses filled with differing shades of liquor on the polished countertop, he noticed they were now hanging by their stems, locked into a metal frame above the bar.

Lise cleared her throat, snatching his attention back to her face. She lifted a gray brow, folded the newspaper, and set it down on the bar with a soft thud. Folding her arms in front of her, she waited patiently as he approached.

The unnerving white of her eyes pinned him. "I suspect you found her in time, then."

"I did."

"Sit, please."

He took a seat next to her and began to idly toy with the lid of a saltshaker.

"I'm glad you did. Her potential means much to me. But"—she waved her hand through the air—"I cannot violate the rules of choice anymore. Either you'll save her or you won't. However, that is not why I asked you here today."

His mind was abuzz and his stomach knotted into a sickening band. *Potential. Potential for what?* It was obvious that Eve's life was in peril; even a normal could sense that. What bothered him, though, was her choice of words. What the hell did "potential" mean? There were a million possibilities. None of which put him at ease.

"No, Cian. I cannot. I know you wish to know, and perhaps I've said too much. The twelve live by a strict code. We cannot alter free will. Not even for an immortal. I've given you the best information I could. Decipher it if you can, but ask me nothing."

He slumped into the seat as a great weight settled in his chest. More mystery. Less truth. What was happening, and why was he the last one to know? Especially when it concerned him or Eve? Damn the immortals and their stupid ethics.

With a bitter twist to his lips, he glared at her. "Who's the twelve?"

"My sisters. I am one of the chosen twelve."

"What is a chosen? You're such an enigma. What are you really, Lise? *Who* are you?"

"Mmmm." She cocked her head to the side. "That is a mystery for another day."

He growled. "I don't know why I expected you to be any different from them."

She only smiled and placed a wrinkled hand atop his, giving his fingers a gentle squeeze. Comfort, like from a mother's hug or that familiar sweater, rolled through him. He took a deep breath, pissed and tired. Weary to the bone.

"I know what you want to ask, but I can't help you."

He shot her a glance. "Who, then? How the hell am I supposed to stop The Morrigan? This is a fool's errand. You know it. I know it…"

She shrugged, slipping her hand off of his. "Maybe. If that's what you feel, then yes. A fool's errand. But even fools get lucky."

He heaved a long sigh, disgusted with all the riddles, all the mystery. Why couldn't someone give him a straight answer for once?

"Because this is not something I can orchestrate. You must have free will to decide it. There are many paths you can take. Only one will lead you where you want to go. You just have to trust yourself."

He rolled his eyes. "I see you can read minds."

She laughed and sat back. "I do have a disgusting habit of meddling, I suppose. Hard not to when you've lived as long as I have. You'd be amazed what I hear."

"I'm sure." His heart grew even heavier as he continued flicking at the salt lid with single-minded diligence.

"Oh, Cian. I wish I had a better answer for you. I do. Really. But I can't help you in this."

"Not surprising. Seems no one has the answers to give."

"Stay the course. Travel the right path." The whites of her eyes shone with ivory brilliance.

He huffed, finally sliding the saltshaker away from him, and dropped his head into his hands. Ideas ran through his mind. *Find Frenzy. Kill him.* Though that wouldn't work, because The Morrigan would only have to send another reaper, and they'd be right back where they started. *Grab Eve and run. Hide deep underground. In some other country. Just away.* But once they started running, they'd never be able to stop, and she wouldn't want that. She had a life here. Not to mention that if he tried it, then his truth would come out, and who was to say she wouldn't rather choose death than trust her life to a hypocrite? His heart twisted in his chest. *One last option, then. Find The Morrigan—*

"Don't you even think it. NO!"

Jerked from his thoughts, he turned to her. "You're not helping me. Dagda's told me nothing. That is a good plan. At least I'd keep her alive."

A fiery blast rippled through him. Her nostrils flared as she vibrated with anger; it flowed from her, quickened in the air, and was like shards of ice ripping through him.

He grimaced and grabbed at his chest.

"Maybe now you'll listen to me."

In his anger he snapped the glass shaker, scattering salt upon the table and floor.

"I said no. Now leave it be. You're walking the true path, Cian. Have faith in my words. Don't give up now, because if you do then she's truly lost. Now…"

He narrowed his eyes as she turned to him with a large smile and snapped her fingers. A goblet of firewater suddenly sat before him on the table.

"Drink. She's not been feeding you, I see. Vampire, is it?" Lise chortled with laughter, shaking her head. "Ironic, that. So close and yet so far."

He snatched up the chalice and chugged the smoky taste of overripe cherries down his throat. "Don't make light of the situation, Lise—"

"Pft. Light of the situation. Me talking about it won't make it any better or worse for you. I find it hilarious."

That was a fine way of describing his personal life. He ground his jaw as anger ate a hole through his chest. "Somehow I don't see how any of this is funny."

"How did your date go?" she asked without batting a lash.

"Are you kidding me?" Was she serious? He glanced up at her over the rim of the cup, then back down, and up again. She was still staring at him, questions blazing in her eyes.

"Really?" he murmured, completely caught off guard. This woman, an ancient…and all she wanted to talk about was monotonous things like his dating habits?

Not that Eve wasn't attractive and didn't make his head spin with lusty thoughts. Honestly he couldn't understand why he wanted to be around her all the time, why, no matter how hard he tried, he couldn't stop thinking about her. About that almost-kiss on her stoop. How even now she made his blood hot. The fact that Lise would care about his love life boggled him.

A soft smile tipped the corners of her pink mouth. "My mind is consumed by so many things; I find solace in the mediocre."

He slammed the cup down onto the table, not able to figure out if Lise was mocking him or not. "I don't know why I came here to-day."

"Hell, Cian. If something as small as chatting throws you into a tailspin, no wonder you're driving yourself sick where Eve is concerned. It's really not that big a deal. Here, let me help you. 'Yes, Lise, the date went fine.'" She gave him a pointed stare.

"Ah," he growled. "It wasn't a date, just a chance meeting."

"Oh"—she rolled her eyes—"I swear you take me for a fool. A chance meeting you orchestrated by making sure to stand outside her shop for hours."

"Minor."

"I'm sure."

Despite himself, he grinned.

"Where are you staying?"

He drummed his fingers on the table. "Does it matter?"

"So in other words, outside her window?"

"If you know the answers, why do you keep asking the questions?" He couldn't contain his impatience.

Lise stretched her arms over her head and yawned. "You need someplace to stay."

"Not really. I don't plan to stick around too much longer."

"Uh-huh, right. Look, I've got a flat in Presidio Heights, Baker Street. Nice little place, nothing fancy. I'll lend it to you for a while. It's already been made over into a bachelor's paradise, so no foolish knickknacks around to blow your cover or make her think you're gay."

This conversation felt very one-sided to him. She kept dismissing him offhand as if what he said was of little consequence.

"No."

She frowned. "And why not?"

"Because."

"Please. Give me a better reason than that."

"Because I don't want to keep lying. Goddess, Lise, I've said too many already. The lies are getting hard to keep track of."

"You haven't lied to her."

"An omission is a lie."

"Pft." She huffed. "Trivial. Valiant though stupid your reasons are, I'll give you one of my own. She believes you a vamp. Vamps have addresses."

"I'm not a vampire, Lise, and that's exactly what I'm talking about."

She narrowed her eyes at him. And he read it for what it was: a warning that that she could and would lash out at him again if he continued dismissing her.

He took a deep breath, completely out of his element where this seemingly frail woman was concerned. He shifted around on the seat, glancing toward the exit, fingers fidgeting on his lap. She made him feel like a wee bairn. He growled and her smile grew wider.

"She's going to ask questions. Wonder why you've never taken her to your home. Things for which you'll have no answer."

"I'll tell her the truth."

"I don't think so. You honestly think this to be the right time to tell her? A day, two days after meeting?"

She paused, and when he didn't answer, she took his silence for agreement with a jerky nod.

He sighed. "I can't keep doing this. All these feelings, and worrying about The Morrigan, Dagda...too much. I'm through, I'm done."

His words were pure bravado. The truth was that the thought of her with another man, gazing up at him with adoration in her liquid-gold eyes made him want to claw and roar and tear things apart. It was a soul-sucking void of heartache and jealousy.

Lise covered his fist with her own, compassion written across her face. "I know you like her. You can't afford to disillusion her, not now. She'll be mad when she finds out. Furious. But if the foundation is solid, then she'll come around. Unfortunately, I'm telling you to continue the farce." She shrugged. "Not a good way to start a relationship, I know. In your case, there is no other option."

"Relationship," he scoffed. "What relationship? I took her out on one date. In four days, Lise, she's dead. What use is there in me binding myself to her? I'm too fucking stupid to figure out how to save her."

He was so frustrated; everything was differing shades of gray to him, so much truth being denied. Who could he turn to for answers? Help? He closed his eyes, a bitter pill to swallow. This had never been anything more than a fool's errand. Which is probably why The Morrigan staved off Eve's death for a few days: in the end, it wouldn't matter anyway.

"Look at me."

He opened his eyes, sick at heart and desperate.

She gripped his arm, her white eyes beginning to glow. "I am on your side, Cian, believe it or not. I want you to succeed. I've told you all I could and then some. Think it over and choose wisely."

He ground his molars, thinking of her sweet scent, her crooked smile, and her glossy black hair. Too late. It was already too damn late. He could no more leave her to her fate than he could walk by a body needing harvesting. He did what he must. He defended what was his.

"Take my home," Lise said, cutting into his thoughts.

"How did you even know to offer me your home? That I'd come and see you?" He scrubbed his hand down his face. "I didn't even realize I was coming to see you until moments ago."

"I know things." She shrugged.

Frustrated, he glanced away. She knew things and wouldn't help. Irony was Lise probably knew exactly what he needed to do to keep Eve safe. He looked up but didn't say anything, just stared.

"Ahh, reaper, I've always sensed in you a great sadness. Recently, I've tasted hope. Faint, but there. Believe me when I say, you'll know what to do when the time comes. Instinct. Remember that. It's instinct. Not thoughts. Now..." She made a grabbing motion in the air, then turned over her fist and opened it, revealing a shiny metal key. "Take my home."

Lise dropped the key in his hand and stood. "Twenty-one sixty-six Baker Street."

He fisted the key in his hand. "I'm not afraid of you, Lise."

She threw her head back and laughed. "You should be."

Chapter 14

"Ouch, that bad, eh, kid?" Celeste grimaced and laid a sympathetic hand on Eve's shoulder seconds after she'd told the truth of how her date went and ended.

"So no good-bye kiss? He just walked off after your, um…garbled good night?"

A rare moment of silence in the store had allowed the sisters time to gossip and poke fun at her expense.

"I know." Eve groaned and bent over the glass display of crystal balls by the cash register. She shook her head on her crossed forearms. Her breath fogged up the glass.

Kill me now. Ground, open up and swallow me.

"Oh jeez, she's got it bad." Tamryn shook the bright-yellow feather duster. "I mean, that was pathetic," she said with a laugh.

Eve stood and glared at her unrepentant sister, who at this very moment was pantomiming her most humiliating come-on line in a singsong, obnoxious, girly voice.

"Thanks for that, Tam. I mean, you're the best sister ever."

Tamryn lifted a red brow and twisted her lips. "Seriously, Eve. It wasn't that bad."

Her heart flipped in her chest. Sleep deprivation and humiliation could wreak havoc on a girl's self-image. She sniffed. "You think so?"

"Yeah. I mean, if he comes back, then you'll know he *really*"—she stressed the *e* long and hard—"likes you."

"Oh jeez." Eve slapped Tamryn's arm and marched into the storeroom. "And here I thought you were being nice. I shoulda known better," she threw over her shoulder.

"Ha. You know me. Never a dull moment."

Both sisters snickered as the bell above the door jingled heralding the arrival of another customer and a temporary cease-fire to the very embarrassing conversation.

Thinking about it still made Eve want the ground to open up and swallow her. Why had she leaned in for that kiss? Yeah, so things had felt right, seemed totally perfect for that first kiss—was she so long out of practice that she couldn't even recognize when a man just wasn't that into her? There were few moments in life she wished she could redo, that had definitely been one of them.

"Excuse me, miss." An elderly man walked up to her, snapping her from her thoughts.

"Huh?"

He frowned. "Some help, please."

Shaking the fog of Cian from her brain, she plastered on a tight smile. "Yeah, sure. How can I help?"

He ticked off an enormous list of items. As she scrambled to fill his order, her mind once again returned to Cian. Seemed like no matter how hard she tried to ignore him, she couldn't.

"...I'll also need some dried dandelions, white willow, and jasmine."

"I'm sorry, what?" she asked, catching only the tail end of what the elderly witch had asked for.

He looked at her, his mouth opened in a small gap of disgust. He then ticked the list of ingredients off on his fingers impatiently. "Arrowroot, dried dandelions, white willow..."

"Yes." She nodded. "I got the rest. Let me go get them."

He lifted a shaggy gray brow.

She turned and headed to the back room, rubbing the tail feather of her still-tender tattoo. Had it only been this morning that she'd made the biggest idiot of herself?

No matter what she did, no matter how many people she'd talked to today, her thoughts kept returning with burning clarity to her good-bye of only hours ago. It also didn't help that whenever Tamryn walked past she'd throw a snicker or snort over her shoulder.

Shoot. Shoot. Shoot. She'd run him off.

It was a Friday night, the busiest night of the week for them. Her sisters really needed her to stay focused, and right now, she couldn't care less. All she wanted to do was go home and forget today had ever happened.

"Seems the witch has a problem," Celeste said, not glancing up from her grimoire, her personal book of spells. A half-filled cauldron sat before her on the workbench.

"Nothing," Eve mumbled, quickly collecting the correct amount of herbs and placing them in glass-stoppered vials. "Same ol' crap Tamryn's been making fun of me for all day."

"Eve, really. Hon, I can feel you projecting that angst all over the place. It really wasn't that bad." Celeste stuck the tip of her tongue out the side of her mouth as she sprinkled some damiana into the concoction.

A bitter, stringent scent filled the room as the viscous fluid swallowed the leaves.

"What are you making?"

"Aphrodisiac. And stop switching the subject."

"I didn't." Eve glanced at the clock, then out the window. The sun was setting. It was now or never. Her stomach was one raging ball of anxiety. She shouldn't have done it, told him where to find her. Because if he didn't come when the sun went down, she'd feel like the world's biggest dumbass.

"Yes, you did. But, hey, if it makes you feel better to lie—"

"Whatever, Cel. I don't care. I'm done. Through. So over it."

"Ha! That'll be the day. So, you still on for the club tonight?"

"With the screaming meemies, wouldn't miss it."

Celeste turned, narrowing bright-green eyes, and smirked. "You know Tam and I really hate that nickname."

"Well, if you guys didn't always live up to it…"

Her sister shook her head with a small smile then turned back to the cauldron.

Eve walked away, the hissing noise of bubbling brew following in her wake.

"Okay. I've got everything you've asked for here. Do you need anything else?" she asked the elder leaning heavily against the wall. He ran a hand down his whiskered cheek, glanced at the vials in her arms, and shook his head.

"No, that should do."

"Okay, then let's go check out."

She couldn't help it: when she walked around the counter she glanced at the clock again. Five 'til nine. This sucked.

"No matter how many times you look at that thing, it's not going to change to your liking."

"What?" she asked, looking at her customer. He reached into his gray coat and pulled out a brown leather wallet.

"Time's a funny thing. Want it to move fast and it won't. Need it to slow down and you can't seem to catch a breath."

"True." She only gave him half an ear, not really in the mood to philosophize.

"And some of us"—he cocked his head and opened his wallet, pulling out a twenty—"don't have the luxury of it. Sometimes it simply runs out."

Her finger remained poised over the zero button, her gaze rolling to his, a chill like frost sweeping through her body and down her spine. "What?"

He had her attention now.

He shrugged, his bespectacled gaze boring into hers. Then he smiled, exposing coffee-stained teeth. "I'm simply saying. You never know when it's your time. Enjoy it while it lasts."

She narrowed her eyes. That was not what he'd meant. She'd swear it. His gaze had been intent with hidden meaning, as if he were trying to convey the urgency of what he said through a look.

"Do you do divination?" Was he trying to tell her some future she was yet unaware of? Her heart clenched.

Tamryn was into divination. Good at it too. She checked the tarots with regularity. Surely she'd have known if there was some black mark over Eve's near future?

Still. There'd been power in his words. She shivered.

He passed her the money, his fingers making the briefest contact with hers. A current like a bolt of electricity traveled from his hand to hers, zipping through her body with the speed of thought. She sucked in a breath as her nerves tingled with a rush of adrenaline. Then it was gone.

She frowned, still feeling unhinged and yet at the same time as normal as she'd ever been. He was smiling.

"Of course I don't, my dear."

* * *

The quickening of ancient power flowed through Cian's veins. In the next instant he was slammed with a mental impression of mind-numbing fear.

He choked on it and took a step toward the shop. He'd sworn not to interfere, not to get involved with Eve again. He stared at the door of the Witch's Brew, indecision warring in him.

He'd told Lise he wouldn't see her again. Given a million weak reasons why he couldn't. But it seemed his feet had a mind of their own. He tried to tell himself he was only seeing to Eve's safety. Yeah. And The Morrigan hadn't really beat him to within an inch of his cursed life; it had all been a serious misunderstanding on his part.

A hunched elderly man walked out the door, a brown bag clutched in his hand.

Cian ran across the road, not stopping to think what he'd do when he reached the man, but reacting on pure, primal instinct. He grabbed the slight man by the neck and slammed him against a green Dumpster sitting against the alleyway between shops. The blow forced the man to drop his bag. The unmistakable sound of shattering glass rang out on impact.

All Cian saw was red.

"Why are you here?" he barked, his frustration and fears for Eve making him brazen and reckless.

A black mist circled in the man's eyes, eating away at the brown until the entire orb was a dark, polished ebony. "Away!"

Cian was thrown to the ground. Needleworks of pain flared through his head. A wet trickle of blood slid down the side of his forehead.

"How dare you touch me like that?"

"What did you do to her, Dagda?" he snarled.

The small, figure leaned over him. A sneer twisted his thin lips. "Dare to touch me like that again, death, and you won't have to worry about Chaos anymore."

Cian got to his knees, holding on to his stomach and glaring at Dagda. "What did you do?"

"Your precious little witch is fine. As much as you might hate it, we're working the same side. The Morrigan's been whipped into bloodlust. She wants the woman, and she'll do anything to have her. I want her safe."

"Why?" Maybe finally someone would give him the answers he desperately needed.

Dagda exhaled, his gaze sharp and assessing. "Lise has told me you've talked. You understand there are some things I can't tell you, but I'm making plans."

"Plans for what? I've prolonged the inevitable. You know it. I know it. Give me something. Tell me *something*." He was begging now. Fine, he'd beg; he'd do anything to keep her safe.

If he was being honest with himself, he knew his desire to save Eve stemmed more from wanting her to get to know him, to see if maybe what he felt she felt too. That perhaps in this life there was actually someone who could look at him the way he'd first seen her looking at her husband. It wasn't altruism that made him want to fight for her, it was desire, pure and simple.

If anyone could help him, show him how. Pride took a back seat to her safety.

"Chaos has plans of her own. The likes of which I'm sure neither of us will spot until it's too late. You've still got time."

"And why should you care, Dagda?" he spat. "Why are you involving yourself in this? Why did you send me to her? Why? What's so important about Eve?"

Dagda glanced away, clenching his jaw as if debating his next words. Cian waited, not breathing, not wanting to kill his chances of finding out some much-needed information.

The king of the fae sighed and rolled his gaze to Cian's face. "There is a prophecy…"

Cian's flagging spirits jerked.

"I don't know everything. However, I can tell you this. An oracle of the chosen came to me long ago speaking of war, destruction…death. All over again. Except this time, all of humanity, normals and supers alike, will destroy themselves."

He frowned. "When?"

"I don't know. Maybe tonight. Maybe tomorrow. Or even a thousand years from now. But it's an absolute guarantee."

Cian's stomach gave a sick roll.

"What do Eve and I have to do with this?" he growled, wondering why the god would think he cared. Then he thought about Eve, his beautiful dark rose, and he did care.

Then another thought intruded. This was impossible. There was no known lore to substantiate this wild claim.

Dagda shook his head. "I tell truth."

"Does the queen know?"

"No. She is goddess of strife. Even if she were to receive the information, she wouldn't heed it. To her it would seem impractical. She was created for the sole purpose of causing disruption. The Morrigan is doing what she does best."

"What do Eve and I have to do with this, then? If the Earth is to be destroyed, me fighting to save her life seems insignificant in comparison."

Dagda clenched his jaw. "The chosen have created one perfect mate for each grim reaper."

"What does that mean? So we each find our mates and miraculously the world is saved?" He snorted. How stupid did the god take him for?

"Yours was the face I saw in the prophecy, Cian. I don't know if Eve is your mate. Or why it's even important you find one. If there's any chance, no matter how slim, that finding her might somehow avert this fate, then I'm going to do everything in my power to see that she is safe."

Something was missing. Some piece to the puzzle. It didn't make sense. How could his finding a mate help the Earth avert a catastrophe of that magnitude? "What aren't you telling me, Dagda?"

"That's all I was given. Remember this. In two more days The Morrigan will strike. She'll be cunning. Keep aware of everyone. Strangers, friends, even her family. I do not know what she plans, but it is coming, and if I know my queen, it will come in a way least expected."

Cian stood, shoving blunt fingers through his hair. The air vibrated with the whistle of a howling wind, and he turned his head for a split second, huddling against the strength of the ripping gale. Then there was silence, an eerie hum of nothing. As quick as the wind had started, it vanished, and with it, the earth god.

An impotent rage filled his gut with fire, gnawed away at his insides. He'd wanted information and yet this was the last thing he'd expected to be told. It was almost too much to take in. This went beyond protecting Eve. And he still couldn't understand what her significance was. To him, she meant everything. But how could one lone witch and death save the world? Learning more had helped nothing, only deepened the mystery.

"Cian."

He snapped around, bent at the knees, ready to tear whatever it was to pieces.

There she stood, his exotic priestess. Her hair was hanging down, long and loose and flowing well past her shoulders. Her golden eyes were huge. Bow-shaped lips turned down into a frown. Her pale skin shone radiant in the light of the moon.

He tried to shut off the emotions. Tell himself that the blood pounding in his ears and the knife twisting in his gut meant nothing.

"What are you doing here?" she asked.

He ground his jaw, then decided. "You said you worked tonight. I came to see you, Eve Philips."

He hadn't meant to stay; he'd had every intention of disappearing before he'd been found, but looking at her now…he didn't want to leave either.

She smiled. It was only a slow curling of the lips, but it put heat in his loins and had him taking a step closer.

"I thought you wouldn't come," she whispered.

He closed his eyes, wishing he had stayed away, wishing he'd never met her, that she could have kept her husband. That none of this ever had to happen to her. All the secrets, all the lies he'd already told. When the truth came out, she would hate him.

He opened his eyes. "I couldn't stay away."

* * *

Eve didn't even try to stop the stupid I'm-so-ridiculously-happy grin from hijacking her face.

I couldn't stay away.

Her heart jerked against her chest just thinking about it. So maybe he had a thing for rambling fools after all.

"How's the tattoo?" he finally asked after a moment of silence.

Without thought she touched the tender spot on her back. "Little sore. Otherwise, it's pretty good. I need to put some more tattoo goo on it, though. It's getting a little dry."

"Hmm…"

She glanced at him out the corner of her eye. He seemed distracted, his thoughts a million miles away. She waved a hand in front of his face. "Earth to Cian."

He looked at her. "What?"

"You feeling okay? You seem bothered."

Exhaling, he ran his hand over his head. She loved that hair of his. It was so long, so out-of-date, and yet it fit. On most any other man, hair that length would be such a turnoff. Maybe because he looked so masculine, but it didn't distract. A wicked desire to have him spread that hair out while she massaged his naked back made her shiver.

"I'm sorry, Eve. I am distracted; I shouldn't be. Maybe I'm not good company tonight."

"No. No, you're fine." There wasn't a chance she was going to let him leave her now, especially because the truth was he didn't seem fine. Not really, and suddenly she felt an urge to do something nice for him. Normally she'd take her friends to a diner and help share their woes over a plate of Mac's famous chili-cheese fries. But with a vamp, that was pretty well out of the question.

Vamps couldn't metabolize regular food; eating anything that didn't involve platelets tended to give them the human equivalent of food poisoning. She'd had to concoct several blood-cleansing potions for untried newbies still unsettled at the thought of feeding.

Which left only one other place at this time of night. Thankfully an Indian summer had bespelled the day, it was unnaturally warm, all the better for what she had in mind, if she had time, that was. She checked her watch. Another two hours before she had to meet the screaming meemies at the club—plenty of time.

"Let's go for a walk."

He frowned. "Isn't that what we're doing?"

Eve glanced around. At nine p.m., San Francisco was packed with tourists. The flashes of several cameras and the happily smiling faces attested to that. Loud music from competing clubs, mixed with the high-pitched chatter of vendors and revelers made it too noisy and crowded. Not something she'd normally mind, but tonight she sensed he might enjoy something a little more sedate and peaceful.

"No, not here. Someplace quiet. Come with me. I know just the spot." She grabbed his hand and led him off the beaten path.

Twenty minutes later they were standing on sand, watching as rolling waves washed up on shore. Salty air filled the night. There was nobody else on Baker Beach at this time of night, and that's how she liked it.

The light of the silver moon danced across the obsidian shore and silhouettes of jagged rock tore through the waters. Dangerous swimming area, but a nice sunbathing spot.

The summers were a mess, especially since this strip of sand also doubled as a nude beach. Gawkers were pretty much everywhere during the day, but there was a certain privacy and eroticism to nighttime forays that couldn't be matched.

She hadn't brought him here to see him in the nude—circumspectly she glanced at the barely visible bulge in his jeans—although…

"This is nice." He inhaled, and in his words she heard a sincere appreciation. For the first time since being around the vamp she sensed him at peace, fully at peace.

She smiled. Maybe he was a nature guy. The city could tend to drive people a little batty sometimes. There were definitely advantages to not being a tourist: knowing the local dives intimately, for one.

He took several deep breaths of the salt tinged air and then turned to look at her. Deep blue eyes glittered in the moonlight. "Thank you, Eve. You can't know how much I needed this."

Biting her bottom lip, she glanced away, her heart thumping so loud in her chest she was sure he could hear it.

C'mon, Eve, remember he's a vamp. Don't want him getting too excited at hearing the rush of hot blood through your veins.

That calmed her immediately. A few nibbles on the neck for fun, sure, but to be fed on…not so much.

The surf was pounding the beach, its navy-blue waves called to her, making her itchy to feel its coolness lap against her heated body.

She gripped his forearm, stopping him in his tracks. He glanced down at her with a frown.

"Hold on." She lifted her leg, hopping around to keep her balance, and slid off first one strappy sandal and then the other. "I've got to go barefoot here. I love digging my toes in the sand."

He stepped closer to her, covering her hand with his own. "Aren't you afraid of stepping on broken glass, or even needles? Beaches aren't that safe anymore."

His worry for her was nearly her undoing. As it was, her heart was in serious overdrive. She'd forgotten what the first blooming of a crush had felt like. And damn, she was thirty, but she was more than willing to admit she was seriously crushing on this thoughtful, sexy as sin vampire.

Memories of her and Michael's first few dates came back to her and with it memories of all the excitement, passion, dread, fear, joy, near-to-tears exhilaration of getting to know someone and knowing you were falling fast. He could be Mr. Right or even Mr. Right Now. Whatever he was, she was feeling it all over again.

She was both terrified and ready to jump for joy. To cover her confusion she lifted her ruby necklace and shook it a little.

"This stone channels my power. With it I can whisper any command and have it come to be. Those within my capabilities, at any rate."

He looked impressed and gave her a soft smile. "I assume you can protect your feet, then?"

"I don't think that's out of my range, no."

There went that stupid grin again, stealing across her face. Could she control anything anymore? Nothing for it; she was a walking free-for-all.

Closing her eyes, she imagined her feet to be as tough as steel and yet at the same time as sensitive as a butterfly's wing.

"Make it so," she murmured and then opened her eyes to see a hazy reddish fog envelop her feet before slowly fading away. The enchantment was wrought. Now no harm would come to her tender flesh, and she'd still be able to feel all the texture of sand and water. Exactly what she wanted.

She dug her toes into the sand, relishing its cool, grainy feel, and inhaled happily. "Why don't you take off your shoes and join me, vamp?"

Cian cocked his head and grimaced. "No. I don't think—"

Eve stood on tiptoe, placing her finger over his sinfully yummy lips. "Then don't think and just do it. Live a little. Don't you know this is how you make memories?"

He trapped her finger between his lips. His mouth was a warm haven and when he flicked her with the tip of his tongue she thought she might die. Or swoon. But probably die, because swooning was just so pathetically cliché.

"I'm sorry," he whispered, shaking his head. "I shouldn't have…"

Placing a finger over his lips she shook her head. "I'm not sorry."

His nostrils flared and with one final kiss to her finger he let it go. She swallowed hard, body pinging like a live wire. Thank the goddess she hadn't eaten anything earlier; her stomach was a hot mess of dive-bombing butterflies.

"You know what. You're right. I should live a little." And so saying, he took off his shoes. Then he grabbed her hand, threaded their fingers together, and resumed walking. The leather of his glove was as soft as baby's skin and pulsed with warmth, which seeped straight into her palm. It was unusual. Unlike the cold feel of leather she was used to.

"This leather…" she said, lifting their linked hands and staring at the black glove, noticing for the first time the runes etched into the leather. "It's so soft. Different from normal cowhide." She traced a finger over one design.

Okay, so she was totally trying to get him to fess up about the glove. At first he hadn't worn one, so she knew his hand wasn't burned or deformed, but he had one on all the time now. Since the moment Indigo had attacked. Not that she didn't like it; it sorta hammered home the fact that he'd lived in eras she'd have given her right kidney and maybe even her left to see. It was sort of regency meets goth and she dug it. But she was still curious.

He grabbed her hand and brought it to his lips, placing a very gentle kiss at the crook between thumb and fingers.

She shivered, her heart taking a nosedive in her chest. Needing to bank the fire scorching between her thighs, she walked toward the water's edge, close enough for the gentle waves to slip over her feet.

The water was frigid, which was what she needed to quench the lust hammering through her veins.

They walked in silence, yet there was no awkward tension. She peeked at him from the corner of her eye.

He was calmly staring ahead.

This felt right.

The water.

The scenery.

And most of all…him.

Chapter 15

So tell me, Cian, how long have you lived in San Francisco?"

An innocent question, but still his heart gave a jolt. It was questions like this that could lead to other more in-depth questions, and that couldn't happen. Especially not now.

Though he had to admit, whether he wanted to or not, this was turning out to be the most pleasant evening he'd had in decades. He couldn't believe he'd done that to her fingers, or the fact that she'd liked it. Being around her made him reckless, crazy to taste her, touch her. He barely knew her, hardly knew what was happening to him. But the only thing he *was* sure of was that he needed to know this woman. Lise had told him to go for it, so there had to be a reason. Maybe this was the key to Eve's ultimate salvation. He had to hope, anyway.

"Awhile," he finally said.

"Mmm." She inhaled and looked to the sky, a dreamy smile on her face. "I've been here for twelve years. Came for college; liked it so much, I decided to stay. You know how it goes."

He nodded.

"There's no place like it. To be able to live free and be who you are without fear of reprisal. It's nice. Home."

Her skin was like silk. The touch of her arm against his, her fingers laced together with his own. He wished he could feel the touch of her hand, without the glove interfering. A burning desire to do the forbidden and slip the glove off, touch her, filled him to the point of bursting. But he couldn't. He wouldn't put her in danger. Ever.

Not to mention the fact that when she discovered the countless lies he'd told, she'd probably hate him forever.

This couldn't be happening, shouldn't be, and yet it was. With one look he'd been entranced and with one smile she'd claimed his heart forever. So fast and so hard there'd be no going back. Eve made death feel. For so long he'd been a machine, moving from one soul to the next, doing his job, not thinking about the person as anything other than a chore. A task to complete. But from the moment she'd poured her feelings into him, she'd sparked something back to life, something he'd thought long dead. She was beautiful and funny, yes, but she made him want more than death. She made him want to live.

So what now? Lose his heart and his mind when she died? He couldn't accept that. Regardless that Lise or Dagda had given him no shred of hope, there still had to be a way. There *had* to be. Because to believe otherwise didn't bear thought.

"Cian…" She bumped him with her hip hard enough that he tripped, nearly losing his balance and falling to the sand.

Eve laughed. Her melodic, sultry sound slithered down his spine and coiled tighter around his heart.

"What?" His lips twitched.

"You, Mr. Man, were ignoring me. I asked where you lived. I've shown you mine, now you gotta show me yours."

He cocked his brow. "Are we still talking about houses?"

She laughed. "You're so dirty. Yes, houses. For now."

Her sultry look gave him visions of ripping the shirt from her body and tasting the breasts she'd teased him with the night before. He grinned.

Lise either could read the future, or she instinctively knew the way Eve's mind worked. He was pretty sure it was a little of both.

Her golden eyes widened and she waved a hand through the air. "Ohmygod, I'm not trying to invite myself over, if that's what you think. Well, I guess that's what it might have sounded like, huh? What I meant was…"

It was mean of him to let her ramble on, but it was qualities like that that endeared him to her. Being and living amongst the fae was always a constant battle of wills, deception, and one-upmanship. Her natural way of being was so refreshing that he almost felt at times lost and unsure. This wasn't normal for him; but then all she'd have to do was smile at him and he felt anchored once more.

She made him feel…alive.

Scarlet had settled deep into her cheeks when he finally decided to put her out of her misery. He grabbed her hand and gave it a gentle squeeze.

Her lashes fluttered shut, and she took a deep, cleansing breath. The anxiety eased out of her, replaced by calm relief.

Heat pooled in his cock. He'd never wanted something so badly in his entire life.

Pulling her into his arms, he laid his head atop hers. She fit perfectly, her tiny hands clutching at his shirt. He knew the instant she felt him, because the gentle flutter flowing from her to him turned instantly to a hot, heavy pulse of sexual desire, so strong it nearly brought him to his knees.

He clamped his jaw shut. At the very least he could control this. If not his desire, then his actions.

"Eve, it's okay." He ran his hands up and down her back in a soothing gesture, and he didn't know what made him do it, but he uttered the damning words, "I live in a flat in Presidio Heights."

"Wow," she said in breathless wonder. "I always heard the ancients were loaded. You'd have to be to live in those million-dollar homes. So how old are you really, Cian? Not that I'm prying or anything."

She raised a black brow.

"Wouldn't you like to know?"

Scrunching her nose, she punched him lightly on the arm and sauntered off, hands crossed behind her back, skirt billowing softly around her ankles. "What can I say, I'm like a hound dog with a scent. I'm gonna get you to tell me how old you are someday."

He caught up, grabbing her hand and pulling her to his side. She laughed and wiggled out of his grip and this time ran off, her black hair whipping through the breeze like a banner.

Excitement stirred his veins, and he took off after her.

Eve zipped around him, graceful as a gazelle, her strong legs eating up the distance along the shoreline. He could catch her, but he enjoyed the chase. The feel of his lungs expanding for breath, muscles in his legs coiling and bunching, pushing off from the sand.

Panting, she finally dropped to the sand—mere inches in front of him—and stuck out her foot.

He tripped over her, landing with a soft thud on the beach. He wasn't even given enough time to right himself when he felt a slight body plop on top of his. Her unique scent filled the space between them.

"Eve," he growled and rolled over, clamping his fingers into her sides. She was glowing with a rush of blood; her pale skin shone luminous. The ruby in the center of her necklace gleamed with flares of volcanic red, swirling with undulating waves of color, rolling into and onto each other.

Their eyes locked and time stood still.

He was aware of only her. The feel of her tiny body on his. Her legs straddling his waist and the steady rise and fall of her chest.

She licked her lips and her anticipation crawled through his skin.

"So bonny." He lifted his hand and trailed a finger down her cheek. The heat off her body seeped through the leather. The gloves were an extension of him. The essence of what he was created the material, it was almost like touching flesh to flesh. Almost. For now, it was enough.

Black lashes, like moth's wings, fluttered shut.

All the reasons why he shouldn't touch, shouldn't taste her, no longer seemed to matter. She was here with him, offering herself in a way no other ever had. For that reason alone Cian couldn't resist.

Placing his hands on her shoulder, he pulled her slightly forward. Her mouth parted in a silent whisper.

So damn beautiful.

He closed his eyes, reaching out with all his senses, wanting to savor this moment, to remember it ten or even a hundred years from now with the same clarity.

When he exhaled, she inhaled. They were one breath, one heartbeat, everything in time and in tune with the other.

She trembled and his heart clenched. Then he closed the final bit of space between them and claimed her lips for his own.

Eve moaned into him. Her fingers curling into his shirt, her soft hair falling around them, shielding them like a curtain.

He tasted, his tongue delving deeper, wrapping hers around his. Warmth spread through his body and centered in his chest. She tasted of apples, sweet and irresistible.

Cian deepened the kiss, his hands roaming along her now-prone backside, kneading, cupping, and committing to memory.

She made tiny mewling sounds, her soft lips pressed tight to his.

Heat, like the warm rays of the sun shot through his pores, a projection of not only her lust, but something deeper. Fuller and much more elemental and with it, a tiny thread of anxiety.

It worried him, but he was hungry for more of her and couldn't reason the why of anything at the moment.

He groaned, wanting to crawl inside her skin and make the warmth stay. Eve was the peace he'd never known.

The lack of air in his lungs was what finally made him break away, and he did it with much regret.

Chapter 16

She was going to call in sick. How in the world did her sisters expect her to make it to their outing after such a high? Nothing could compare to what she'd experienced with Cian.

Absolutely nothing.

It had been an earth-shattering, mind-blowing—so much for not giving in to clichés—kiss. Actually it had been so powerful that she was more frightened than excited.

Never in her life had she doubted her absolute love for Michael. He'd always been *the one*. She wasn't looking for love, or even a long-term relationship. Been there, done that. All she'd wanted was someone to hang out with. Keep the loneliness at bay, so to speak.

Instead, what she'd felt had gone deeper than any emotion she'd ever known at her husband's hands or touch. Michael had been fireworks, where Cian was lava. Nothing Michael had ever done in their ten years could compare to what she'd felt with the vamp. The merest contact of lips on lips, bodies pressed against bodies. Right there in that moment she'd have done anything for him, and that had scared the ever-living daylight out of her.

Confused, she'd mumbled a pathetic apology and had run off, demons of her past chasing at her heels.

The look on his face right before she'd run off—brows lowered and blue eyes glittering with doubt—made her ache.

What had she done? Now he was going to think she was either really crazy or not worth the time and effort. Neither thought brought an iota of comfort.

More miserable than ever, she groaned, dropping her head into her hands, and leaned back deeper into her couch, the gentle flicker of an aromatic candle the only light in her apartment.

What the hell was wrong with her?

She'd all but begged for that kiss. Had wanted it from the moment she'd laid eyes on the sinful temptation of his body.

Painful memories filled her head. Michael, broken and lifeless, smiling and always teasing her about being such a nerd for liking history the way she did. But those thoughts were turning fuzzy, unclear, and unfocused.

Pictures of Cian kept crowding her mind. Dazzling blue eyes, ridiculously long ebony-and-frost-colored hair, a body to make a wicked heart melt.

"Oh goddess. This wasn't supposed to happen. Not so fast. Not so soon."

She couldn't shake the sense of betrayal, that somehow her enjoyment of the kiss, of his touch, had lessened the beauty of what she and Michael had shared.

He'd been her first love. Reckless, wild passion—they couldn't get their hands off each other in the first year. It had all been so perfect.

So why did that pale in comparison to the stolen moment on the beach? She ground her jaw, feeling sick at heart. It had been her idea to take Cian to the beach, to play with him the way she had. She was responsible for that kiss happening, had very nearly orchestrated the entire thing.

The cold, harsh truth was she wanted Cian more than anything she'd ever wanted in her life.

Love charms never brought about this type of bottomless passion, only lust that, once sated, went away almost immediately. She'd be tempted to think magick was somehow involved. How else could she explain the immediate attraction and feelings that veered more toward love than lust? Charms couldn't do this. It just wasn't possible.

And no matter what, she refused to believe in love at first sight. That was hokey romance babble, nothing more.

So if not first sight and not a charm, then what?

The shrill ring of the phone yanked her from her thoughts. She yelped and, with panicked fingers, picked up the phone, nearly dropping it in her haste.

"Hello?"

"Eve, honey, Tam and I are waiting at the apartment. You coming or what?"

The static of female laughter and melodic music filtered through the line.

It was Celeste, and suddenly the idea of spending a Friday night alone, and only at ten thirty at that, made her feel lousy. She also wasn't in the mood to go to any clubs and make polite chitchat with drunk men whose only concern was whether they'd get into her pants or not.

"Can we change plans and you guys come here instead?" She twisted the cord around her finger, hoping her sisters weren't too dead set on going to the club tonight.

"Honey, what's wrong?" Instantly Celeste's voice turned from jovial to worried.

She shook her head, staring off into space. "I'm just a little bummed is all."

"Eve, you stay there. Tam and I are on our way. We'll be there in ten minutes. You just hold on." Then the line went dead.

She hung up the phone and walked to her window, gazing out at the starry night, wondering where Cian was and what he was thinking.

* * *

Cian punched on the light in Lise's flat, squinting to adjust to the sudden brightness. What had just happened? Everything had been going well, at least he'd thought.

He'd tasted panic inside her, known something was happening, but for the life of him he couldn't begin to explain what had made her turn from sultry sex kitten to frightened colt between the span of two heartbeats.

"Bloody fool," he spat and shoved blunt fingers through his sand-encrusted hair. How was he supposed to know what to do or even say anymore? This wasn't something he'd ever expected or believed could happen.

Shedding his clothing with a swipe of his hand, he stalked toward the couch and plopped down. He could still taste her. Smell her all over him. She was on his skin. Tongue. The woman had crawled into his brain. Denying that he felt something for her was a joke; it was more than just something…it was all-consuming.

How the hell did mortals do it? Why would they fall in love when it brought nothing but angst and misery? Worst part was no matter how much he might want to walk away and forget Eve and anything closely associated with her, he still had a job to do. Keep her safe.

He ground his jaw from side to side. Already he sensed a madness creeping around the corners inside him, a shadow coming to life and breathing down his neck.

His nostrils flared and he scrubbed a tired hand down his face.

Regardless of what Eve felt—or didn't feel—for him, he'd see her safe or die trying. That was a vow sealed in blood.

First things first, he needed a shower and as cold as possible, to not only get the sand off his flesh but the lust out his veins.

Maybe this was for the best. At least now he could concentrate on how to see her safe, rather than the lush curves of her body.

He stood and stalked toward the hallway, raging hard-on clearly evident and making him cranky. Blue carpet muffled his footsteps; he passed a bedroom, glanced inside, and moved on. It took a second for his brain to process what he'd seen. When it did, he narrowed his eyes and backed up.

No, no trick of the light.

There, lying in the center of a windowless room, sat a gray stone coffin. Nothing else around it, no knickknacks, bookshelves, cluttered desk, nothing. The room was bare save for the casket. He walked up to the tomb. The preternatural strength of his eyes seeing things humans could not. There were Celtic runes inscribed along the length of the pewter-colored stone. Markings of death and blood.

He passed his hand along the top of the coffin. Tendrils of heat saturated his palm. A dull greenish glow encased the stone. This was a genuine, honest-to-goddess vampire's sarcophagus. Not the kind normals bought to bury their dead, but the kind used for the soulless living.

His lips twitched. Damn if Lise didn't think of everything. On the off chance Eve decided to test the coffin's magick, she'd feel the radiating pulse of it vibrate straight to her bone. He frowned. Not that that mattered now.

He stalked off to the shower, shoving his hand over his cock and trying to get it to go down. Already his balls were beginning to ache and drive him crazy.

He stepped into the shower and turned the faucet on as hot as it would go. Steam gathered around his ankles, circled up to his head. Visions of Eve swam in his brain.

The feel of her body on him. Desire coursed a dangerous trek down his veins and into his already-engorged cock. Grinding his jaw, he took himself in hand and began rubbing.

The way she'd tasted, like candy and a hint of wine. Exotic appeal. He leaned his free hand against the wall, his muscles clenching and his breathing turning ragged.

That sultry smile and lioness gaze. He pumped harder, the pressure building. His body was on fire and quaking. Close. He hissed, on the verge of a violent explosion.

Ebony hair. Pale porcelain skin. The feel of full breasts pushed against his chest. His legs trembled and he gnashed his teeth.

He couldn't help but wonder what she'd taste like. Would she be wet for him and only him? He rubbed harder. The way he got hard only for her. There was no one else, nothing else that could do to him what she did.

His back spasmed and his fingers clenched the warm tile. He imagined the spray running down his back was her fingers, that it wasn't his hand on his cock but hers. He pumped harder. Faster. Dizzy with his lust, mad with desire, he pumped and pumped until his seed poured from his body.

"Eve," he groaned, the rushing tide of his orgasm made him weak. He leaned against the wall panting for breath. The hot water scalded his skin. He turned the tap to cold. Frigid enough to burn her from his mind, but her mark was already imprinted on his soul.

Chapter 17

Two—heavy on the Cuervo—margaritas and nearly a whole bag of chips and salsa later, Eve was still no closer to feeling better.

"I really screwed up."

"Gah, Eve." Celeste rolled her eyes, the coral-pink mask on her face making her look more clownish than aggravated. "You're killing me. If you like this guy so much, go find him, have sex, and get it over with. Put us all out our misery, please."

"Jeez." Tamryn punched Celeste in the arm.

"Hey!"

"Your sympathy is so heartwarming, Cel. I think we could all learn a thing or two from you. Sheesh." Tamryn lifted a red brow, disgust thinning her rose-colored lips. "Listen, Eve. If you like the guy, call him."

"It's not that simple. I never got his number. Just an idea of where he lives." She twisted her lips, dipping yet another tortilla chip into the chunky salsa. The tip snapped off into the bowl. Growling, she shoved the dip aside and laid her hair-rollered head back down onto her body pillow.

"I'm sorry, guys. I'm pathetic. Since when did I become so mopey? I hate people like that!"

Celeste laid her hand on Eve's and gave it a gentle squeeze. "Look, I'm sorry for being so cruel"—she shot Tamryn the evil eye—"I was only playing."

"You know, Eve..." Tamryn scooted closer, the cotton between her painted toes looking ready to fall out. "I think this might be guilt—well, heck, I don't think, I *know*. You don't have to feel guilty about falling for someone else. It's been two years...."

"I know that." Eve rubbed her hand down her arm, a nervous habit she'd picked up trying to hide her projections. Like it really did any good. "It's more."

Violet eyes huge with understanding stared up at her. Tamryn gave a slow nod. "I see."

"What? See what?" Celeste narrowed malachite eyes, and confusion pinched her brows.

Eve blew out a tired breath and sat up, clutching the pillow to her chest and staring at the black-and-white Humphrey Bogart on the screen. *Casablanca*, one of her all-time favorite movies, was playing on mute. Didn't matter; she could almost recite every line of that film by heart. Now, *that* was a love story.

She reached into her brown paper sack of old taffy, pulled one out, and thought of Cian when she bit down into the Neapolitan.

"Celeste, are you sure you belong to this family? You sure can be dense sometimes."

Tamryn reached over to the coffee table, grabbed the remote, and shut off the television, forcing Eve to concentrate on their conversation and not tune them out the way she really wanted to do.

"It's stronger, Eve, isn't it?" She paused, searching Eve's face. "The bond with him is stronger than Michael."

Celeste frowned and glanced toward her. Eve rolled her eyes but nodded.

"Well, so what." Celeste stood and began gathering the empty glasses and bowls and headed into the kitchen. She tended to get tidy when discussing Eve's love life. "Eve, we all know how much you loved Michael, him most of all, I'm sure." She dumped the dishes into the sink, grabbed the tea kettle, and filled it up with tap water. "It's okay. You're one of the lucky ones to find not only one but two great loves. Or Cian might be a rebound and that could be where these feelings are stemming from. But you're a smart girl, and I think we all know that's probably not the case."

She twisted her lip, nibbling on it. "You guys wanna hear something pretty heavy?"

"Yuh-huh," Tamryn nodded, wavy red hair bobbing up and down, "you know I do."

"I just bet you do, busybody." Eve snorted.

Celeste placed the kettle on the stove and walked back into the living room, plopping down on the floor Indian-style.

"Whew, okay." She lifted her hand, her eyes glazing over for a second. "Remind me never to move that fast when the room's spinning."

They laughed, the alcohol beginning to make even the ordinary funny by that point. Breathless and lighthearted, Eve hiccupped. It was always so good to be around her sisters. They had a way of showing her things were never really that bad, life went on, and what happened today need not rule your life tomorrow. Good to be reminded of that sometimes.

"So, you were saying?" Tamryn asked when they finally quieted down. She pointed her blackberry-colored toenails toward the ceiling and waved her hand over them, trying her best to speed up the drying process.

Pressure was starting to build inside the kettle. A low-pitched vibration rattled the stove.

"I think what totally freaked me out about the whole thing was that in that moment I realized Michael could hardly begin to compare with the vampire. And might I add"—she widened her eyes, holding up a finger—"a perfect stranger at that. That's so unlike me. I'm careful. Play it safe. I don't fall in love at the drop of a dime. This is different, as if I don't have a choice in the matter, and it's all happening so fast, my head's spinning. I feel like this is totally out of my control, and I'm not sure I like that."

Heavy silence met her statement. Tamryn could only blink. Celeste didn't bat an eye, just stared.

The teakettle whistled. Its shrill scream snapped them out of their trances.

Eve leaped, heart nearly jerking from her chest.

Celeste jumped up and ran to shut it off. The ice-pick-stabbing-in-your-brain noise died with a pitiful little wail. Then she began piddling around in the kitchen, opening drawers and slamming cupboards.

"Then you shouldn't ignore that, and as a witch you know this," Tamryn chided, not missing a beat. "Sounds to me like you're trying to be the control freak again. We all know life is predestined. What will be will be. You learned that with Michael."

"I know." She huffed a stray lank of ebony hair out her eye. "But what if I'm wrong? I could be. I have been in the past."

Celeste came in carrying a tray with three steaming teacups on it. She handed one to each of them, then took her own and sat in the recliner. The warm, relaxing scent of chamomile circled the room.

"And what if he is?" Celeste asked, taking a tentative sip of the brew. "We can play that what-if game forever. You know it, I know it, so let's do ourselves the favor and not."

"You know I hate to agree with anything Scrooge says, but she's right, Eve."

She gazed into the amber liquid in her cup. Her sisters were right. This was all beginning to give her a headache. The back-and-forth and freaking out. Over what? That she found a guy stimulating, not only physically, but mentally. He was a mystery and yet at the same time there was this innate sense that she knew him. He was one of the good guys, vampire or no.

"Well, it doesn't matter anyway. I never got his number or address. And I seriously doubt he's going to be looking up psycho chick any time soon."

Eve took a sip of her tea but wrinkled her nose at the heat scalding her tongue. She'd never liked tea hot, preferring it tepid or even on the cool side. Something her sisters had always called a disgusting habit.

"That's what you thought the other night, and he came back. I think you'd be surprised. If this really is predestined, then nothing under the sun can stop it from happening."

"Whoa, getting all existential on us now, are you, Cel?" Tamryn teased, tossing a pillow at Celeste's head. It landed with a soft plop, dribbling tea over the cup's rim and onto her shirt. Her pink face twisted into a frightening mask of cracks.

"Tam!" she shrieked and threw the pillow back, missing by a good yard. "I swear you act like you're fifteen instead of twenty-five."

Eve shuddered. "I think you should go take that stuff off now, Cel; it's starting to drop into your tea. Yuck."

Indeed little pink flecks were falling into the cup.

With a growl Celeste stalked to the bathroom, slamming the door in her wake.

Tamryn snorted, making Eve laugh and remember the look on Celeste's face. One of loathing and uppity snobbery. Her sister was a hot mess.

She held her stomach and wheezed between bouts of giggles, "That was really mean, Tam."

"Bah. She's too serious. Needs to lighten up. Anyhow, I was thinking—"

"Oh, I can't wait to hear this one."

The sound of rushing water filtered through the hallway. Eve tasted the tea again; this time it was cool enough to be drinkable.

"What if we did a séance?"

"For what?"

"To find out his address, of course."

"Yeah, well"—she set the cup and saucer down—"not that I don't appreciate it, but isn't that a little Hollywood? I mean, we can find it without the hocus-pocus. I'm sure he's in the phone book."

"I'm sure we could, genius." Sarcasm dripped from her words. "But you're forgetting the little matter of not knowing his last name."

Eve opened her mouth then snapped it shut, frowning. Come to think of it, she'd never learned his last name.

Celeste huffed and entered the living room. "What's this about a séance?"

"Bionic ears..." Tamryn shot Eve a quick she's-so-weird look. "I was just saying that we should do a séance to divine where this hot vamp lives."

At that Celeste perked up and nodded, planting her hands on her hips. "Sounds good. We haven't done anything in a while, feeling a little rusty. How 'bout it, sis?"

"If everyone else wants to, then I guess when in Rome, right?"

"Uh-huh." Both sisters nodded.

Eve sighed, stood, and walked to her cupboard full of candles and herbs. Not that she didn't want to do this—okay...who was she kidding? She didn't want to do this.

Yet somehow she would, always did whenever her sisters were involved. She grabbed five tall white candles and one thick black one. The dark candle was inscribed with the ritual symbols of power, in its center a pentagram. This would consecrate the magick circle. Finally, she also grabbed a premeasured packet of sage, cedar, mugwort, and sweet grass, cleansing herbs to make them ritually ready to enter the world of spirits.

Tamryn jumped up and ran to the bedroom, she came back out a moment later with a gem-encrusted dagger. Celeste pushed the coffee table and sofa farther back.

All three came together. Eve placed the white candles at strategic spots, lit them, and then stepped inside the center of the circle, holding on to the dark candle still. Tamryn lifted the dagger and drew a five-pointed star through the air.

The room grew heavy around them, dense with power. It rippled like the tides of the sea.

"I'm not as good with the ley lines as you are, Eve. But I think this'll hold just fine," she said, the tip of her tongue poking out the corner of her mouth. With a nod, she sat and the rest followed.

"Now, let's cleanse ourselves and then do this," Celeste said with a happy smile.

Eve sat the black candle down between them and pulled the dried, bunched herbs out the packet. Four separate knotted herbs fell out. With a regular cigarette lighter, she lit the tip of the sage first. A dark curl of smoke ribboned through the air.

"Sage to drive out the evil and keep out negative thoughts," all three said, voices going deeper with the invocation of magick.

Eve waved the herb through the air, allowing the smoke to filter under noses. They didn't want to breathe it in, only have the essence pass along their skin. The rest would take care of itself.

"Cedar to bless this home."

She repeated the same process, then lit the sweet grass.

"Sweet grass to welcome in good influence."

Lighting the mugwort, Eve didn't wave it under noses, but rather let the plant burn down in her hand. Its smoke was a hallucinogenic; not much was needed for its effect. This was what opened the portal between the physical and spiritual realms.

She closed her eyes, already light-headed from the drinking and now becoming a little groggy from the herb. One last step, then the spirits would speak with them.

"Light the black candle, Eve," Tamryn hissed.

A chill zipped up her spine. Already Eve felt the spirits around them; she couldn't hear or see them, but they were definitely there.

The air itself was thick with the presence of beings. The room was growing steadily cooler, making her break out in goose bumps. What if Michael showed up?

Her heart lurched. He might not, there was no way to know who would and wouldn't show. It all depended on the whim of the spirit.

"Won't this make me look stalkerish?" Eve asked—anything to stall and give herself a little more time to gather her courage.

Celeste laughed. "A little."

That was the last thing she wanted. Maybe there was another way, one that did not involve the possibility of seeing her dead husband.

Fingers yanked the lighter from out her hands. She opened her eyes to see Tamryn lighting the black candle. "Too late to back out now, Eve. You'll thank me later."

The last wick flared to life and the room gave a loud shudder. Floorboards groaned and a spiraling helix of iridescence opened before them. Many nearly translucent bodies spewed forth.

Old, fat, young, thin. Boys, men, girls, women. They all came. Some yawning, others glaring murderously at the women.

"What do you want?" a woman looking to be in her midtwenties demanded. Fat curls bounced around her head. She was dressed in colonial period garb, an old soul. Usually only the more recent dead chose to speak, and they tended to be the most unreliable sources.

Spirits were naughty, no other word for it.

If there was one thing in life Eve was good at, though, it was her magick, and speaking with the dead was a particular specialty of hers.

She narrowed her eyes. "One thing. Where can I find the vamp called Cian?"

"And what do I get in return for this bit of information?"

Always tit for tat. You'd think the undead wouldn't be so stingy. Greedy little buggers.

"How 'bout bespelled into a doll, wench?" Celeste snapped. She'd never had patience for the folly of the spirits. What was so ironic was that Celeste actually loved to séance.

The spirit huffed and stomped a dainty foot, her skirt flouncing with the movement. "I don't like you, witch. You get nothing from me."

The air was growing colder, crisper, as more and more spirits surged through the portal. Eve's teeth chattered. She was ready to get this thing over with.

"Don't pay attention to my sister, spirit," Eve said. "What is it that you want?"

The spirit turned cold blue eyes toward her, her austere face impassive. A harshness twisted the delicate features of the woman. She opened her mouth to speak, then paused before uttering a word and cocked her head.

"You're Michael's, aren't you?"

Eve's heart felt like it literally was going to rocket through her chest. She forgot the cold altogether. "You know him?"

The woman bobbed her head, her curls bouncing becomingly. "He's nice."

"Does he…does he talk about me?"

Tamryn squeezed her fingers, in sympathy or to urge her to hurry it up, she didn't know.

"Not much. A little. He likes Cian."

Shock didn't even begin to describe it. This conversation had gone from weird into the *Twilight Zone* category.

"Because of that, I won't charge you. You can find your Cian at 2166 Baker."

* * *

Eve was putting away the candles, her mind consumed by the conversation with the spirit.

"Man, that went surprisingly smooth tonight, didn't it?" Tamryn asked, placing the dagger on the coffee table and then helping Celeste to right the furniture once again. Already the apartment was warming. "Guess it helped that we happened to bump into a spirit that knew Mikey, eh? Wish we could have learned more about him."

"Yeah," she mumbled, only giving her sister half an ear. The only thing she could think about was the fact that Michael liked Cian. Was this a sign? Had Michael somehow known that she needed to hear that to free her from her doubts, panic, and fears?

Celeste grumbled, pointing to the window. "How long were we entranced?"

Eve looked. Sunshine was creeping under the blinds. Daylight already? That was the problem with the spirit world. What felt like one or two minutes could actually be five or six hours in real time. It was part of the reason why she hated entering that world. It was so draining.

She walked to the window and drew up the blinds. Startling bright light poured into the room, nothing but blue skies as far as the eye could see.

Crushed, she stepped back. She'd hoped to go to Cian's as soon as possible and try to explain, make things right and really give this thing—whatever it was—a chance. She frowned. Now she'd have to wait all day.

"It's seven o' clock," Tamryn wailed, sleepiness threading her voice. "We have really got to do that more often or we're gonna lose our touch altogether. Goddess, I can't believe we stayed with the spirits so long."

Celeste shook her head, blond hair curling around her face. "I've got to open the shop in like the next ten minutes. Look, Tam, I still feel fine, so I'll run first shift. You can relieve me at two. Sound good?"

"What about me?" Eve asked.

"You think we're gonna make you work after what you found out?" Celeste gave a wicked smile, green eyes shining bright. "You can have today off, tomorrow too if, you know…things start to get hot and heavy."

"Oh brother." She chuckled. "I swear you guys must think I'm some sort of nympho."

"Umm, yeah." Celeste gave her a duh look, then shrugged. "Look, dolls, this has been fun and all, but I gotta run. And, Eve, since I'm sure you'll be in hiding most of the night tonight and probably even tomorrow"—she grinned wickedly—"don't forget the gathering, okay?"

Of course Celeste would go into mother mode, changing from teasing to serious so fast it gave you whiplash.

"The gathering." She frowned and glanced toward the calendar hanging on her wall. "Ohmygod, that totally slipped my mind. Yeah, for sure, I'll be there."

"Good. Well, then. Kissy, kissy, and all that jazz, and Tamryn remember to wake up, please. 'Cause if you don't I'll turn you into a dung beetle." With a finger wave, Celeste was out the door.

Tamryn turned back around, bloodshot eyes wide with humor. "There is something seriously wrong with that woman. You think we're really related?"

"'Fraid so."

"Yikes." She shook her head and shuddered, her lips curled into a crescent-shaped smile. "Anyway, all right if I crash here? I'm wasted and if I gotta go relieve the queen B, then I'll need all the rest I can get."

"Fine by me. Pull out the couch bed. I'm going to bed too."

"Mmmhmm. Yeah, okay. No doubt thinking about that handsome hunk of a vampire." She bit her lip, a grin spreading across her face. "Word of advice. Make sure to pull the door all the way shut if you're gonna play with Blue Thunder."

"My god, Tam! You're as nuts as Celeste." Eve marched back to her room. Exhaustion crept into her vision, her sister's tinkling laughter trailing behind.

The fact that she'd been thinking about doing just that was what embarrassed her the most.

What would life be without her sisters?

Chapter 18

Frenzy stood, exhausted. Heartbeat slowing down from the frenetic thumps of earlier. So many souls in one small area, he'd been bombarded with the fiery rush of shifting to reaper throughout the entire night.

His arm ached with a deep throb in the very tissue of his muscle. What the hell had they been doing to call so many spirits to them?

He growled and flexed his hand, now fleshy and hopefully for good this time. Never before had he been forced to shift so often. Regardless that the souls were no longer tied to bodies, being around them brought out the death in him, and the ire.

"Witches."

The creak of shifting floorboards and patter of movements that had gone late into the morning hours suddenly stopped. He narrowed his eyes, giving them a second, seeing if it was truly over.

He grabbed hold of the brass bedpost and closed his eyes. Instead of three, two steady pulses reverberated through his eardrums. One sister had left.

The heartbeats slowed into the gentle cadence of deep sleep. With a swipe of his hand he drew out some of his essence and covered himself in stealth, then opened a portal between his bedroom to Eve's.

Rosebud lips parted in a tiny gap. Black lashes fanned against the perfect paleness of skin. One leg wrapped around a body pillow stuck out the corner of a purple velvet blanket.

The blinds were closed, but couldn't contain the sun filtering between cracks. He walked forward and stopped at the edge of the bed. Did she know how close to death she lay? Was there any awareness in mortals that each second was precious? That life could so easily be snuffed out?

The thought that the next step, next breath might be the last crippled them.

Frenzy pulled the leather glove off his still fleshy hand. He wasn't going to harm Eve physically. Fine. There were other ways to hurt and he was a master at that.

Lashes fluttered against her cheek like a moth's wings. She was entering the first REM cycle. There would be no waking up now. He smiled, walked around toward the head of the bed, and hung his hand inches from her forehead, so close her body heat seeped into his palm.

The point today was to harm not bodily but emotionally. Leave her scarred and scared. Draw her into despair, panic. Break her will and leave her numb.

"Sleep. Sleep," he chanted, filling her mind with memories drawn from his own. They were the nightmares of an immortal.

Bodies, diseased and wasted. Children, infants staring into the great void, mouths opened in soundless screams as their village burned to a cinder behind them. Flies buzzing around heads. The rotten stench of decay heavy in the air.

She whimpered, tossing her head.

The Great War. Witches staked at the cross, guts and intestines drawn from still breathing victims. Humans shaking their pitch-forks; swords and daggers held tight in their fists. Faces of women and men—blue bloods and laymen alike—twisted into masks of ha-tred, contempt.

Her breath grew labored, chest heaving up and down. The room grew heavy with the sharp crack of agony. Tangible pain tore at Frenzy's face, chest, and back. He frowned. Pressure drew against his skull like the sharp rake of claws.

His gaze flicked toward Eve. She moaned, twisting the sheets be-tween her fists. Of course. It made sense now.

Cian would never fall for anything less extraordinary than him. This woman was more than witch. Her emotions were a corporeal force.

He slammed more into her. Fury from his past crept into his vision, fragmenting her thoughts with anguish, his anguish. Me-mories of his fourteenth-century Middle English beauty, Adrianna. His beautiful Adrianna, beaten, raped, and tortured.

Rich mahogany hair covered in blood.

Eve's pain ripped into him and he accepted its twisting, knifing ache. He growled, remembering and throwing it all at her.

Mud and dirt caked on Adrianna's royal-blue gown. Nails torn off in her struggle to escape, and gasping for air when there was none to take in.

She was left for dead on the side of a muddy road like so much garbage, and all because she'd rejected the advances of the duke for his.

Hate boiled inside him like a festering wound. The infection of his soul spewed over.

The gown he'd bought for her, shredded beyond repair, exposing her long, lean crimson-stained thighs.

Eve cried out—low, desperate cries. Tears rolled down from the corners of her eyes.

"Hell," he snarled and ran from the room, from the memories. The sounds of Eve's whimpering ripped into his back.

His nostrils flared, the murky haze of madness crept into his vision. Opening the portal with a swipe of his hand, he made ready to step through when the sound of rustling sheets caught his attention.

He turned. On the couch and curled into a ball lay a petite redhead, hair much like his own. But where his was pure fire, hers was a deep bloodred. One hand lay tucked under her chin. She had fragile, elegant features. He drew from Curtis's memories, searching for the name of the sister.

Violet eyes. Redhead.

Tamryn.

Whimpers and moans spilled from the other room. With one final glance, he left.

* * *

Eve sat at the kitchen table, nursing a cup of tea going on one hour now. She couldn't shake the dream from her head. Three hours after lying down she'd woken with the sounds of screams and battle cries thundering in her head.

She stared without seeing at the wall and bit her lip until it throbbed like the beat of her pulse. The babies lying broken. Women fallen to their knees, wailing and screaming in absolute heartache. Fire eating the huts, destroying memories.

She winced and took a sip of her lukewarm drink. The nightmare had been so real, vivid and terrifying, to the point that she could recall scent—unwashed bodies, the sickly sweet smell of blood. Sulfur odor of ash and fire. Crushed grass and horse sweat. Her hands shook and she dropped them to her lap with a heavy sigh.

An admitted history buff, she devoured books dealing with war and the ruin of empires. But she'd never before suffered like this. Her dreams had never been so fertile or realistic.

And the woman. Dead, raped. The horror she'd been through trapped in the eternal stillness of her gaze.

Eve swallowed hard around the lump in her throat and looked away, blinking. Bringing much-needed relief to the grit locked behind her eyes.

"Well, I'm a memory." Tamryn walked out of the bathroom, dressed in one of Eve's old scarlet-and-black baby-doll dresses. She looked down and then up. "You don't mind, do you? Cel would kill me if I relieve her late."

"No." She waved her hand, stood, and walked toward the kitchen sink, pouring out the rest of her tea.

Tamryn grabbed her arm and turned her around, eyes narrowed and searching. "Eve, you okay?"

She sighed and rubbed the bridge of her nose. "Fine. Didn't get much sleep. Just tired."

"You sure?"

Her lips twitched into a half smile. "Yeah, but you'd better go before Cel starts hounding me, trying to figure out where you are."

Tamryn frowned, doubt glittering in her eyes. She didn't believe her. That much was evident. But she didn't push it either, only shrugged and walked to the door. "It's okay, Eve. Sometimes it's better to keep things to yourself. I won't pry. Don't forget the gathering," she reminded her again.

"I won't." She shook her head.

"Good. See you tomorrow, and give that hunk of yours an extra nibble for me." She winked and slid out the door.

Eve smiled, but didn't feel it, and walked toward her window. The sun was still hours from setting, hours until she could see him again. It was sick how much she was coming to not only enjoy her brief moments with Cian, but eagerly anticipate them. Something about the man called to her, made her feel desirable again, safe. She sighed, knowing sleep would be almost impossible now that she couldn't stop obsessing over how many hours were left in the day.

Chapter 19

It was night, finally. Eve threw on a pair of faded blue jeans and a black turtleneck, tucked her keys and wallet into her pocket, and ran out the door.

She only hoped he'd be willing to listen. She raced down the flight of stairs.

Please, god.

So consumed was she by thoughts of talking to Cian that she barely noticed Curtis until it was almost too late. She came to a screeching halt, nearly running over Samhain in her haste. Curtis reached out, his hands gripping her by the shoulders and holding her steady.

Her heart thumped loudly in her ears. "Oh my gosh, that was too close." She gave a weak laugh, grabbing her chest. "You seem to be saving me an awful lot lately. Sorry about that, Curtis."

"Ah"—he shrugged her off—"no worries. You seem to have a lot on your mind."

She nodded, shifting from foot to foot. Antsy to go. What if he was already gone, doing whatever the heck vampires did at this time of night? It was getting late.

"Yeah, I do."

His warm gaze stared into her own. She was getting ready to turn away when she caught a flicker of color burning in his eyes. Startled, her heart tripped in her chest. Had she seen what she thought she'd seen or only an illusion of light dancing inside them? She blinked, but all she found was a sea of deep brown. There had been something, she was sure of it.

Ridiculous, nothing there. Stop being silly. She was just nervous at the prospect of seeing Cian. That was all. Threads of the dream were still unnerving her, obviously. It was not a good day for her. Conspiracy theories would abound if she wasn't careful.

Curtis gave her one last squeeze then dropped his hands. "You take care, there, Eve." And then he walked on, tugging ever so slightly on the cat leash in his grip.

Samhain gave a small meow before finally deciding to follow.

She frowned, turning to stare at Mr. Lovelace's retreating figure heading into his apartment, and dismissed the odd moment. There were other, more pressing matters to attend to at the moment, like getting to Cian's posthaste. With that thought in mind, she raced outside to find a cab and head toward Baker Street.

Thirty minutes later she threw some bills at the cabby and got out, staring at the brick-faced Victorian home with wide-eyed wonder.

"He lives here?" She could hardly believe it.

It was beautiful. Classic.

Two-story home in the gothic style. Filigree black railing circled the top of the house. Stone gargoyles facing the street and sitting on the porch, their mouths open in wide Os, brows lowered and faces twisted into a glower. She shivered and rubbed her hands down her arms. Just the type of place she'd imagine a vampire living in. A wild storm, jagged lightning piercing the sky against a black backdrop, was the only thing missing to make this place really have that creepy, perfect vibe.

She glanced up and down the block. Pink and yellow azalea bushes lined the steep sidewalk. Elms, maples, oaks, and a variety of other trees littered the area. This was so different from the norm. San Francisco was pretty much one house or shop on top of another as far as the distant horizon. Baker Street was suburbia in the big city. Strange that in all her years she'd never been down this way. It really was beautiful.

She bit her lip, adjusted her top with nervous fingers, and walked forward. Now that she was here she wasn't exactly sure what to say. This was going to look really weird no matter how she approached it.

Eve walked up to the door, hand poised and ready to knock. She didn't see any lights on. *He's probably not even here.*

"No chickening out," she whispered.

At the least he deserved an explanation for yesterday.

Taking a deep breath she shook her hands and shoulders, psyching herself up. "Okay, okay. I can do this. I am woman, hear me roar."

Oh, that was really stupid.

She ran cold fingers over her face and nodded. Nerves twisted her gut in knots and threatened to make her sick. "Okay. One. Two. Three…"

The door flew open and she yelped, startled to see Cian headed out.

His blue gaze widened then narrowed. He looked from side to side and frowned. "Eve?"

Words left her. She was drawing such a serious blank it was a crime. Her hand was still fisted and poised to knock. She slowly brought it back down to her side.

This was mortifying in the extreme and not the entrance she'd hoped to make, that was for sure.

"What are you doing here?"

She gave a crooked grin. Now was as good a time as any to reassert herself. Straightening her back, she decided to face this head-on rather than become the cowardly mouse. "I came to find you, Cian."

He lifted a brow, confusion glittering in his eyes.

She took that moment to study him. Goddess, but he looked good. White button-down shirt tapering to his broad chest, blue jeans fitting snug on his thighs. Not so tight as to reveal the package, but definitely enough to outline the smooth, firm muscle of his legs. That dark and light hair and those blue eyes. Perfection.

Yeowza!

He stepped back, ushering with his arm for her to enter. He still looked as confused as ever, but at least he was gentleman enough not to let her flounder on the stoop forever. The man was classy, she had to give him that. Relieved that he hadn't decided to slam the door in her face, she leaned in and kissed his cheek. Well, she'd *intended* to kiss it, but at the last second he turned and their lips wound up meeting. Just that brief contact sent heat zipping down her spine and she was smug enough to enjoy seeing his eyes widen in response. The man wanted her, even though he might not be ready to admit it. He was as helpless to this thing happening between them as she was.

Clearing his throat, he walked toward the kitchen area as if he needed space. She might have been hurt by his abrupt departure if it weren't for the fact that she was feeling a little frazzled herself.

Her eyes widened the deeper they went into the house. Polished, hardwood floors. Bearskin rugs, boulder-style fireplace in the living room. Leather furniture of the deepest brown, mahogany entertainment center. Plasma-screen TV on the wall. "Loaded" did not even begin to describe this house. It was a bachelor's paradise.

The kitchen was gorgeous, with the same polished floors, but all the electrical appliances were a futuristic silver—stove, fridge, even the toaster. The countertops were black marble.

"Take a seat." He pointed to the breakfast nook. She slid into the diner-style table.

"Want something to drink?" he asked and turned toward the refrigerator, opening the door.

He was humming with curiosity. It was obvious in the tense lines of his shoulders.

"Got OJ?" She shrugged.

"I think so." He reached in.

From out of nowhere, lancing spikes of pain arced down her skull. She winced, squeezing her eyes shut as fire raced through her body.

The same thing that had happened the other day was happening again, and this time returning with a vengeance. Eve winced, pressing her fingertips to her temples. It was like somebody was pressing her head from both sides. Pressure was building. Tears filled her eyes. This headache was worse. Much worse.

Like breaking a leg, puncturing a lung, and finding out you had cancer all at the same time, worse.

"Eve!" Cian grabbed her shoulders. "What's wrong?"

The timbre of his words echoed in her head like the gong of bells. Her limbs turned sluggish as fog crept over her vision, and then there was black.

*   *   *

Cian kept applying a wet towel to her forehead. The slithering madness inside him had snapped at his seeing her slump in her seat. Fear bubbled through his veins.

He still trembled from the aftereffects of so much psychic energy being blasted at him. It had been so powerful he'd dropped to his knees in agony and could still taste the adrenaline on his tongue. The incessant pounding in his skull was nothing compared to the fire stabbing through his brain earlier. Once she'd passed out, all the symptoms had faded; still, it scared him.

He glanced at her, his heart in his throat. She was pale white, her lips a light shade of blue. It was like the mark of death, but her pulse was strong. He couldn't make sense of it.

Had she been suffering with those long? He ran a worried hand across her brow. She wasn't feverish.

A healthy glow was settling back into her cheeks. He closed his eyes, his nerves unsteady and his hands shaking. Relief was a soothing balm to his tormented mind.

Gently he picked her up and walked her to the guest bedroom, which, thankfully, had a bed. He adjusted the pillows. Long black hair fell like shadow against the cream pillowcase.

"Lass, can you hear me?" he asked in a soothing, rocking tone. He framed her face in his hands, searching her for any sign that she was coming to.

A muscle in her cheek twitched.

"Wake up. Come on."

She moaned.

"Eve." He grabbed her hand and brought it to his whiskered cheek, expelling a long breath.

Her lashes fluttered and then slowly she opened her eyes, the golden depths bright with unshed tears. "What the hell happened?" she croaked.

"You passed out."

She wrinkled her brows. "What? When?"

"Don't you remember? Just a second ago." At her blank stare he rushed on. "Eve, you were projecting so hard I nearly joined you."

She sat up, bringing a hand to her forehead.

"I'm not sure moving is the best thing for you right now." He held her around the waist, trying to draw her back down.

"Cian, I don't know what happened, but I feel fine now."

He frowned. "How is this possible? Don't you remember the headache in the kitchen just a second ago?" Surely she couldn't have forgotten that.

She gave him a weak smile and pushed her hand against his chest, freeing herself to sit up. "I, ah…" Her gaze shifted around the room, confusion settling like a mask on her features. Exhaling sharply, she looked to him. "Last thing I remember is you asking me what kind of drink I'd like, and then it's pretty much blank from there."

Narrowing his eyes, he studied her. Was she lying? Would she even have a reason to? But there was no denying the honesty in her golden gaze. She really didn't remember.

This wasn't normal. People didn't go from near death one second to looking perfectly healthy and fine the next. "How do you feel now?"

She shrugged, a crooked grin on her face. "I feel fine. Never better actually. Little confused, to be honest, but otherwise…"

He gripped her shoulders, forcing her to stare at him. Being death had its advantages. Knowing what afflicted a spirit for one. Be it human, plant, or otherwise. All he'd have to do was pass someone on the street and he'd know immediately if they suffered a life-threatening disease. A physical manifestation of the malady would present itself. The low throb of cancer eating away at organs, or the rush of HIV through blood.

The sharp pains Eve had experienced made him scared that it could be a tumor, something pressing against her skull. All the symptoms fit.

Heart hammering in his chest he lifted a gloved hand and ran it along her head, feeling not for the hair beneath but the gentle hum of disease. He could hardly swallow around the lump in his throat.

Nothing.

No hum. No betraying vibration. Silence.

His nostrils flared, even more confused than ever before. With the exception of what had happened, Eve was as healthy as an immortal. No mortal sickness lay waste to her body.

Her eyes were like wide saucers in her face. "Cian, what are you doing?"

He dropped his hands. "I feel like I should take you to the hospital."

She gave a tiny shake of her head. "I really feel fine. I doubt they'd find anything. I mean"—she threw out her arms—"do I look sick?"

"Well, no…" He couldn't shake the feeling that something wasn't right, but neither could he put a finger on what that something might be. For the first time in a long time, he felt helpless. Not a feeling he relished where Eve's safety was concerned. "Has this ever happened before?"

"Seeing as how I don't even remember *this* ever happening, I can honestly say no." She bit her lip, a sultry gleam filling her eyes. "You're cute when you do that."

Her words were so unexpected he couldn't stop himself from smiling. Warmth shot through him at her words. "What?"

"That. Worrying about me the way you do. It's cute." She smiled that crooked smile of hers.

He really wanted to get to the bottom of whatever that was, but she seemed fine and reluctant to keep talking about it. What else was there for him to do but move on? Obviously she was fine; maybe it was some quirk of the witch he was unaware of. So he took a deep breath and tried not to think about how his heart had nearly stopped in its tracks.

Cian stood and walked to the door. "Yeah, well, what can I say?"

She lay back down on the bed, pulling a pillow under her cheek and smiling. This tiny woman was lying in the center of a massive bed. And yet the bed seemed dwarfed by the size of her personality. From the moment she'd entered the house, it was like she shared a part of her soul with the home, blotting out the shadows and darkness, filling the space with her light.

He swallowed.

Nothing had ever looked so right or made him feel so warm.

"I guess, umm..." She gazed at him, a question in her eyes. Whether he wanted her to stay or go.

"Orange juice, right?"

That endearing smile lit her features again, erasing the strain from her brows. She nodded, and he turned to get it, his heart an aching thing in his chest. Seeing her here, in this house, felt so right. Natural. These emotions she brought out in him sometimes worried him, because with each passing hour he got to know her, the more he needed her.

The reasons for her coming and how she'd found him in the first place crowded his thoughts with each footstep.

Chapter 20

It was still dark out when Even opened her eyes and leaned back against the pillows, frowning and thinking. Had she really blacked out the way Cian had said? It was probably true; there was a chunk of time just gone. Which was sort of frightening.

Last things she recalled were sitting at his kitchen table and then waking up on his bed. She worried her bottom lip. Her thoughts a little fuzzy, lethargy began to creep into her limbs. Due to the nightmares, she hadn't gotten much sleep. What was it about Cian that made her feel so safe? Despite the fear she'd suffered at home, all she wanted to do now was draw the sheets over her head and fall asleep.

She shifted and stared out of the open bay window, inhaling the fresh sea air wafting through.

The other morning she'd suffered a terrible headache, but it was nothing serious. It seemed the same had happened again tonight, only this time coupled with a complete lapse in memory. Truth was she felt a-OK aside from the sleepiness.

She blew out a breath. How weird that she couldn't remember.

Was he exaggerating what happened? She rubbed her temple. There wasn't even an aftereffect of lingering pain. If it'd been that bad, shouldn't she have recalled something?

Footsteps alerted her to Cian's presence seconds before he entered the room. Worries fled at the sight of him carrying a serving tray with a tall glass of orange juice and a plate of toast. All that was missing was a cute little vase with a rose inside it.

She laughed and sat up, giving him room to set the tray across her lap. "You didn't need to do all this."

There were tiny saucers filled with a variety of jams and a small tab of butter.

"Well"—his gravelly voice rolled through her veins—"after what happened, I figured putting something in your stomach couldn't hurt."

She smiled and buttered her toast. "You sure do own a lot of food for a vampire. I can't understand how the sight of this stuff doesn't turn your stomach."

"Yeah." He snorted.

The flavor of sourdough burst inside her mouth with the first bite. "Oh," she moaned, "this is so good."

He grinned and sat on the edge of the bed. "Glad you like it."

Eve devoured the toast and drank more than half of the orange juice before she spoke again. She pushed the tray aside and sighed, placing her hand over her stomach. "Jeez, I just realized that's the first thing I ate all day. Thanks, I really needed that."

Now that she'd eaten, she was really starting to feel sluggish, and his bed was so comfortable, the comforter thick and plush. All she wanted to do was kick off her shoes, curl into him, and fall asleep.

"So, how'd you find this place?"

"Right"—she rolled the *r*—"I kinda forgot all about that, didn't I?"

He cocked his head, twisting his lips.

Now came the part that she'd dreaded. Her stomach knotted all over again. "Truth is, after I totally wigged out on you at the beach yesterday…"

"Hmm"—he nodded—"what was that all about? I thought we were having a good time."

The guy didn't pull punches. Blunt but honest, at least he didn't beat around the bush or pretend like he didn't know what she was talking about. She admired him all the more for it.

"We were. I was." She sighed and gave an apologetic shrug. "This is so hard to say without sounding totally weird."

She couldn't look at the open confusion in his deep blues any-more. It was just making her too nervous. So she allowed her gaze to roam the room, coming to rest on the burnished cherrywood ar-moire. "Two years ago I lost someone really dear to me. And it's crazy, but in that moment I got so carried away"—she paused, tak-ing a deep breath—"and, I dunno… I just panicked."

He grabbed her cold hands, warming them. She looked at him. His touch seemed to fill that empty space inside her, like the seam-less joining of two souls.

She drowned in his bottomless eyes. He wasn't judging her but comforting, and she felt herself falling deeper and harder. Her heart gave a tiny jerk.

"You still didn't tell me how you found this place."

His fingers slowly stroked the small of her back. It felt good, and she relaxed into his touch.

"That's it? You're not pissed at me for acting like such an idiot?"

He kissed her knuckle and said, "Who am I to judge?"

The movement of his firm lips against her flesh made her tingle, and desire coursed a turbulent path down her body, making her ache low in her gut, her nipples tightening into hard, painful buds.

She shook her head and patted the spot on the bed next to her. She hardly knew him and yet it felt like they'd known each other for years. There was something very calming about that.

"My sisters forced me to do a séance."

A grin split his face.

She rolled her eyes. "I swear I'm not a stalker, but you never gave me your number or address, and I wanted to find you and tell you that…I was sorry."

He crawled next to her, draping his arm around her shoulders and pulling her close. "It's okay. I am glad you came."

Stomach fluttering at the tenderness in his voice, she laid her head on his chest. The steady beat of his heart, a song in her ears. The soapy scent of his body filled her senses. She sighed. This was so nice, so perfect.

With a flick of his wrist, Cian turned off the lights, and several candles around the room burst to life. A soft golden glow filled the room.

"This is nice," she murmured, closing her eyes. Sleep crowded her mind, becoming harder to ignore.

"Eve."

"Hmm?" She could stay like this forever.

"Do you want to stay the night?" His voice was a soft whisper.

A small thrill raced down her spine, and she nodded, nuzzling his chest with tiny moans until she finally fell asleep.

* * *

He watched her. It seemed that was all he could do anymore. In repose she reminded him of a sylph. Angelic and ethereal. Reaching out, he touched the sable polish of her hair. It was silky soft, and he rubbed a strand between his fingers.

She moaned, and he trailed a finger down her cheek. It was warm to the touch. He wasn't sure what she liked to sleep in, but he was certain the turtleneck had to be hot. With a swipe of his hand, he replaced her jeans and turtleneck with a soft white tank top and a pair of cotton sleep pants. Her clothing reappeared by the sitting chair in the corner, draped over the top.

"Rest."

"Didn't know you vampies could do that." A soft smile graced her lips before quickly fading into a loud yawn.

Goddess, how he wanted to tell her the truth, that he wasn't a damn bloodsucker, he was a fae, a death dealer, and absolutely, irrevocably ensnared by her.

But the moment passed and she was too exhausted for this kind of conversation. He would tell her, when the time was right. Cian wasn't tired, rarely needing sleep the way a human body craved it, but he didn't want to let her go either. She rolled onto her side, her backside firmly spooned against him. The white tail feather of her tattoo peeked out the bottom of her shirt.

He reached out, dragging his finger along the design. It was healing nicely, barely pink anymore.

"You are so bonny, lass," he whispered.

It was getting close. Their days were numbered. This was the third day. He had two more left. Two more days to figure out how to stop this. It didn't seem possible that time was moving so fast. But it was, and Cian was no closer to figuring out how to keep her safe from The Morrigan than he'd been at the beginning.

He closed his eyes, the weight of her body a comforting presence. In such a short period, he'd come to care for this woman more than he'd ever imagined possible.

Smirking, he shook his head. To think she'd gone through a séance to find out where he lived. She fascinated him, everything about her. Eve was fire and passion, a woman with a dark past who'd come so far.

Her soft, even breathing warred with the mechanical rhythm of the grandfather clock in the hallway. The hands of time were ticking away, and all he could do was helplessly stand by and watch it move on.

Sometime later, he wasn't sure how much, she rolled over. Her moans growing louder and louder. Hearing those mewls, seeing her body undulate and move, he had no doubt what she was dreaming about. His lips quirked. His cock twitched.

To touch her, to taste her—he'd give almost anything to have her now.

As if sensing his gaze, her eyes fluttered open. "Cian." Her voice was so soft, tremulous.

"Lass?"

"Do you feel it?"

He wasn't sure what she meant. He looked out the window. "Feel what?"

"The fire. Do you feel it?"

His heart stuttered. He licked his lips. His balls ached so badly he could barely remember a time they hadn't anymore.

She dragged her foot along the length of his calf, her touch sizzled. It burned, made him crave. Want. His breathing grew sharp and heavy.

"I feel it," he muttered, secure in the shadows crawling around them to utter the truth. Sensing the dark would take his words, hold them sacred, keep them safe.

Her eyes were liquid pools. Golden drops of brilliance. "I want you so bad. More than I've ever wanted anyone else."

He sucked in a sharp breath. She had no idea, no clue how much those words made him tremble. Like his world had tipped on its side. He'd known how much she'd loved Michael, how much a part of her still did. That she could say that to him…

"Eve." Her name on his lips was a promise, a whisper of something he could not put into words.

She crawled on top of him, her breasts smashed into his chest. Goddess, he wanted this so badly: to rip the clothes from her body, bury himself in her warm haven, and forget.

"I need you, Cian. I have from the moment we met. I need you to touch me, to ease the fire in my blood." She kissed his neck, and her scent wrapped him up, made him dizzy. He groaned. His fingers dug into her firm backside, kneading, petting.

He couldn't believe he was about to say this. She was everything he wanted, she was throwing herself at him, and, goddess, if it wasn't tempting, but…"Eve, you're half-asleep—"

Her tongue flicked at his neck. A moan rumbled from his throat, from the deepest pit of his soul. "Eve…"

"I'm not asleep. I'm awake. Alive. For the first time in a long time. Kiss me, Cian."

"Lass." That was all he could say; there were so many reasons why they shouldn't do this. Why they couldn't. But her pants, her moans, drowned out all reason. He'd show her she wasn't the only one feeling the fire with his tongue, his body.

Cian growled and rolled them over, pinning her beneath him. She wiggled, squirmed, and he ground his cock in between her thighs. "Is that what you want?"

He wanted her, this woman, with a desperation that bordered on madness, and he hoped to the goddess that she wanted it too, because he wasn't sure he'd be strong enough to back down now.

She threw her head back, her lips parted in a tiny O. "Yes, goddess, yes."

He was pure instinct now. She was a feast laid out for him, begging him to taste, to suckle. Cian crawled down her body.

"No, Cian…please."

No sex. He couldn't cross that line, but there were other ways to gain pleasure for them both.

His hands were rough as he ripped her tiny shorts down the sides. She gasped and then smiled when he yanked on her thong.

"Ohhhh," she moaned.

He grunted. Any other moment he would have taken his time. Not tonight. He'd whip her up slowly, hot kisses trailing a path down her neck, her breasts, teasing her navel, and then maybe laving the sensitive skin between her thighs. He was hungry, crazy for the sight of her. The taste of her in his mouth.

He ripped the flimsy thong off and then sat on his knees, stunned to silence for a moment. She was shaved. There wasn't a hair to hide the peachy perfection of her dewy slit. She spread her legs and stuck her finger in her mouth. She was unashamed of her nudity; her eyes glinted with lust and something nameless, foreign. She stared at him as he stared at her, but he couldn't rip his gaze from the sight of her naked flesh.

"Eve." Her name ripped from his throat like a benediction.

"I'm all yours, Cian." Then, slowly and with practiced ease, she took the finger she'd been sucking on and traced it up her slit. "All yours."

He was an animal. Cian took her finger, sucked on it hard, tasting her sweet essence. Letting it settle on his tongue like nectar, but one taste wasn't enough. "I'm sorry, lass," he crooned, "I canna be gentle. So sorry."

He shoved her legs down hard on the mattress and settled between her thighs, taking her swollen nub into his mouth, and sucked. Hard.

Her nails were tiny claws scraping at his scalp, and she lifted off the bed, her thighs trapping his head as she rubbed herself on his face. "Don't want gentle," she panted. "Want you."

Then there were no more words as he sucked, tasted and devoured. Running his tongue down the long, wet length of her. She was a wild, crazy thing, her groans growing in pitch and intensity.

Cian couldn't stop from touching himself. He pulled back just enough to take his cock in hand and rubbed hard, his vision growing blurry.

"I'm coming, Cian." She keened, her knees trembled, and then she was spasming on him, giving him everything she had and Cian roared as his seed blasted from his body with the force of a tsunami.

They lay there stunned, breathless. Her hands were gentle, rubbing his hair. "Come here."

Exhausted, he crawled back up her body, wrapped tight around him. His lips found hers and she kissed him back. But it wasn't possession or lust; this kiss held something both were too afraid to whisper but felt to the depths of their souls.

He rolled over with a sigh, and she snuggled into his chest. Then her breathing grew heavy and he knew she'd fallen back asleep. He smiled and joined her.

Chapter 21

She was beautiful waking up, a lazy dance of limbs stretching out and back arcing up. Eve reminded him of a petal opening to face the sunlight after a long sleep. And it made him desperate for more. Three days wouldn't be enough; five wouldn't be either. He needed more, a lifetime, an eternity of this. Of waking up and finding her beside him. His jaw clenched. Was it selfish that he wanted it all?

Her lashes fluttered a second before finally opening. She blinked a few times and then turned to look at him, sleep still in her eyes.

"Good morning. Or should I say good night?"

He knew the moment she remembered what they'd shared last night, her cheeks filled with pink. Her lips twisted and she glanced to her right. She bit her bottom lip, and though he'd tasted her once, he knew in that moment if she wanted to, he'd be more than happy to oblige. He would never get enough of Eve.

"Last night was, ah…" She licked her lips, still unable to look at him.

"Me too." He grabbed her hand and placed it against his chest.

She finally looked at him. Within her eyes he read that same foreignness he'd read last night. That gentle flutter of something both infinite and profound. He trembled and she shook her head.

"So, umm…how long were we out?"

He turned to look out the window. Navy-blue and violet streaks raced across the endless expanse of sky. "Pretty long."

"Huh?" She glanced at the bedroom clock and then gasped, sitting up and clutching the sheet to her chest. "I slept for almost ten hours? I gotta go. I gotta…" She jumped to her feet and ran toward the door. "The meeting! Oh my god."

She was a vision, bare breasts bouncing with her hurried steps. Full swell of her backside flexing with each stride. His blood hummed.

"Hey. Hey." He caught up to her and grabbed her elbow. "Calm down. You should probably wait to put on something a little warmer. And what meeting?"

"What?" She glanced down, eyes going wide, finally noticing she was nude. She blushed again and if she didn't seem to be in such a panic to leave, he'd be pulling her back to the bed for the sequel. "Where are—"

He jerked his thumb behind his shoulder. "Hanging over the chair. You looked a little uncomfortable last night, so I—"

"I thought you tore my clothes." The blush was still firmly settled in her cheeks. She bit her bottom lip, and he couldn't stop himself from touching the spot with his finger.

Hunger replaced the panic in her gaze. "More time. Goddess, what I wouldn't give for more time," she moaned.

It was obvious that she needed to go. With a sigh he stepped back. "I tore some shorts and a shirt I put you in. The thong's gone."

She raised a brow. "Changed me in my sleep, you dirty boy. That's okay. Commando-R-Us, that's me." She winked, and he growled.

"More time," he said.

"More time," she agreed with a nod.

Eve walked to the chair, grabbed her clothes, and slipped them back on. The jeans and turtleneck once again hugged her curves. Very luscious curves at that.

His eyes traveled the length of her, a slow, heated perusal, no longer having to imagine what that body looked like beneath. Her desire coiled inside him and he grinned, staring at her face. Blood rushed to his cock, making him instantly hard and ready.

She narrowed her eyes, pulling her lower lip between her teeth. "What I wouldn't give to know do what's going through that mind of yours."

"Might frighten you."

"Hmm. If that's a challenge, I think I'm up to the task."

He inclined his head, an answering grin on her face. "So what's this meeting?"

"Just a gathering held each month where every species has a delegate speak on their behalf and give the happenings of what's going on in their territories. A must attend for business owners. It keeps us up-to-date, and it's a good place to mingle, make trades. That sorta thing. I've never missed one." She smoothed out the flyaway curls gathered around her face and grinned. "Anyway, Cian, thanks for letting me crash…and that other stuff."

She was so cute when she got shy. How a woman could be so wanton and sexy in bed and then shy about it afterward confused him but also made his blood hot. She'd never be boring.

"It's not a problem."

She rocked back on her heels, shoving her hands down her back pockets. "It's getting pretty late. I really need to go."

He ground his jaw and took a step forward. Though he really didn't want to do what he was about to suggest, neither was he willing to let her walk away.

"Take me to the gathering with you."

She shook her head, her eyes narrowing into slits. "Seriously? You want to go there with me? It's a boring meeting."

"I don't want you to go alone. It's dangerous at this time of night."

Eve reached out and patted his cheek with a soft smile. "That's really nice of you. But I'm a big girl and I can tell you don't really want to go." She touched her ruby stone necklace. "I've got this. I'll be fine."

He turned his head, planting a kiss on her palm.

She sucked in a breath, golden eyes growing soft. Sexual tension arced through the air like electricity. The rich scent of patchouli filtered under his nose, and he inhaled and nodded.

"I just want to be with you."

Currents of warmth flowed through him.

"You're sure?" she whispered.

He nodded.

"Okay, then." She walked toward the bed and picked up her fallen boots, sat on the edge, and pulled them on. "You wouldn't happen to have a spare toothbrush lying around here, would you?"

He pointed to the bathroom. "Under the sink, there's a couple."

She smiled and walked toward the bathroom. Rushing water warred with the sound of a scrubbing brush. The strong scent of mint filled the room.

Why couldn't he shake the feeling that this was a terrible idea?

His gut was a nervous mass of knots. Eve was losing time. Not only that, but he still hadn't come up with an answer to their dilemma. Now they were headed to a gathering full of the undead and supernatural. This was going to be trouble. Nothing but trouble.

* * *

Eve ran through the streets of San Francisco, Cian right on her heels. And they weren't the only ones. Others were coming out the woodwork, slinking away from shadow and flying as fast as the wind could carry them toward Presidio.

It might have been faster to take a cab, but there was a strict rule: no normals allowed within ten yards of the monthly meets. Ever. More for their safety than anything else.

Panting and sweating profusely, they finally arrived at the historical military keep—now a transformed park reserve—with little time to spare. She'd always tried to leave for the gatherings with at least an hour to spare, but not today.

Freaking sexy vamps.

She'd cut it way too close and now looked like a drowned rat. She wondered what Cian thought. Just thinking about him made her remember what she'd done last night. What he'd done. What they'd done.

Her stomach flopped and she couldn't stop the grin from stealing across her lips. Goddess, but the man could…

He chuckled, and she knew she'd been projecting again. She rolled her eyes, casting him a dirty look. "We're here." She pointed to the cream-colored four-story abandoned complex covered in chipped paint, cut with nicks and grooves in the stucco wall. It looked in shoddy disrepair, but it was actually very solid, able to withstand years' worth of earthquakes.

"So I see."

Cian pulled her to his side as a group of vampires walked inside. "Stay close to me, Eve."

She laughed at his protective gesture. "I'm fine. These monthly gatherings began long before my birth: there's never been any bloodshed. It's perfectly safe."

His jaw set and he eyed a group of stalking pumas. Sexy Cian was gone, brooding Cian taking his place. "I'd feel better knowing you were close."

Smirking, she nodded.

Men. Well, okay, so maybe he was still kind of sexy in a broody Bruce Wayne kind of way.

"Eve, holy hell. Get your butt in here."

She turned and spied Tamryn gesturing frantically for her to hurry inside. Grabbing Cian's hand, she walked in. The cavernous room was more than big enough to hold the variety of creatures gathered.

Large tiers of candles lit the otherwise darkened room. There were no decorations, only chairs, a few benches, and the head table up front, in which sat the delegates of each race.

Iah, of the moon clan, spoke for the vampires. Severe and austere, he was nonetheless pleasing to the eye. Hawk-beaked nose, chiseled cheekbones, and dark eyes the color of polished ebony. Rich Egyptian skin glistened purest copper.

Next to him sat the were liaison, Lootah of the Kohana pack. Regal and proud, he gazed at the group. The burned red of his face a fine map of wrinkles and scars. He was an ancient. Old wolf, and well versed in the matters of his kin. It was good to see him up there. He brought to the talks a wisdom of age very few could match.

Last, but certainly not least, Edlyn of the briar thorn coven. Frail of body but strong of spirit. Salt-and-pepper hair caught up in a braid, tendrils curling around her tired face. Deep into her eightieth year, she'd seen more than many mortals in her time and was the perfect delegate to speak for the witches.

"C'mon…hurry, before this starts." Tamryn pushed past several rows of bodies, leading them toward a bench in the back corner of the room.

Eve squeezed through the narrow openings, following her sister and throwing Cian a grateful glance. Now that he was here, she was thankful.

She'd never been able to share this part of her life with Michael, and being here with Cian felt right. He truly understood what it was to be different. They shared a bond she'd never had with her husband.

Chatter rose to cacophonous levels, drowning out the noise of any one individual conversation. It was all just buzz to her. Mostly the species stuck to their own, forming tight bands of vampires, wolves, hawks, panthers, and so on. But a few, like herself and Cian, intermingled.

Mingan and Celeste were deep in talk when they finally made it to the bench and dropped down beside them.

"So we made it." Eve glanced at Mingan. "Good to see you."

He nodded, a distracted frown on his face. "Yes, you too, Eve." He patted Celeste's sleeve in a farewell gesture then marched off.

She frowned, casting a quick glance at Cian, his face a mirror reflection of her own. "Oddly dismissive. What was that all about?"

Celeste shook her head, a worried gleam in her moss-green eyes. "Rumors been flying about a murder."

"Murder? What murder?" First she'd heard of this.

"Vampire. Found this morning staked to a cross. Body burned beyond recognition."

Shocked, she blinked. "When?"

Lootah stood, spreading his arms wide and quieting the crowd with a glance. "The meeting will come to order."

It was like a light switch had been turned off. A crowd of hundreds instantly fell silent. The delegates spoke for the groups for one reason. You respected them enough to listen.

Hard thing to command in a room full of predators.

Brown eyes full of knowledge and centuries' worth of sorrow landed on Eve's face for the briefest of moments. In the eyes, she read truth. The rumor of murder was rumor no more.

"I'm sure you've all heard by now that Indigo, of the clan thrive, was found dead this morning."

Instantly buzz exploded through the room.

"Indigo," she hissed and looked at Cian.

He frowned. "The vamp in the alleyway two nights back?"

Her eyes grew wide and she nodded.

"Not that I ever cared for that hothead much, but ohmygoddess." Celeste shook her head. "The turd's gonna hit the fan now."

"Quiet!" Iah shot to his feet, quelling them all to silence. "Thank you, Lootah, but I think I can take it from here."

Lootah nodded and sat.

"Indigo was killed in the most despicable of ways. Strapped to a cross and roasted to cinders by the sun. How could this have happened and no one noticed?"

He pounded his fist on the table. A wicked gleam filled his black eyes. She could feel his rage simmer just below the surface and everyone leaned forward a tiny bit, breaths indrawn and waiting on tenterhooks.

"Her death was an earmark human killing."

The room broke into a violence of voices. This was big news, one that held many connotations.

For one, the shaky pact between normal/super relations. Supers were given the right to live out in the open, in freedom, without fear of retribution. The law stated that no human should come to harm at the hands of the supers and vice versa.

In her heart, she knew this would irreparably damage the fragile peace between supernaturals and normals.

Iah pointed to a vampire dressed all in black. "Mia, is this not so?"

Mia stood, her pale, perfect skin gleaming, her rich sable hair caught up in a severe knot. Her face lacked the lines and wrinkles of the elders; she was youth personified. But it was the eyes, the malachite gaze that gleamed with the eternal mark of age, that gave her away. This was an elder. Well past her four hundredth year.

"Yes." The gravel of her voice reverberated through the room and brought chills to the back of Eve's neck.

"This is an outrage!" Another vampire toward the rear of the room jumped up and shouted, punching his fist through the air. "One that must be dealt with swiftly and fiercely. Lest all normals forget who's really the weaker of the two."

"Aye!"

"Yeah."

"...lest they forget."

The room erupted in an ear-piercing chorus of voices, several of them vamps, but a few weres, or even witches. Eve clamped hands over her ears, wincing at the cacophonous pitch buzzing through her eardrums.

Their faces were angry and contorted, the ardent predators inside them demanding reparations. She knew what they thought; she could feel the resentment rolling off them. They'd lived by the rules, and so too should the normals.

Bloodbath, Tamryn mouthed.

Mia turned, a sinister smile playing on her bloodred lips. "We'll band together and find the killers. Then we'll do to them what they did to Indigo."

Rage. The emotion more intense than even the sight of blood, transformed others into their Mr. Hyde personalities. Fangs began ripping through mouths, fur sprouted from knuckles. The room grew heavy with tension, like a rubber band seconds before it snapped.

This couldn't happen. Somebody had to stop it. She glanced toward the delegates. They each wore calm looks, hands crossed in their laps, and none looked ready, or willing, to break up the angry crowd.

Heart racing, adrenaline surging through her veins, Eve jumped to her feet. "No! You do not understand." No one stopped talking. "Stop," she shrieked, "and listen!"

That caught the group's attention. It was a rippling tide of faces turning to stare at her, an eerie silence filling the hall. Iah frowned. The room grew tense with expectancy. "Enlighten us, then, witch."

"Indigo killed a human that night."

"Lying witch. She would never!" Mia screamed, her green eyes narrowing with ire.

Cian stood, standing so close to Eve they shared body heat. She was grateful and her heart gave a tiny flutter in response. He gave her the strength to plow on.

"I arrived at the scene to hear her feed off the dying man."

Mia's nostrils flared as her fists clenched by her sides.

It was unnerving to have so many eyes on her, boring holes into her. One wrong move and she'd come under attack by the full weight of all the others within.

"Are you certain this was Indigo?" Iah asked.

"Yes. I saw her with my own eyes. She was high off blood."

Iah snapped his mouth shut. Eve knew what she'd just done. She'd put the blame square on the vamps. The humans had retaliated, but the fangs had struck first. Very, very bad mojo. The truth was the vamps had broken a sacred pact. The innocent victim suddenly was not so blameless.

"How can we trust your word?" Mia pointed a violet-painted nail at her. "You're a known normal lover. Michael, was it?"

She sucked in a breath. Fury boiled through her veins. Cian placed his hand on the small of her back, rubbing soothing circles into the flesh.

"Because I was with her that night." Cian's voice cracked through the room. Her knees shook; it was a surprise no one noticed them clacking together. She leaned slightly into him.

The voices started back up again. There were cries of shock and confusion, but mostly anger. The ceiling rattled with the high-pitched vibrations of so much noise.

"Enough!" Edlyn made her way to shaky feet. "We shall investigate this matter further. Until then, there is to be no retaliation."

"NO! You'll believe a witch's word over mine?" Mia was shaking, not only from anger but something else, something deeper and more powerful. This wasn't just anger; it was primal and debilitating pain.

Eve frowned, remembering her own pain when Michael had died.

"I demand justice for her."

"Sit down, Mia," Iah snarled and exposed the bright ivory of large fangs.

"Screw you! Screw everyone one of you damn delegates. I won't take this mortal's word over what I saw last night. If you won't give me justice, then I'll do it myself. Who's with me?" She turned, holding out an arm. The heavy silver armband she wore and the power radiating from her reminded Eve of the Valkyrie of legend. A maiden warrior of death.

A small band of vamps, weres, and even one witch toward the front of the room jumped to their feet.

"Good." she smiled.

"Weres, step down," Lootah growled, gray fur ripping from his forearms and face. "I don't care what you do, Mia, but my cubs go nowhere."

Two weres surrounding Mia dropped their heads and began to tremble. A third stood defiant, head held high. Low rumbling vibrations coming from the back of his throat.

"Surely he doesn't mean to challenge Lootah right now," Celeste breathed, casting a worried glance to her sisters.

Eve was spellbound. She couldn't rip her gaze away from the train wreck unraveling before her. The gatherings had always been peaceful, a promise of mending the past and looking toward the future. Everything was falling apart before her eyes.

A sinking feeling of despair filled the pit of her stomach.

The room overflowed with kinetic energy, a whipping, lashing torrent of rising anger. The pink-haired, punked-out were hissed and crouched into a fighting stance, transforming instantly to grizzly. A massive ten-foot bear replaced the man.

Lootah turned fully wolf, jumping onto the table, yellow fangs exposed and dripping saliva, muzzle pulled back, and an angry snarl twisting his face. Lootah should have looked puny compared to the bear, but he was the alpha and the entire room knew it. It was the way he carried himself. Head high, tail sticking straight up like the handle of a pitchfork.

The bear charged, his burly body crashing against the table. The other delegates scattered. Everyone knew better than to interfere in pack business. You didn't do it. Period.

Lootah, for all his age, was spry and agile, gracefully sailing over the bear's head and snapping his fanged jaws into the bear's furry hind leg.

The bear howled, manically swiping his paw through the air and twisting around, but his bulk brought him crashing to the ground. Lootah moved so fast, Eve hadn't even seen it. One second he was piercing the thick hide of the bear, the next his taloned paw was pressed against the bear's throat, his muzzle mere inches from a life-sustaining artery.

Lootah transformed his head to a man's. It was unsettling to see that on the body of the wolf.

"You will listen to me!"

She waited on bated breath. The rise and fall of the bear's chest and tension still flowing from out his body made her think he might try to attack again, but in the end the bear conceded, shifting to man and turning his head aside. Shamed. Size had been no match for speed. Lootah still had many years left as delegate. And Eve could only hope that whoever challenged him for alpha dominance in the future and won would have as keen a mind as he did.

"He may have authority over the weres, but he does not decide our fate!" A gothed-out vamp—wearing a spiked collar and black face paint—yelled, crowding closer to Mia's side. Several other vamps, who'd earlier been sitting, now stood and gathered around the lone female figure.

Edlyn held up her hands, and the amethyst amulet hanging around her neck began to glow deepest purple. "Please, brethren, heed Lootah. Do not ride into the night with your fury and hate and sever the weakest ties we have to our human counterparts."

Vampires and weres both stood. A shuffling mass of bodies co-alesced into one tight unit of discontent and angst. Fury was so evident in the faces of some, they began to push and claw at those not of their kind.

Eve's heart picked up in cadence, pounding like a solid block of stone against her chest, threatening to rip a hole. Cian sidled close. The body heat off her sisters crowded her from behind. Things were getting ugly. And the sad truth was that in some ways she sympathized with the self-disgust of cowing to those inferior to them. Could the normals not see that it was the supers, and not human words of war or death, that kept the so-called thieving murderers in line?

Iah nodded, his obsidian hair swinging behind his back. "The witch is wise. Knowing what we know, we can only pray the death is satisfactory to the normals and that they will not choose to rescind the order of peace. We broke the pact first." The melodic strains of his Egyptian accent filled the room with a mesmerizing resonance.

"Pathetic!" Mia spat. "Is this what we've become? A pack of mindless drones, willing to take handouts from the normals?" Her voice cracked and she took a deep breath. "I won't. I can't do it anymore."

Iah clenched his jaw, pain glittering in the depths of shadow-filled eyes. "If you leave now, you will be dishonored and an outcast. A pariah to the clan. You'll have no name. Is that what you want?"

Eve wanted to cry. Mia had snarled at her, sure. But the woman was grief stricken. Anyone short of a blind man could see that. What she felt Eve understood keenly. This was the loss of a lover, and her madness would make the decision.

Tears that refused to fall glistened in the vampire's eyes. "It is."

With those words bedlam exploded. It was like a dam had broken loose. Monsters who'd bottled up all that hatred toward their lot suddenly had a figure to emulate, model themselves after. Those that had barely toed the lines of polite society before now wanted war. Dominance.

Weres turned on witches. Witches on vamps.

She cursed and gripped her amulet. "C'mon, now! We need to leave." A jetting stream of ruby light shot from her amulet, encasing all four of them in an iridescent lined shield.

No matter how much she might sympathize and in some ways revile the normals, she was in no mood to be drawn into a battle that was sure to leave her a bruised and bloody mess.

Rumors of another Great War had been around for centuries. Everyone was always gloom and doom when it came to the supernatural state of affairs. And this gave her a sickening feeling of anguish in the pit of her stomach.

Everywhere they looked shuffling, shifting bodies pounded in on them, attempting to draw them in. Hands grabbed for her but bounced back when they touched the shield. Bursts and crackles of searing orange light shot out from Tamryn's fingers. One shot hit a werepanther square in its nose. It howled and screamed a frightening mix of human and monster that only a panther could make.

She stumbled several times, knocking into Cian's back. He turned but didn't stop, and grabbed her by the elbow, pulling her along faster and faster. Eve panted. The panic seized up her throat and her ability to breathe correctly. She was sweating; droplets stung her eyes, making her lose her focus and concentration. The shield protecting them from the melee grew thinner and thinner. Soon anyone and everyone could overtake them.

She happened to glance to her left and noticed a bright shock of gleaming red hair. Her eyes widened, remembering the specter of the man standing next to the demon the other night. She stopped, nearly knocking Cian to the ground. Tamryn and Celeste barreled into her from behind with loud muffled oaths. Her heart jerked violently in her chest. Between one blink and the next, he, it—whatever the hell it was—was gone.

Cian bellowed. The part of the shield he'd stood under fractured and a vampire managed to pierce his arms with bramble-thick claws. He slammed his fist into the brunette's nose. A crimson geyser exploded on impact.

He turned and grabbed Eve's hand and with his mass created a thin path for them to run through and out of. Cool wind slapped them in the face, bringing instant tears to her eyes. She glanced back for a split second, expecting to see the red devil behind them.

"C'mon, Eve!"

That was all the reminder she needed. Fire scorched her lungs, every muscle in her body bloated with adrenaline as she pumped her legs faster and harder than before.

"Run faster, damn it," he yelled, practically throwing Tamryn and Celeste ahead of him and bringing up the rear.

She wanted to stop. Scream. But she didn't. Bloodlust would soon set in with the creatures. There was only one thought hammering away at her skull: *Get to safety, get to safety, get to safety.* It was a running mantra her feet kept rhythm to.

Finally they reached the safety of cabs and humans. Ironic that suddenly she felt safer around the normals than she did with her own kind.

"I gotta stop," she croaked, halting immediately and bending over, palms flat against her knees, sucking in air like it was mother's milk.

Cian stopped but didn't struggle for air at all. That beautiful body of his was in perfect physical shape. Damn him.

He shoved his fingers through his hair and glanced back. "Okay. A taxi, then."

"Thank the goddess," Tamryn groaned, holding on to her side and wincing.

Celeste was completely white around the mouth and could only nod her approval.

Cian signaled for a cab, and when one pulled up, everyone clamored in, sitting back with a sigh and a groan.

Chapter 22

Cian paid the fare despite not having any real cash. Lucky for him, no one noticed. He'd pulled an old trick and paid with essence. The money looked real, felt real, but by tomorrow morning would be nothing more than a memory.

Eve kissed her sisters good-bye on the stoop and then turned when they headed inside, rolling her neck from side to side with a tired-hound-dog expression.

They walked in silence. Abandoned streets echoed with the sound of their footsteps. The darkened sky glittered with the light of a trillion white jewels, like a glittering sea of diamonds. The night uncharacteristically fog free.

"Thanks for being there tonight, Cian," she whispered so low he even had a hard time catching it.

He nodded and shoved his hands deep into his pockets. Tonight had been a numbing terror for him. So many bodies. Hands reaching, clamoring, clawing like some apparition of a Hollywood horror. Then there'd been the scent, that unique odor of death, and every nerve in his body had screamed to get her out of there before the stroke of midnight. Gone before Frenzy could reach her.

He closed his eyes, sick at heart. Nightmares of this day would stay with him forever.

"Goddess, I hope the delegates got it under control. Especially Mia. I've never seen this happen before." He opened his eyes as she kicked at a pebble with the toe of her boot. She was distant, faraway, and remembering. "I'm sure everything will be all right by tomorrow," she murmured more to herself than him.

"You really think so?" he drawled.

She twisted her lips and shrugged. "No. I don't." She shook her head and continued to speak without blinking. "It all felt surreal, like I was watching a vision, or a premonition of what's to come. It scared the crap out of me."

Finally she blinked—several times—then gave a slight shake and glanced at him as if recalling where she was and with whom. She flashed him a weak smile and took a deep breath. "Let's talk about something else."

He nodded, but the thoughts were never far from his heart, not only the violence of tonight, but the very real fact that Eve was in mortal danger. Every time he thought on it, it only made him more angry. Anyone else and he would have thought of a solution by now. A way to keep her safe and with him, but he was beginning to suspect that perhaps death could never find true happiness. Maybe that was the crux of the problem: happily ever after was never supposed to be in the cards for someone like him.

She frowned, eyeing him, somehow aware of his inner turmoil. Not right now. He wouldn't allow himself to spoil these last moments with her. Not like this. So he plastered on a fake grin and said, "Like what?"

Eve stopped walking and turned toward him with an unspoken question in her eyes. She placed her hand against his chest and smiled, really smiled, one of those smiles that come from deep within, a pureness of soul.

He stepped closer, nearly crowding her. Welcoming flutters of heat wrapped around him, pulling him even closer. How could she do that? This woman, with the power of one glance, could bring him to his knees.

She lifted a dark brow, peering deeply into his eyes. "A strange man visited me in the shop a few days ago."

He tensed, knowing immediately of whom she spoke.

"He said the weirdest thing."

His fingers twitched. "What was that?"

"It wasn't so much what he said, but how he said it." A noticeable shiver traveled down her spine. Their eyes locked as she wet her lips. "He said that life is not a given and to enjoy it, because it won't last."

Dagda had been bold. Eve couldn't know how close to the truth that statement had been. She looked like a fragile doll with her black hair caught up in a ponytail, small strands curling around her face. Her face was free of makeup and had a scrubbed, pink tint to it. The effect made her look so vulnerable, childlike even.

He couldn't help himself. He touched the crook of her arm and pulled her slightly closer. Now they were breath on breath, body heat to body heat. The air around them charged with the snapping force of their desire.

"And what do you think about that?" he asked. He knew what

he thought about it: Dagda should have stayed away from her. Every second around him only brought her deeper into danger, but as much as he wished he could turn off these feelings and walk away from her, he couldn't. She was his drug, his addiction, and crazy as it was, he needed to be with her. Because no one ever made him feel the way that she did.

"At first"—she licked her lips—"that he was crazy. But there was power to those words, a conviction that stopped me from dismissing him."

Eve slid her hand up his arm. His body screamed. His nerves strained from resisting the urge to yank her into his arms and crush her to him.

Though he'd had a taste of her, it wasn't enough, he wasn't sure he would ever have enough where she was concerned. He wanted this woman with a ferocity that rivaled the queen's bloodlust.

"Do you want to come home with me tonight?"

His mind running on feelings and not on thought, he said the only thing he could.

"Yes."

* * *

Cian walked around Eve's living room. He didn't know what he'd expected. Maybe something dark and more in keeping with her witchy trait, but the room was primarily shades of white and tan with the greenery of plants adding a splash of color here and there.

She'd excused herself to the bedroom to change; leaving him alone with thoughts that had turned suddenly crippling.

When she was around him, flashing that smile, it was as if all common sense fled. It was so easy to forget that he was something other than death.

That he wasn't the vampire she thought him to be, a man free to tie his heart to hers and, if it didn't work out, also leave them able to go their separate ways. No harm, no foul.

Their predicament laid heavy on his mind. And again he came to the only possible conclusion he'd come to the other day while talking to Lise. He knew what she'd said: Don't do it. Don't even contemplate it. He couldn't see how she could deny the idea had merit. Dangerous. Stupid, yes. But it had merit, nonetheless. And with the way time was running out, his options were incredibly limited. What did he have to lose? Nothing. And in return, Eve would have a lifetime to live. That was all he wanted. All he'd ever wanted for her. Happiness.

Eve had given him a gift: the rare peace he'd sought his entire existence. It was his turn to return the favor. Only with Eve had he ever felt a true connection. The fact that he cared whether she was mad, happy, or sad spoke volumes.

Tomorrow all hell would be unleashed. The truth of who he was would have to be revealed. All he wanted to do was forget, have this final night with her. And yet he couldn't let her find out by accident. As much as the thought galled, he had to be a man and tell her himself.

He rubbed his chest, a bitter taste in his mouth. If he could give her back her old life, her husband—regardless of the numbing pain that thought caused—he would. He'd do it all to see her as happy as he had that very first day.

She walked into the living room wearing a pink tank top, black silk sleeping pants, and a smile. "Sorry I took so long. My sister called. I swear that woman has a sixth sense about me. She knew I had a visitor and wanted to know who, when, and where." She ticked it off on her fingers.

Goddess, but she took his breath away when she looked at him like that, a sexy beneath-the-lashes glance.

"Aye? And which sister was that?" His voice came out thick and heavy with Irish inflections. It was a sure sign that he was slowly losing his composure.

She bit the side of her lip. "Have I told you how sexy that burr is? I've always had a fascination with accents."

"Did Michael have one?"

He clenched his jaw the second the words left his mouth and the light went out her eyes. There he went again, self-destructing. But it was all he knew. His kind didn't mingle. They didn't show emotion and *never* fell in love. There was no room for that; it couldn't happen. And he was dangerously close—teetering on the edge of the cliff.

Truth was, for another night in her arms he was tempted to forsake his heart and spend an eternity berserk with grief.

"No. He didn't," she said and shook her head. Then she turned toward the kitchen. "I'm gonna make me some chamomile tea. I've got a baggie of blood in the fridge. Take it if you're hungry. I'm not squeamish about that stuff."

He couldn't help but smile. She'd been prepared. "I've fed. Thanks."

She grinned and set the kettle to boil. "No problem."

A conflicting miasma of emotions assaulted him. He wanted to both stay and leave at the same time. He was no fool. Tonight was more than games on the beach or holding her while she slept or even having a taste of her passion. There'd been heat in her eyes, the tension between them demanding they make a decision. Eve was making her move, and he was tempted—more than he'd ever imagined being possible. He needed to stay busy and focus on something other than her.

Shadow boxes filled with a sculpted menagerie of mythic creatures lined the walls, from dragons to unicorns, mermaids to centaurs. He picked up a figurine of a mermaid perching on a rock, prisms of light shooting through its amber-colored skin.

He sensed her behind him before she said anything. It was like every nerve in his body was attuned to her, sparking and crackling when she came near him.

"I'm ridiculously addicted to amber." Her soft voice was a mere whisper.

He heard the ticktock of a clock, the bubbling steam building in the kettle and the inhalations of her breath. He turned, misjudging how close to him she stood, and knocked into her.

She stumbled back a step and his hand shot out, grasping her elbow and keeping her steady. She placed her hand against his chest, her lioness gaze holding his.

"Thanks."

He nodded and set the figurine down on the television stand, never breaking eye contact.

Her hands slipped up his forearm. Fire raced a path across his flesh at her gentle touch.

"Eve." Her name came out a throaty whisper, full of longing and desire.

She bunched the fabric of his shirt beneath her fingers and drew up on tiptoe. She brushed her nose against his neck, her breath created a warm, tickling sensation. Hot shivers coursed through his veins, turning his blood to molten lava. He hissed and drew her closer, molding her body to his.

"What is it about you?" she whispered into the hollow of his throat and then nipped him. "One taste just isn't enough. You're an addiction, a craving I can't get out of my system."

His heart thundered. Rolling vibrations traveled through his veins, making him alive and needy for more. He growled low and traced a path down her spine.

She flicked out her tongue, tasting him with just the tip. "Mmmm."

His hands shifted to her backside, his burgeoning erection heavy between them.

"Ah. Goddess," she moaned, her head on his shoulder. "It's been so long."

Adrenaline spiked through his brain. Eve was giving voice to everything he felt but couldn't say. He picked her up; his hands gripped her backside and he reversed positions, pushing her against the wall and pinning her in place, his legs planted shoulder length apart. She was at his mercy.

Eve slanted her lips against his, tasting, touching. Then she bit down. Dull pain bloomed at the contact. A wild heat traveled through his blood, bringing out the monster, the whipping lust.

He tore himself away from her. She opened fog-filled eyes, staring at him in confusion. A rumble tore past his lips as the slithering madness crept in. He hadn't known a woman in centuries, and the loss of that touch made him feral with need.

He trembled, his breathing haggard. She didn't know the truth.

If they did this now, she'd never forgive him. He fought the wild animal inside but couldn't pull away. Not just yet.

He dipped his head, tasting her throat.

"Cian." She massaged his scalp. His body flared to life, the nerve endings sensitive and excited. "I love your hair. I want to roll in it," she moaned.

He scraped the side of her neck with his fangs and inhaled the sweetness of her flesh, closing his eyes in ecstasy.

She pulled the leather thong from his hair. The heavy strands fell free. She gripped tight and pulled him even closer. Pain flared down his skull at her rough grip, heightening his excitement all the more, to see her need so raw and exposed. His stomach clenched and his muscles quivered. Everything inside him was aware of her, of her scent, her taste, her touch.

Their lips were so close breath passed between them. His lungs filled with her scent of mint. If he were a good man he'd stop this. But he wasn't a man, and he'd never confessed to being good.

With a growl he covered her mouth with his. He licked and nibbled her lips, coaxing her with his tongue to let him in. She opened a fraction, her hum of approval shooting straight through his chest like an arrow.

The world narrowed down to just them. Nothing existed outside of them. He was aware only of the roar of his blood. The rapid beat of his heart, and her soft purrs of approval.

Her tongue darted into his mouth, dueling with his.

His hands roamed her body. Grabbing her breasts and kneading, rolling the nipples between his fingers until she groaned. The leather of his glove yet again came between the touch of flesh on flesh. Frustrated, he snarled, "Tell me what you want, Eve?"

Her hand snaked a path down his chest, over his stomach, and lower still. She was so close to his engorged cock that he could feel the heat of her hand poised above him. He grabbed her wrist. "What do you want?"

"You. Goddess, I want *you*." She panted, slamming her mouth down on his again.

He growled with approval, knowing she'd be able to handle the primal and aggressive nature of mating with death. Also knowing she wanted this as fiercely as he did. Grabbing the edge of her shirt, he lifted it up and over her head, throwing it to the ground.

"Take the gloves off," she whispered against his lips, grinding her hips down harder.

It was like a slap of cold water. A reminder. He clenched his jaw. A shrill, discordant whistle peeled through the room, startling them both and making him jump, almost dropping Eve in the process. Only through sheer will was he able to keep a tenuous hold on her upper arms until she firmly regained her footing.

His muscles strained, every nerve exposed and raw. One touch of her hand over his cock and he'd have spiraled into orgasm. It took him a moment to get back into the here and now. He heaved for breath, trying to regain control.

Her eyes were wide, her lips bee-stung, and her cheeks a crisp pink. Tendrils of hair framed her face, giving her a disheveled, thoroughly ravaged look.

The tension between them was hot, vibrant, and alive.

His arms felt heavy for want of her, his body crying out for release. Her pink tongue slid along the edge of her bottom lip.

"The water," he said as the piercing wail continued.

"I don't care." She slid her arms around his neck. "Kiss me again."

The plea was not one he could ignore. As he lowered his head the quicksilver recognition of his ilk traveled along his flesh and made the fine hairs on the back of his neck stand on edge. He gripped her arms, staring out the window that led into the fire escape. The night was thick with darkness, but he knew. He'd sensed death. She still had time, damn it. She still had time.

A loud knock sounded on the door.

He stiffened and she pulled back with narrowed eyes. "Who would be knocking on my door at eleven thirty at night?"

The tingling rush of reaper was gone, but the tight band in his chest didn't loosen its grip. Something still felt wrong. "Let me answer the door, Eve."

She nodded mutely. Pulled on her top and patted at the flyaway curls.

He stalked to the door and opened it.

"Oh!" she cried, startled.

A set of brown eyes stared back at him.

"Curtis?" Eve rushed up, grabbing onto the back of Cian's shirt.

Cian glanced around the low-lit hallway, a sense of unease eating away at him. He had to investigate. Search out Frenzy. It must be him. Death was lurking. In his gut he knew it to be true, even though he could no longer sense the reaper. He knew. He just knew.

"I should go…"

"Oh no, wait. Umm, Curtis…"

It pained him to leave her side, especially now. But he couldn't stay here while a killer lingered. He had to find Frenzy. He leaned in and planted a whisper soft kiss against her lips. "It's okay. I'll see you tomorrow."

Empty promises.

* * *

And just like that she watched him walk away. Her heart shattered. Why had he left that way? The incessant wail, like a colicky infant, drummed through her ears. She stomped toward the stove, finally shutting the stupid kettle off.

"I'm so sorry," Curtis said, taking a step in.

She wanted to snarl, to snap at him. Here he was saying he was sorry and yet he'd still walked in, ruining what had promised to be the best night of her life.

Ready to verbally rip him a new one she glanced at him and instantly felt her anger deflate. He looked pale and white around the mouth, unshed tears shining in his eyes.

For the moment Cian's abrupt departure took a back seat. "Curtis, what's wrong?"

"I can't find Samhain anywhere. There's a storm coming and I'm worried," he said, voice cracking.

It took everything she had in her not to scream. She was a witch and sensitive to the witch-familiar plight, but it didn't mean she had to like the fact that Curtis's knock had sent Cian running for the hills. What the hell was that all about? She was tired. Sick at heart. Horny. Damn, she was really horny.

She took a deep breath, resigned to another lonely night. "Hold on, let me get my coat."

Five minutes later Eve commanded her ruby stone to illuminate. It flared to life, immediately lighting the darkened alleyway behind her apartment.

Green Dumpsters and brackish puddles of water filled the air with their own unique aroma.

"I can't tell you how much this means to me, Eve." Curtis glanced at her.

"Don't worry about it. I'm sure you'd do the same for me."

He frowned. "Yeah." There was an echoing sadness in his voice. With a slight shake of his head he turned and cupped his mouth. "Samhain, come here."

"Samhain," she called, joining in the hunt.

Empty boxes and crates full of rotted foodstuff were the only things she could see. "Samhain, come." She made kissing noises, trying to drive the cat out if it was indeed hiding somewhere in there.

The slow rumbles of thunder could be heard off in the distance. The rain she'd smelled earlier was fast approaching. She glanced toward the sky. A thin vein of light blue pierced the sky and clouds glowed with lightning. This one was going to be a doozy.

She hugged her jacket tighter, rubbing her hands up and down her arms. "C'mere, kitty, kitty."

Curtis walked deeper into the alley, throwing boxes around and calling out to the cat, desperation in his voice.

A soft meow caught Eve's attention. She turned around and there, standing on the sidewalk and gingerly licking her paw, was the missing tabby.

"Samhain," she hissed and marched toward the cat, picking it up under its fat belly. "You gave us a scare." She scratched the orange cat between its ears. It purred, long and low.

"Oh," Curtis cried and ran toward her, relief spread across his face.

Eve held out the cat, ready to switch it over to the rightful owner. Curtis grabbed the tabby by the scruff and pulled it into his arms.

Samhain hissed, kicking out its paws and flailing around until Mr. Lovelace hugged the fluffy cat to his chest.

She frowned. Since when had he started grabbing the cat that way? She wasn't one to judge, but she hadn't liked that one bit. A witch must always treat their familiars with respect. That had been rough and unnecessary.

"Thank you, Eve. I can't begin to thank you enough." He rubbed his cheek against the tabby's face with a grateful smile.

Okay, so maybe that had been a quirk. "It's not a problem, really," she said and turned to head back to the apartment as the first drops of rain landed on her nose.

They walked the ten yards back to their apartment in silence. The wind was really picking up now, whipping her hair in her face. This was promising to turn into a gale. Not an uncommon thing for living so close to the coast.

Curtis unlocked the door and held it open for her. She ran through, shaking herself once she got out of the nipping wind.

"Getting a little frosty out there," she said. "Well, g'night, Curtis."

"Wait. I'd really like to repay the kindness if I could."

"That's really nice, but you don't have to."

"I know I don't." He hugged Samhain to his face. "But I want to. How does breakfast sound tomorrow morning? My treat."

She grimaced. "I don't know. I think I might actually have to work tomorrow. If I take another day off, Tamryn's liable to have my tail."

He chuckled. "No problem. I'll just bring it over before you go to work."

It seemed she was going to have a breakfast date whether she wanted to or not. She shrugged. "Okay, what the hey. Sounds like fun. I'll meet you at your apartment say sevenish. Deal?"

"All right," he nodded. "I'll come to you. My pad's a little messy. Woman sensibilities and all that, you know."

She smiled and reached out, ready to give his forearm a squeeze with her final good-bye, but he stepped out of the way so fast it almost gave her whiplash.

She blinked, unsure of what to say or do.

Curtis gave her an apologetic shrug. "I've got a cold, don't want you catching it."

She narrowed her eyes studying him. Good color to his cheeks, nice even breathing, no fatigue lining his eyes. He didn't seem to be sick at all. As a matter of fact, he looked fit as a horse.

"Sure, Curtis." She nodded, beginning to rethink the whole breakfast thing. "I guess I'll see you tomorrow, then."

He nodded and walked to his apartment, slipping inside with one final wave. She shook her head.

A bath. That's what she needed right now. She huffed and stomped up the stairs. Her night was totally ruined.

Chapter 23

Frenzy slammed his fist into the wall. Anger rolled through his veins because of the position he'd been put into. He clenched his jaw as another perfect opportunity was wasted. This was the day of her death. He should have done it. He'd had every intention of taking her. Forcing her into the street after the cat he'd conveniently lost. She should have been run over. He would have swiped the soul and all would be done.

He'd taken off his amulet long enough to port by her window and let Cian catch a small glimpse of him. He knew the reaper would run after him, try to find him, maybe even try to pound him to within an inch of his godforsaken existence.

He walked into the kitchen, placing his hands on the countertop, and stared at the orange tabby.

His hands shook as the rage built inside him to a dangerous level. He should have taken Eve tonight. Cian was running around looking for him, for a ghost that had vanished. It would have been simple. Perfect. And then Cian had glanced at Eve with that wild look of determination. A look that said: *Nothing will happen to you. Not while I'm around. I swear.*

Frenzy shook his head—memories (always the memories) haunted him. Of his Adrianna and that very look he'd flashed her, only to return and find her dead. The horror of that night had become his living nightmare.

He closed his mind and hardened his heart. Eve would die, and by his hand.

Boom. Boom. Boom. The strike of the grandfather clock snapped him from his trance-like state. He jerked up and stared at the timepiece. Witching hour.

With a growl, he swiped his hand, opened the portal and stepped through into his queen's chambers. She glanced up. Her multicolored hair was caught up in a knot, the tips fanned out to resemble the tail end of a bird's feather. The red and black gleamed like fire and shadow.

Her lips were a deep shade of crimson, her eyes painted moss green, as was the gown tapering to her body. She reminded him of spring.

"Well?" she asked. "Are you ready?"

He ground his jaw and nodded, though not without a sickening twist to his gut. "I am."

The Morrigan raised a black brow, red lips thinned into a razor-thin line. "It's fifteen past midnight."

She was asking. Wondering why he hadn't taken the mark's life yet. "Cian hasn't left her side. I haven't had an opening."

There was not a flinch or flicker that she'd heard him, but he could feel the gentle prod of her power. She was tasting him, reaching out with her essence, searching for deceit.

Posture relaxed, he eyed her. The force of his gaze screaming that he told the truth and not a lie, hoping that by sheer force of will she might believe him.

After a tense minute of silence she crossed her legs and said, "Fine. I don't care how small the window of opportunity is: you strike at the earliest possible moment. No more mistakes." A lashing rain of power punctuated her words, like the sharp nicks of a blade—piercing his face, his flesh.

He counted slowly to ten as the anger snapped inside him like a piston. "There will be no more mistakes."

The queen narrowed her eyes, a swirling red beginning to overtake the blue. "See that there aren't."

There wouldn't be. Not anymore.

"Good. Now go, before Dagda returns and finds me scheming."

* * *

Cian ran all around her block, frantic with worry, searching for Frenzy. Leaving Eve that way, that hurt look she'd flashed him, had pierced his heart. What could he tell her that wouldn't send her into an immediate panic? Nothing. And so he'd done what he thought right.

He'd followed her and Curtis, waiting in shadow, watching them. Knowing that if Frenzy was going to attack, it would be right then in that perfect moment. He'd expected a trap. Nerves alert and high, tense, sure that at any moment death would pounce at her.

But they'd found the cat and walked back inside. He'd closed his eyes, listening to the sound of her heartbeat, determining that it wasn't flying erratic, that she was safe and he'd continued searching. For nigh unto an hour and still nothing.

It was as if Frenzy had simply vanished. He began to doubt himself. Question whether he'd really seen that flash of red. Or whether it was stress making him see what wasn't there at all. How could stress make him feel that tug of the reaper deep in his chest? It had to be real. Maybe it was a test, or simply a reminder. Frenzy was definitely stalking and letting Cian know that with every chance he got.

A sound like the gentle tap of wood against wood caught his attention. He paused, barely breathing.

A quick shuffle. A shallow breath.

He ran like a blur, following the faint noise deep inside a labyrinth of alleyways, then the sound died. The light from the moon cast crazy shadows along the brick exteriors as he stopped and watched.

Tap, tap, tap.

He twirled, the sound coming from behind. Disbelief almost choked the air from his lungs. A big squirrel sat on a crate tapping a rotten walnut against the wood. He sighed and the animal glanced up, went stiff for a second, and then took off, its thick tail whipping through the night like a rust-colored flag.

"What's wrong with me?" He shook his head. I'm chasing ghosts, looking for something that wasn't there. He had to trust his senses. He'd made the right decision leaving earlier to find Frenzy. Now he had to trust himself again and head back to her. The reaper was gone, vanished into the dark embrace of night.

He swiped his hand and opened the portal, arriving back at her apartment within seconds. He stayed out of sight, careful to keep his distance. Eve was too sensitive for him to get any closer to her than across the street. She paced back and forth in her living room for a bit, until finally retiring to her bedroom.

He felt her as surely as a wick to flame. She buzzed through his veins, an intoxicant to his senses. He clenched his jaw as the first sprinkles of rain fell down around him. A cold wind swept through the bay area. Lightning followed a rolling clap of thunder, filling the night with electrical currents of danger.

No one wandered the streets. Cian had only the howl of wind as company. It was a melancholy opus reflecting his torment.

Rain fell in a drowning deluge. The chill saturated his body and he began to tremble, unable to rip his gaze from the golden drop of light behind the curtain of her window.

Eve was encased in darkness, a lonely silhouette staring out at the world. He could picture her eyes watching the fury of the storm, entranced by the strikes of lightning, protected and safe within the warmth of her apartment.

He felt her everywhere, in his mind, her emotions twining with his own. Her sadness became his; her loneliness bloomed as a thorny rose inside him, gouging and bleeding him dry.

Cian closed his eyes and hunched into the wind. His hair tangled around his head like a charmed cobra, the strands lashing and tearing at his cheek with sharp slaps.

This wasn't fair. It shouldn't be happening to her. She was too young. Too full of life. Out of sheer frustration, he roared, "Dagda!"

The driving wind ripped the name from out his mouth. More lightning crashed: jagged tears through the navy-blue fabric of night.

"What?" A deep, familiar voice punctuated his thoughts.

He twirled, blinking away the deluge. "How can I save her? How?"

Dagda was encased in undulating shadow. They curled around his body, spreading throughout the area. The ebony of his eyes should have remained hidden, he should be a blank face full of darkness, and yet they glowed with earth's power as he fed off the storm. This was the earth god, and he was in his element.

"Go to her, Cian. You haven't much time left. Don't look for shadows. Find her and you'll save yourself."

"I don't want to save myself!" he yelled, rain filling his mouth, nearly making him choke on it. "I don't care about myself. I need to save her."

The creeping shadows surrounding the god began to fade, the substance of his body becoming ephemeral and unclear. Dagda's voice rolled through the wind. "Isn't that the same thing?"

Then he was gone and Cian knew what to do. The answer became so clear. He'd enjoy these last moments with her, savor them and keep them close. Her love had saved him. And now he'd do the same for her. He'd carry this night with him and in the morning, he'd go and find The Morrigan and trade his life for hers.

Lise had told him not to even think about it. But Dagda had confirmed it. He'd vowed to save her and he'd meant it. A great burden lifted from his shoulders. She was safe. Finally, he'd figured out a way.

One last look at her darkened window and he let his feet lead him to where his heart had belonged all along.

Chapter 24

Eve heard the knock like a resounding boom through her skull. Scowling, she stalked to her door. *Who the hell can it be this time? I know I'm not this popular.*

She gave serious consideration to not opening it. It was almost one in the morning and the only thing she wanted to do now was lie down. She was physically drained and even a bit on the angry side. She couldn't understand the fluttering of the heart, twisting of the gut compulsion to open the door. She pulled it open.

There he stood. Her fantasy. Her desire. Almost as if by thinking about him she'd conjured him up.

He was dripping wet, his long multihued hair hanging in his face, drops of rainwater falling to a puddle at his feet. His clothes clung to his body like a second skin, highlighting the sharp grooves and flat planes of muscle.

Deep blue eyes sparkled with pain, and she felt it. For the first time she experienced what it was like to feel another's pain. It was a wrenching entity filling her with a choking sense of loss. Tears filled her eyes at the ferocity of it, and her heart responded.

"I thought you weren't coming back."

"I have to find out what's happening between us." His voice broke with need and unspoken desire.

Her lashes fluttered and liquid heat crashed between her thighs, making her instantly hot and ready. The need was elemental and primitive, surging from some deep recess inside her. It was more than lust; it was ancient and deep, twisting inside her and forcing her to obey.

She knew she should be mad at him for ditching her the way he had. But she couldn't. Not now. Not seeing him like this.

Stamp SOFTIE on her forehead and get it over with.

She stepped into his arms and from there it was bedlam. She lost herself to the glorious madness.

Cian picked her up, forcing her to wrap her legs around his waist, and he stepped inside, kicking the door shut. A mimic of what they'd done only an hour earlier. Would they finish what they'd started this time? Goddess, she hoped so, prayed so.

The scents of rain and salt filled her head as she licked at his exposed neck, sucking and biting. Her hands were frantic as she tried to rip the shirt from him.

He growled, the sound animalistic, and she responded by raking her nails down his back. Hard.

"Eve. Eve," he whispered in a rush in her ear, running his hand down her hair and dropping to his knees on the ground.

She exposed her neck to him, lost to the liquid heat of passion burning through her veins. He scraped long fangs down her neck, biting but not piercing the flesh.

She hissed, her skin tingling and sensitive. Her nipples hardened and scraped against the lace of her bra, which suddenly felt too confining. Eve moaned when his hand grazed her breast and she wrapped him tighter in her embrace.

"Feels so good," she whispered.

His fingers were clumsy as he tried to shuck her tank top over her head. She ran her fingers through his wet hair, scratching the scalp and wriggling her ass on his engorged cock.

"Rip it, Cian. Tear it off, I don't care," she panted. Only knowing the damn thing needed to come off now!

He fisted the shirt in his hands and tore. It came apart with a muffled ripping sound. Her body was as soaked as his; a wanton rush of adrenaline hummed through her as she yanked on his shirt.

Meanwhile his mouth slammed down on hers, teeth colliding and tongues dueling in a kiss of fierce possession. Her head swam with fuzz; her body burned with flames.

Still she pulled on his shirt, but it was so wet it hardly budged at all.

"Damn it!" She exploded with frustration and pulled back to try and somehow shuck him out of the thing.

"Forget it, Eve." He hooked his finger behind the clasp of her bra and snapped it off, throwing it behind her head. Where it landed, she didn't care.

She pressed her breasts flat against the freezing wetness of his shirt. The combination of heat and cold had shivers traveling down her spine.

He lowered his head, grabbing one breast and beginning to knead while his tongue flicked at the nipple of the other. The cold leather against the warmth of her skin had goose bumps running a race down her arms.

She wished he'd take the things off. But it didn't matter. Not right now. Not while he was touching her and looking at her with dark heat in his eyes. Maybe later.

A grunt fell from her lips as pleasure tightened its hold inside her. Blood rushed through her veins. She wanted him, everything he had to give, and nothing would stop her this time.

To ease the ache building inside of her, she rubbed herself against his leg.

His tongue circled her nipple, the heat of his mouth making her jerk in response. He twisted the other between his fingers and she screamed, her mind and body exploding with sharp bursts of warm pleasure. A heaviness settled between her thighs. She needed to be filled, possessed.

"Oh, Cian. Now," she said as she somehow managed to unzip his jeans. The velvet steel of his shaft almost leaped out at her. Her fingers grazed the warm flesh, and she licked her lips in anticipation.

She wrapped both hands around his cock, fingers barely meeting. He was thick and long and perfect. He hissed, tremors traveling his body. His breathing was hard and heavy.

Cian tugged at the elastic band of her pants. She lifted herself up enough for him to shove them down and, unable to wait even another second, impaling herself on him.

He hissed, cupping her with his palm. She felt stretched, filled almost to the point of pain. But with that pain came incredible pleasure, and she rode him hard, her cheek pressed against his. Wet hair clung to her brows.

She closed her eyes and lost herself in the movement. Their scent. He pumped into her harder, forcing her slick heat to pound up and down on him at a furious pace.

Their bodies slapped together and heat rushed to her core. She gasped and hugged his neck. White stars danced behind her eyes. Muscles contracted, reaching a crescendo. A spiral of pleasure traveled down her spine, filling her limbs, and had her on the brink of orgasm.

He bit her neck, and that was her undoing. A frenzied explosion of exquisite fire. She arched back into the blossoming flames. Her breathing came in short gasps and her nails dug into his arms.

"Eve," he roared, his cock contracting with the tide of his own climax.

It took a second for her to come back to herself, but when she did she smiled and nuzzled the side of his neck, feeling more whole and complete than she ever had in her life. Reluctantly she opened her eyes.

He sighed and embraced her, holding her to him like a fragile doll. There was such strength in his hands, and yet he was gentle, his fingers idly trailing a path down her back.

"I guess this is the part where I say, hi, Cian."

He laughed, a deep, throaty sound filled with inflections.

"I'm glad you came back."

"Me too."

"Why you'd leave?" Seemed kind of dumb to ask this question now, especially after what had happened, but she was still a little confused and hurt. He'd left without an explanation, just a good-bye and so long.

He twisted his lips, running his hand through her hair. "I thought I had someplace to be. Then I realized it wasn't as important as being here with you. I'm sorry, Eve. I'm so sorry."

His words nearly brought tears to her eyes. Not so much what he said, but how he said them. A deep, wrenching heartache poured from his lips. It still didn't explain why he'd left. But hadn't she done the very same thing earlier? Maybe he had skeletons too. Painful secrets buried deep. And like Cian had told her before, who was she to judge? She understood all about those skeletons. In the end, she was grateful he'd come back.

Maybe someday he'd feel comfortable enough to share his secrets with her, but in the meantime she wouldn't hold it against him.

She smiled and placed a tender kiss against his lips. He sighed, leaning his forehead against hers, and they sat that way for a while. Just holding on. Two wounded hearts seeking and finding solace in each other.

After a moment she felt a cold drop of water slide from his hair to her chest, which made her glance down and become embarrassingly aware of her clothes. Or rather the torn remains of them. Her breasts were hanging free. Her shirt was gone—or the tatters of it anyway—hidden only goddess knew where. She felt like a floozy compared to the still-dressed Cian.

"Jeez. I'd better put something on," she laughed.

He looked at her, the wild lust gone but the heat still glittering in the depths of his royal-blue eyes. "I think this look suits you." He ran his hand down the curve of her breast.

Warmth fluttered anxious wings in her belly. Even after that she still wanted him. He rocked his hips. She smiled. He wasn't as hard as before, but he was definitely getting there. The air between them sparked with eroticism.

She bit her lip. "You keep that up and I might have to have my way with you again."

He chuckled, kissing the tip of her nose. "I don't think I'd mind that at all."

Though she didn't want to rip herself away from him just yet, she also didn't want him catching chill. He was soaked to the bone and her right along with him. She stood, hugging her shirt shut.

"First things first, you need to get warmed up." She couldn't help but glance down at his cock. A greedy smile played on her lips. Butterflies dipped and dived as she remembered the feel of him inside her.

"I'm fine." He grinned, noticing her gaze as he slipped himself back inside his pants. He stood and grabbed her hand. "But if you insist, I know something that can warm me."

She snorted, slapping her palm against his chest, unable to resist giving the firm muscle beneath a small squeeze. "You vampires. Think you're so tough. Even you guys can't walk around with soaked clothes all night long. For one night, let me baby you."

Chapter 25

Hearing her call him a vampire yet again made the full weight of his lies crash down around him. There wasn't much he could do for her, but he could give her truth. And maybe in the end, when he was gone, she'd remember that at least he'd done that for her. "Eve, I have something I need—"

In a matter of seconds he watched the smile on her face slowly slip and the golden eyes lose their luster. She gave a crooked smile and placed cold fingertips against his cheek. "First we get warm. Then, if you still need to"—her mouth turned down—"we'll talk."

Tendrils of her confusion and fear skated down his spine. Eve was procrastinating. As if somehow she instinctively knew this conversation was one she wouldn't want to have.

A hollow ache spread through his chest. Each time he put this off, it made it all the more difficult. Yet he couldn't ignore the entreaty in her gaze.

"All right. Later, then."

Relief smoothed her brows. "Good," she sighed and walked toward her bedroom, stopping at a closet and tossing him some clothes. "Put those on. They should fit. Give me a second to get out of this and meet me in my bedroom in say…two minutes?"

He nodded, and she walked away.

There was a time and place for everything. What sense was there in rushing to tell her? She'd find out soon enough, and it didn't seem like she was in a hurry to know at that.

Looking down at the carpet, a vision of her slick skin sliding along his burned his sight. The hairs on the back of Cian's neck tingled. Now she wanted him to join her in the bedroom, and there was no way he'd be able to stop himself from making love to her again.

He closed his eyes for a brief moment. She'd said two minutes. It was nearly that. He glanced down at his wet clothes, quickly stripped, and put on what she'd tossed him—a baggy pair of lounging pants and white shirt.

"Cian, you coming or what?" Eve asked walking out into the hallway, wearing a navel-baring top and short white shorts. She stopped, her mouth tipping at the corners, golden eyes turning round with delight. "Nice."

Her obvious perusal heated his veins.

"I've never seen you dressed so casual. It's a great picture."

Eve sashayed up to him, dragging her hand across his chest. His nipples pebbled at her touch. Heat coiled long fingers around his heart, the feel of her was like fire, branding him and making the flesh prickle.

Slowly she walked around him. He dragged her perfume deep into his lungs.

"Oh, very nice." She grabbed onto his bicep and squeezed. "I think you should wear these shirts more often."

Cian grinned, but then stiffened when she walked behind him. Curiosity and excitement lapped up against him like the gentle waves of the sea; she was remembering something. And he was sure he knew what it was.

"You once told me you have a tattoo. Where is it?"

He ground his jaw.

She lifted up the edges of his shirt, exposing a tiny sliver of his skin, but it was enough. A loud gasp and then she bunched the shirt the entire way up his back.

"Wow. You weren't kidding about having a tattoo. This thing is massive. So intricate." Her warm breath rippled along his skin.

He didn't move, allowing her to touch him. He felt raw and exposed. What must she see when she looked at him? At the hideous mark of his shackles?

"Can you take your shirt off?"

His heart trembled. He closed his eyes and in one swift motion took it off. He felt like a caged animal that'd been beaten and manhandled. On the defense and edgy. "I despise it."

"What? Oh no. No, It's beautifully done. The black is so vivid and bold." The warm press of lips touched the center of his back.

The design, a symbolic manifestation of the servitude he was forced to endure, and she'd kissed it. He turned, pulled her into his embrace and wrapped his arms tight around her, wishing he could crawl inside her skin, where it was safe and warm and good.

She meant everything to him. Her actions made him realize he was making the right choice. This was a life worth preserving. The world had to see what he saw, had to know her, because Eve was someone worth loving.

"Thank you."

She giggled. "For what?"

"Just"—he shook his head—"thank you."

She pulled back, a happy twinkle in her eyes. "Come with me." She grabbed his hand and, walking backward, pulled him down the hall and into her room.

* * *

Eve bit her lip, glancing at him from beneath her lashes. A nervous flutter of wings lit inside her throat. Her bedroom was bathed in the flickering golden glow of candlelight. The woodsy scent of incense undulated through the air.

Now she was a vision of sultry seduction, but a second ago he wouldn't have recognized the madwoman kicking socks and panties under the bed to hide them from sight. She crossed her fingers behind her back, hoping he wouldn't encounter a bra or two she might have overlooked.

With the rest of the house, she was such a clean freak. Not a speck of dust left to gather anywhere. But when it came to her bedroom, for some reason, she never worried about dropping a bra or panty on the floor and leaving it there until laundry day. Probably because she hadn't been laid since the wheel had been invented. Who would see her room to care?

"I'm sorry the bed's not made. Kinda ruins the whole seduction thing, I know." She gave a self-effacing laugh. "But I only had two minutes, so you'll have to forgive me this time."

His gaze stole her breath. Mysterious eyes, full of pain and hurt, but when they looked at her it was different. It was a gentle caress, a twisting, knotting perusal that she felt all the way to the tips of her toes. And after what had just happened in her living room, she shouldn't be so nervous. But that had been all fire and brimstone. This was so much more.

She led him into the room and sat him down on her bed.

"Lie on your stomach, Cian. Please."

He turned to her, a question turning his lips.

"Trust me." She smiled and placed a quick kiss on the side of his mouth.

"Hmmm, I don't know."

She swatted him and he jumped. She threw her head back and laughed at his wide-eyed shock. "Lie down, you, or I'll have to bust out my kung fu moves."

He chuckled, lying facedown on the amethyst comforter. "You've got me."

"So trainable. I love it," she teased and straddled him, sitting down and pushing his hair aside. Maybe later she'd give in to her other fantasy of rolling around in the thick strands.

She ran her hands along the contours of his chiseled back, fascinated with the dark lines of his tattoo.

The skull itself was frightening, but the intricacy of the artwork was beyond reproach. She narrowed her eyes. Man, the thing looked really fresh. The ebony ink darker than any shade she'd ever seen, with none of the typical green tint to a fading tattoo. The color reminded her of shadow.

"You're gonna have to tell me who gave you this thing, Cian. I think even Mingan would be jealous of this one."

He only grunted as she reached over to the end table and grabbed her oils. She opened a stopper, poured a generous amount onto her hands, and rubbed them together.

A rich herbal scent filled the room.

He moaned even before she started the massage. "What is that?"

Eve dug her hands into the tight muscles of his back and began to knead out the kinks. "It's Balsam Peru I mixed with ylang-ylang. You like?" She slid her thumbs along his spine, rubbing deep and pushing hard.

"Mmm."

The vibrations of his groan shooting between her thighs made her whimper in response. Liquid heat pooled inside her crotch. "I'll take that as a yes."

"Yes," he grunted. And then, "You have magic fingers." Every word he said rolled through her body, stoking the already-growing fire.

Slicked-up hands made it easy to drive out the knots. The shimmering substance made his skin glisten. The powerful scent filled her head, her nose. She sucked it deep into her lungs, smelling not only the oil but the musk of his body. The effect was making her hot and twitchy. Her lower stomach clenched, and she could only hope he was feeling half as good as she was right now.

"I feel it, Eve." He rolled over, making her slip from his back and falling onto her side. He gripped her waist, a devilish smile played on his lips.

"I'd swear you were reading my mind," she chuckled, sliding her hands along his chest.

"No, just your emotions."

She bit her lip, burying her nose in the crook of his neck. "Goddess, that's so embarrassing." Heat settled in her cheeks.

He tipped her chin back and shook his head. "Don't be embarrassed. It's one of the things I love about you. You make me feel at ease. I know who I am when I'm around you. I love you."

Wow! Brain cells went dead. Her stomach flopped and blood thundered in her ears. She melted. Warmth crept into her limbs. And it felt right. Fast or no. "I love you too."

He closed his eyes, a painful expression twisting his face. He slid his arm beneath her body and pulled her tight to him. She could feel the beat of his heart; it felt like it was going to fly out his chest.

"Eve." More than just her name came out his mouth. That one word encompassed a coiling need.

"Make love to me, Cian."

* * *

His heart constricted. The peppermint warmth of her breath tickled his cheek. He itched to trace her lithe curves like a figurine and devour her mouth with his own. Cian closed his eyes and tried to breathe.

All he got for his effort was the tantalizing fragrance of scented herbs and flowers. It tugged like an invisible magnet, demanding he crush her to him and give into the passion that hadn't yet been sated. But he wouldn't do this fast. He would take it slow and savor her like a fine wine.

She nipped at his neck. "Kiss me, Cian. Make me yours." The hot, kittenish whisper speared his heart.

Golden eyes full of want blinked back at him. Slowly, deliberately, he lowered his head, brushing his lips over hers in a gentle caress.

Eve wrapped her arms around his neck and pulled him down, forcing him to lie upon her completely. He touched his lips to hers, tongue sliding along the seam of her mouth, asking without words for entrance.

She parted on a sigh and he darted inside, tasting her sweetness and moaning deep in his throat. He slid his hand along the length of her naked thigh, and when he encountered the cotton of her shorts, he tugged gently. Then he flicked his wrists and both their sets of clothes were gone. For the first time they were body to body.

"Whoa. What was that?" She gasped. "Did you just take our clothes off?"

He bit his lip, fighting the grin.

"Didn't know vamps could do that."

"There's a lot about me you don't know."

"Another challenge, eh? Mmm...I like," she moaned, moving underneath him. "Take off the gloves, touch me everywhere."

He stiffened. The temptation was like a powerful magnet, demanding he do it. Demanding he finally feel her. "I...I can't."

Her brows lowered as he crawled back off of her and sat up. It would only take one time...a cockroach to die in her apartment and he'd turn reaper. If even one digit on his hand grazed her she'd go comatose. A frozen corpse. A soul trapped in a dead body. Just like the man Indigo had killed the other night.

"Hey. Hey." She grabbed his hand and brought it to her lips, rubbing her mouth against the leathered knuckles. "It's okay, really. If it's a disability or anything, I hope you know you can trust me. I won't force you."

He dropped his head, closing his eyes as the beauty of her words ran through him. So much deceit. So many lies. That's why he wanted to tell her the truth. To show her who he really was. He wanted the lies to end.

She placed his hand against her breast. His eyes snapped open and she smiled.

"I always thought Christine should have gotten with the Phantom." She reached up and touched the side of his face. "Nothing you could show me would make me love you any less. But please, don't let my ignorance ruin this night. Let's finish what we started."

She grabbed him by the shoulders and rolled him down on top of her. He forgot his worries, his fears, everything fled as he stared into the beauty of her face. "I don't deserve you, Eve."

"Shh." She gently bit him on that spot between collarbone and neck. Fire raced through him. His gaze grew hot, hungry.

He grabbed one coral-colored nipple and rolled it between his thumb and forefinger.

Eve hissed, arcing up and running her fingers through his hair. "Cian!"

Smiling at the sharp desire piercing her voice he took the nipple into his mouth and suckled. Her flesh tasted sweet and salty. He laved the same kind of attention on the other breast before moving down.

He rubbed his cheek against the creamy smoothness of her flat belly. A violent wave of desire slammed through him, making him dizzy for want of her. Eve was projecting, writhing, and moaning beneath him, her lust and her need raining through his veins.

Wanting to taste everything, he went lower still, his face between her legs and staring at the very essence of what made her a woman. He'd tasted her once; now she was his addiction. He needed more and he would have more.

He kissed his way down her thighs, biting gently and imprinting a trail of red upon her skin. She dug her nails into his scalp, her salty-sweet scent wafting through the air. He ran a finger down her wet slit, exposing the engorged flesh.

Eve hissed, bucking up.

"So bonny," he breathed, then lowered his head and took her swollen nub into his mouth, sucking, tasting, and inhaling all of her. She was sweet and tart and he couldn't get enough of her.

Groaning, she slammed herself deeper into his mouth, grinding her swollen nub on his lips and demanding he take more. He swirled his tongue around the silky smoothness.

A raspy moan expelled from her lungs. He grinned as he finally came up for air and licked his lips.

Her eyes were glazed and a wicked grin rolled across her face from ear to ear. She held out her arms. A repeat of the other night. Obeying without hesitation, he moved up her body. Inches separated his lips from hers.

Then she claimed those lips. This was no gentle kiss. It was a blistering fire, scalding, teeth colliding, tongues dueling, breath-leaving-lungs type of kiss.

Her rumbles of approval vibrated straight through his chest. Elemental need tore him up.

She pulled away first, her face flushed, her lips full and cherry red. Eve pushed against his chest, forcing him off so that she could sit up. His body throbbed, ached for her. It was a desire so sharp it was painful, like a thousand razor blades slicing through his skin.

The rosy flush of her face was even more obvious against the wealth of black hair cascading down her back. "I want to ask you a favor." Her voice came out a husky, throaty whisper.

He could deny her nothing. "Anything."

His black-haired priestess. Her powers held him enthralled. Her desire for him poured over his body like waves of thick, warm honey.

"Undo your hair."

Immediately, he pulled the leather thong from his hair. The long strands fell heavy to his shoulders. Her throaty laughter filled the room. She pushed him down, splaying the black-and-ivory tresses across his back.

She laughed as she ran her fingers through it. "Goddess, it's so soft. I've wanted to do this since the moment I laid eyes on you."

He was content just to have her touch him. To see the delight sparkling in her eyes and the laughter playing on her bow-shaped lips.

"I've never seen anything like your hair. Polished sable and ivory. So long. And yet, I can't imagine you any other way." She stopped and stared at him. "You're so beautiful."

He trembled and pulled her onto his chest. "Eve, you make me feel alive."

She sighed, nuzzling his neck. He rolled them over, his hands framing her face. The beautiful vixen in his arms was more than he'd ever imagined.

"I can't wait anymore. I want you now."

The words touched off a wildfire of passion. *Now.* He had to have her now.

He grabbed her by the hips and pressed the long length of his cock against her slit. She was slick.

Excited tremors moved through her body. Wanting to give her exactly what she asked for, he gripped her waist. She growled and arced her back, pressing herself against his erection.

"Oh yes."

Not able to withstand her temptation another second, he slipped his cock into her warm haven.

Cian pumped into her. She hissed, her pelvic muscles milking him, clenching him in a vice grip. A wild groan spilled from his lips. Her hands fisted the sheets.

He couldn't take it. This hellcat. This witchy woman of his heart. He didn't just want her body. Cian wanted all of her. "My gothic rose."

Eve increased her tempo, matching him drive for drive, the sharp slap of their bodies a testament to the crazy passion between them.

"Yes," she cried.

Her pale skin began to glow purest white, while his turned darkest ebony. He sucked in a breath, not so lost in his haze as not to notice what was happening between them.

He stopped moving and pulled out. Eve gave an inarticulate cry, her eyes widening at the colors of their bodies. Like ice on shadow. She lifted her hand and traced an invisible line between them, her light banishing his darkness.

The pain, anger, it all washed away with the pulsing white light.

"Cian…" she breathed. "What?"

"I don't know, Eve. I don't know." Whatever it was, it felt good. The dark stains inside his soul faded, banished by the beauty of her gift.

He entered her again, her beautiful eyes turning soft. There was no rushing of bodies but rather a silky melding of hearts.

She wrapped her legs around him.

"Eve," he whispered, awed by the gift she was giving him.

The lightness and darkness spread like liquid throughout the room. Her legs trembled, and she cried out.

He clenched his teeth, tasting her passion. Her climax. She was spiraling through a sexual haze, dragging him with her. A slow burn inched through his veins before she burst. An eruption of energy so strong the room shook. With her release came his, and he roared as his seed exploded inside her.

Then all was calm. Two hearts beating in unison. Arms and legs wrapped around each other. Eyes closed, he took a deep breath and willed his heart back to normal as the colors slowly evaporated back into their pores.

She broke the silence with her trademark throaty laugh. "I can't feel my legs."

"Eve. You've bewitched me."

She kissed his forehead and smoothed back his hair. "I think it's the other way around."

He wrapped her in his arms, content to just hold her.

She sighed and a moment later asked, "Why did we glow? That was bordering on sci-fi territory there. And I know magick."

He shook his head, burying his nose in her hair. "I'm not sure."

They settled against each other, his fingers drawing lazy circles on her arm. In this moment, in this hour, everything was as it should be. Perfect. And they continued to enjoy each other for several more hours, lost in the wonder of new love.

A static burst of radio shattered their lovemaking. He glanced at the alarm clock sitting on her end table and his eyes widened with the wild beat of his heart.

It was six thirty a.m., and the responsibility of who he was, the truths he must tell, came crashing back with brutal reality.

Chapter 26

Oh jeez, how did I lose track of time like that?" Eve sat up and shut off the alarm with a dejected sigh. She looked at Cian with a sad-puppy-dog frown. "I have to start getting dressed for work. I wish I could stay here with you instead." She walked her fingers up his chest. "But I guess you probably need to get going yourself. Sun's gonna be up in another half an hour."

He grabbed her fingers, closing his eyes and taking a deep breath. He was so quiet. A sudden tension began to twist and grow through the room.

She swallowed hard. The sexual high she'd been on plummeted. She thought back to the I-have-to-tell-you-something moment a few hours ago, and a crushing sense of loss slithered down her spine.

It wasn't that she was a mind reader, and honestly, she couldn't explain the leeching feeling of dread seeping through her skin, but she knew something terrible was about to happen.

"Eve," he started and opened his eyes. Their blue depths glittered with sadness.

She ground her jaw and snatched up the green terry cloth robe hanging over the footboard of the bed, covering her body like a shield.

"Cian." She stopped him, lifting her hand and shaking her head. "Don't...please."

He sat up, running a finger down her arm and she couldn't stop herself from enjoying his touch.

"Eve," he pleaded. "You've got to listen to me."

She closed her eyes. "Let me preserve this beautiful memory. If you're leaving me"—her voice cracked—"then I won't stop you. But let's not taint what we shared with ugly truths."

"What I have to tell you, you'll eventually learn on your own, and you'll hate me even more for finding out by someone else."

Pain tore through her heart. Was he married? A murderer? What?

Her hands shook as she stood from the bed and walked to her closet, pulling out a skirt and top. He sighed behind her and she leaned her head against the door, closing her eyes for a split second.

She didn't want to know, and yet curiosity poisoned her thoughts. She pulled on her clothes and then turned to him.

He was propped up against a pillow, the blanket covering his nude torso. Worry lines marked his forehead, and he looked at her in silent appeal.

Moments ago she was the happiest she'd ever been. Now she felt nothing but dread. "If you insist, then at least give me enough time to get ready for the day. I have a sickening feeling that once I find out, I won't be able to do much of anything."

He lowered his eyes and she ran to the bathroom.

* * *

Eve sat at her kitchen table, the sound of a running shower filtering from her bathroom.

Her gut churned with anxiety, wondering what he would say. She closed her eyes, pain spearing her heart.

A loud knock on the front door made her yelp and clutch her chest. She glanced at the clock. It was seven.

"Who..." Then it hit her, the breakfast date she'd made with Curtis. She groaned. Now was definitely not a good time for that.

She marched to the door and opened it. Curtis inclined his head with a bright smile. "Good morning, there, Eve. Brought us some bagels and tea." He held up a white paper sack. There were two steaming Styrofoam cups in a holder in his other hand.

"Curtis, I'm so sorry. I totally forgot about this, and I don't think it's such a good time."

He frowned, and the light shining in his rich mahogany eyes turned dull. "I'm sorry to hear that. You know what..." He gently pushed his way inside and walked to her kitchen.

Her eyes went wide. Had he just barged in after she'd told him no? Shock rooted her to the spot.

Curtis placed the bag and tea on the counter. "You keep these, then. Maybe some other day."

Eve waited for him to leave, but he stood there, smiling. She kept the door open and walked toward him, trying to formulate in her mind the best way to ask him to leave. He flicked his eyes toward her, and a burning flame of amber undulated in their depths.

Instinctively she recoiled.

"I'm sorry, Eve. I didn't want it to happen this way," he said and grabbed her wrist.

A surge of vertigo shot down her skull, into her neck, and through her limbs, turning them numb. Nothing made sense. A murky haze descended over her mind.

"Come closer," he demanded.

And she did. Like a puppet being pulled by its strings. She tried to fight it, told her brain to stop. But it was like a virus had infected her mind. Nothing worked. She thought harder and harder. *Stop. Please stop. What's happening? My goddess, I'm still moving. I can't. I can't...*

She was outside herself, watching this all happen like a movie on a screen. Inside she wailed, screamed. A shiver of panic stole her breath.

He looked at her, squinting his eyes. His nostrils flared and any internal thought she possessed, any ability to realize this was wrong, dissipated.

"Pick up your cup." It was Curtis speaking, but the voice wasn't his. It was ancient, filled with incredible power.

She watched her hand reach out and pick up the cup.

"Take off the lid."

Trembling fingers tore the lid off.

"Now"—he opened the paper sack, pulling out a small white canister—"add some sugar." He opened the lid.

Small yellow flecks filled the jar. She blinked. The label on the side read WOLFSBANE.

"It's not sugar," she whispered. Eve tried hard to think, to remember why that wasn't good. Deep down, she was aware that something was terribly wrong.

"Of course it is," he said and pushed it toward her, dipping a spoon into the jar and pulling it out to show her the white granules.

She sighed and smiled. Of course. Harmless. "Sugar for my tea."

"Yes, that's right. Put some in."

She dropped two spoonfuls of sugar into her cup.

"Good. Very good. Now stir it, Eve."

She stirred.

"Drink it."

She brought the cup to her lips, steam curling under her nose, liquid barely sliding against the skin of her lips. Ready to swallow, to take her first taste of the brew. But...she couldn't. There was something inside her. Something that stopped her at the last minute; all she could do was hold the cup against her lips.

"Drink it, Eve. Drink it now!" Curtis commanded. Then he sucked in a breath, his gaze darting to the hallway. He swiped his hand through the air and vanished.

"Eve!" Cian roared, running into the living room and breaking her from her trance.

Startled, she screamed and jerked, pulling the cup away before the first taste. A small splash of hot tea spilled onto the front of her shirt. She hissed as it scalded. Then she frowned at the blank slate of time lost.

She stared at her hand. Confusion clawed at her throat. She couldn't remember. What was she doing holding tea? When had she made it? She looked at the Styrofoam and her eyes widened. Dazed, she set the cup down on the kitchen table.

What the hell was going on?

She looked to Cian and her jaw went slack.

"Are you okay?" he asked, running up to her.

"What's happened to your hand?" she shrieked, staring at the macabre ivory of bone.

He closed his eyes and hugged the skeletal hand to his chest. "This…was what I needed to tell you."

Chapter 27

This wasn't how he'd wanted to tell her. But when his hand had shifted, all reason had fled and he'd run to her with one thought in mind—keeping her safe.

He glanced around the room. There was nothing. No feeling of death lingering in the air. He was sure of he'd felt it. Where was Frenzy? The reaper had to be around.

"Cian"—her voice shook—"what is going on?" Distress sparkled in her golden gaze.

Something he'd like to know himself. These circumstances puzzled him. How could he always sense another reaper but never see him? *Think, Cian. Think. C'mon, c'mon, c'mon. If you can solve this riddle, you can figure out how to save her.* He knew that. Instinctually he knew that.

"Tell me." Her voice was a tight thread of anxiety.

She wanted answers. He wanted answers. His mind was split. He couldn't focus on two things at once. And the thread of doubts concerning Frenzy became hazy, foggy. He lost his train of thought.

"Eve, I'm…"

"You're what? Tell me. Get it over with. Who are you, Cian?"

"I'm not who you think I am," he growled, refocusing on her.

She flinched, and her fear stabbed through his heart.

His nostrils flared at the metaphysical pain. This was the hardest thing he'd ever had to do.

"I…" *Do it, damn it! Tell her now.* Panicked, he said in a rush, "Eve, I killed your husband."

She didn't make a sound, but the chill of her pain encased him in burning frost. It was like licking flames eating at his flesh, tearing him apart from the inside.

"You weren't the one who ran us over. I saw him." Her voice cracked.

His blood pumped harder with anxiety.

"I am death, Eve. What humans call the grim reaper." He held up his hand.

She was silent. Barely breathing. Hardly moving.

Her stillness unnerved him. If only she'd say something. *Do* something. He spoke into the quiet, not able to stop now that he'd started.

"My hand turns to bone when a soul is ready to be harvested. As it did on the day of your husband's death. But I wasn't just there for him. You were supposed to die too."

The static of her energy tormented him.

He frowned. "I…I couldn't do it. I tried." His gaze dropped to the floor, unable to stand the vacant look in her eyes. "You were a fighter, and even though I hardly knew you then, I already loved you. You saw me, for the first time in my existence. Only you."

Through all of that, she didn't make a sound.

There was one last confession that had to be made. He took a deep breath. "I belong to the circle of fae. I'm no vampire."

She inhaled sharply then. Her breathing began to come in hard and heavy pants.

"You killed Michael." There was a hollowness to her voice he'd never heard before.

He reached for her hand out of habit.

"No!" She pulled away, hugging her arms to her chest. "Don't touch me ever again."

Her words slid over his skin like burning oil. His heart shattered at the look of repulsion on her face. A bluish-green vein on the side of her neck pulsed with a rush of blood and adrenaline.

Her lips pulled back, exposing her gums as she sneered. "Why? Tell me why? What possible reason could you have for taking his life?"

He scrubbed a hand down his face. "It was my duty. It was his time."

"Time? Time! You talk to me about time. What the hell would you know about that? We were trying to have a baby. Our lives were finally settled." She touched her flat stomach.

Her torment snapped through him like the angry slash of The Morrigan's whip.

"Eve, please try to understand."

"No! I don't want to ever hear you say my name again." She shook, her fists clenching by her sides. "So was I a great lay, Cian?"

He winced and shook his head. "Please don't do that. I wanted you. I…Eve, I know what you must think, but…"

She gave him a sarcastic, evil laugh. "Oh really? You do, huh? I'll tell you what I heard. One…" She lifted her hand and ticked off a finger. "…you killed my husband. Two, you tell me it was out of some freaking sense of duty, which, let me tell you, is no consolation. And three, you're a god—"

She snapped her mouth shut. A muscle in her jaw ticked.

He knew what she'd been about to say. That he was a goddamned fae. His grief turned to anger and desperation. "No. It is my duty. Just as it's my duty now to protect you. There's still a bounty on your head. The Morrigan will not rest until she sees you dead. Don't you get it? I'm here to protect you. I love—"

"Don't"—she cut him off with a swipe of her hand—"even say those disgusting words to me. As if I'd believe you anyway."

Tears were shining in her eyes, her face scrunched and she was on the verge of tears. "You used me."

"Not a chance! It was real."

"I was such a fool. So what is it, Cian? Do the beautiful ones find you revolting? Do they look at you with pity, or disgust? Or maybe both? How long has it been since you've been laid that you'd be willing to screw the wife of a dead man?" Tears were streaming down her face in a rushing torrent that she didn't even bother to disguise.

"I resent your accusations." He clenched his jaw. She was swinging below the belt. In his anger he said the first words that came to mind. "What hurts worse, Eve? That I killed your husband, or that you sullied your lily-white hands on a fae? That you let one touch you? That you actually enjoyed it?"

She swung her head to the side, her eyes widening with rage. "How dare you try to turn this on me? How dare you imply that?"

"You think I'm stupid enough not to know your disgust where the fae are concerned? Imagine if all your friends were to find out we screwed and you loved it. You think any of them would ever look at you the same way again?"

"Damn you."

He regretted his words, but they were out there and could never be forgotten. "It was never about the sex for me. And if I could bring your husband back I swear to the goddess I would, if only to see you happy again."

Her whole body jerked in response. "You're so good, I almost believe you. But guess what…"

This was worse than he'd imagined. In some misguided way, he'd hoped she'd forgive him. That in their time together she'd actually seen the truth of who he was. He'd been wrong, and lost his soul in the process.

"…you've lied to me before." She picked up her purse and turned toward the door.

She opened it and with her back to him, whispered, "You can see yourself out."

Then she walked out without so much as a backward glance.

* * *

Eve didn't care where she was headed, only that she had to get away. Having to look at the face she'd thought she'd fallen in love with for another second would have killed her. Did he have any idea, any clue? Did he even care how much it hurt?

She was rippling with energy, begging for anyone or anything to cross her path. Eve wanted to fight, to rip and claw and tear stuff apart. At the same time she wanted to scream and fall to the ground in a puddle of tears. But all she could do was run.

Before she knew where she was headed, she was already there. Club X. It never even crossed her mind to find her sisters.

She ran up the stairs, passing all the floors until she reached the mixed flock and entered, her gaze frantically searching for the one being able to bring her any kind of peace.

Under a dim blue light sat the hunched form of Lise. Her white gaze locked on to Eve's.

She walked to the booth and stopped, trembling and unsure of herself, only knowing death couldn't be worse than the ache in her heart.

"Sit." The word was like a rushing wind, powerful and full of unimagined strength.

It never crossed Eve's mind to refuse. She sat down, clasping and unclasping her hands in front of her, her leg keeping up a nervous rhythm.

"Why did you run away, Eve? Why did you leave him? Do you know how stupid that was, especially now?"

She frowned. She'd expected sympathy, not judgmental scorn. She was the wounded party, not him. He'd lied to her, killed her spouse. Why would Lise even care?

"He killed Michael."

Lise narrowed her eyes. "He was only doing his job!"

She snorted, not wanting to hear this. "No. No."

"He could no more control his actions than you can help being a witch. That is who he is. It is his function. One he has done over a millennia. Do you know the pain he's carried? Do you even care?"

The exact words she'd thought earlier, now flung back in her face. "I'm the wounded party here, Lise." She touched a finger to her chest directly over her heart. "He hurt me. He lied to me."

"Me. Me. Me." Lise sneered. "You're so self-centered."

She inhaled, deeply stung. Never before had Lise turned her anger on her like this. It was inexcusable. Wrong. "I've done nothing..."

"Spare me, Eve. You are listening with your heart, not your brain. You want to be hurt. You want someone to blame. Make him your scapegoat, everyone else does. The reapers are so easy to hold responsible for all of life's woes. They do the job no one else will, day in and day out. They die from the suffering they must endure. You were saving his soul, bit by bit, hour by hour."

She closed her eyes, not wanting to listen to Lise anymore but unable to block out the deep truth of her words. It was a dull knife piercing her soul.

"I blame myself." The chosen one pounded her fist onto the table, the guise of frailty snapping irrevocably for Eve. This was an immortal, not a frail woman, not a friend. She would not baby Eve, and this time Eve wouldn't be able to run away.

"I did everything but tell him you were his chosen. He tried over and over to resist you. You want to know why?"

Eve glanced up as burning tears slid down the corners of her eyes.

"Because he didn't want to lie to you. To make you feel as if he'd betrayed you." She clenched her jaw, her eyes began to glow, and her rage transferred to Eve, filling her with disgust and shame.

"He's fae." She didn't know what made her say it. She felt herself grasping at straws, desperate to get Lise on her side and understanding her pain. She succeeded only in whipping the immortal into a frenzy of fury.

Lightning quick, Lise latched onto Eve's hand squeezing it nearly to the point of crushing the bone. She hissed, tendrils of pain spiraling from the grip.

"And that should matter why? Has he treated you with contempt? Spite? He worshiped you. Yes Eve, he's a fae. He participated in the Great War." Her hold on Eve's hands didn't relent. "And not that this should matter, but he had no part in the treachery. He was little more than the cleanup crew. I thought you were smarter than this."

Lise threw her hand away in disgust. She brought the throbbing wrist to her chest and huddled over it protectively, for the first time truly knowing the power of Lise. Her heart hung in her throat. Eve tasted the fear on her tongue.

"The night you almost died, the night your husband was taken, it was because of him, Eve. He made a choice, and he chose you. That choice cost him dearly."

Eve swallowed hard, remembering that night with perfect clarity, as if it'd just happened yesterday.

"He's done nothing but protect you."

The chosen one sat back, her look of fury now replaced by a mask of calm. "To be sure that no one is blameless, he should likely have told you the truth before now, forced you to understand. But coming here and looking for my sympathy, you'll have none. If you cannot see the fault that lies within you, then you do not deserve him."

Lise stood, her white gown rippling around her body like a living entity. She touched Eve's cheek and Eve jerked in response, expecting Lise to slap the crap out of her this time.

"Make peace with this, Eve, and with him. Sooner rather than later." She reached into the air, a white slip of paper appearing in her hand from nowhere. "You might be able to reach him here."

Eve looked at the paper. A phone number was scrawled across it. The chosen one nodded and walked away.

The pain, the fear, the anger and hurt—it all washed over her, drowning her in emotions. The connection she felt with Cian was more than lust or friendship. It had been magickal, mystical. *Meant to be.* She'd been helpless to him from the moment their gazes locked. Her soul had always craved her spiritual other, and as much as it felt like a betrayal to admit it, Michael hadn't been it.

She dropped her head into her hands, the paper crinkling in her tight grasp. A cloying wash of grief rippled through her. Not for Cian's misdeeds but her own. For her stupidity and childish behavior. The words she'd flung at him. Pain ripped through her heart, as she remembered the wounded expression in his eyes.

All she could think of in that moment was to hurt him as much as he'd hurt her. To make him feel what it felt like.

She clenched her jaw, an emptiness consuming her soul.

What had Lise said? *Make peace with this.*

Hope, faint but there, shot through her. *It might not be too late.* Maybe he was still at her apartment.

She shoved away from the table, uncaring that she resembled a slaughtered raccoon with mascara dripping black down her face. Her only thought was of Cian. His arms. His quiet, gentle manner. So much he'd endured and the strength it had taken to come clean. Looking back she could see all the times he'd tried to tell her, to open up and be honest. She'd sensed it and had always shut him down, preferring to hang on to the lie. Lise was right; she'd been just as much to blame.

There was probably no chance in hell that he was still there. Likely he was long gone. But she had to try. She had to make an attempt. He couldn't leave thinking she hated him.

Chapter 28

Cian was broken. Shattered. He'd done his part and told the truth. He couldn't say he honestly blamed Eve. Everything from the moment they'd met had been a lie, except his feelings for her. He'd never deceived her about that.

He'd hoped. Goddess, he'd hoped Eve would have accepted him. Understood he was a man who loved her and who also happened to be fae. That his race did not define him as a person.

He swallowed hard. All that was water under the bridge now. There was nothing more for him to do here.

Still he followed her, all the way to Lise's. He had to make sure she was safe, regardless that she didn't trust him anymore. He couldn't allow harm to come to her. Not a creature or reaper tried to stop her. Assured she was safe, he swiped his hand, opening the portal between the here and there.

Steeling himself, he walked through, landing back on Alcatraz Island.

Rusted, ramshackle, abandoned prison cells were a perfect analogy to how he felt on the inside. Empty. Soulless. He walked toward the tree, covering himself in stealth so that none of the chattering, filming tourists would catch sight of him.

He was never coming back. His time as reaper was over. His heart and soul were now irreparably bound to Eve's. Despite that, in the end she'd rejected him, and he was lost. And he couldn't fade knowing the queen would stop at nothing to take her. So he went now to offer his life for hers. The death of an immortal would more than make right the balance to order and chaos, allowing Eve to live the life The Morrigan would deny her—that of marriage, kids, and many happy memories.

That would be his penance.

* * *

Eve plowed through the door, throwing her purse on the ground and calling out his name. There was only silence. Hope died inside her. As she'd suspected, he was gone; not a trace of him remained. Her nostrils flared and she ran to her phone. She might still be able to reach him.

The thought crossed her mind to go to his house, but if he'd seen who was at the door, would he have answered? Probably not. At least with a phone call he was more likely to pick up.

She closed her eyes. If he turned her away, or even refused to listen, then it was all her fault and there would be no anger. The things he'd said, the malicious words he'd thrown, had cut her to the quick, until Lise made her recognize her prejudices for what they were. Disgusting, awful truth.

Fear of the unknown, a hatred for all things fae, had kept her from listening with her heart, and look where it had gotten her. Anxiety constricted her chest, twisting her stomach in on itself.

"Damn it, Eve. Damn it." She picked up the phone and walked to her kitchen table, sitting down and staring at the white headset like it would suddenly sprout fangs and snap her head off.

What made her sick the most was that deep down she'd suspected he harbored a secret. Being so comfortable around food, not leaving her side until the very last moment—sun creeping over the horizon—and those gloves. Those ever-present gloves. If she'd opened her eyes instead of refusing to see the truth, she'd have known him not to be a vampire. Vampires didn't make flame, couldn't take off clothing with just a thought. But she had pretended not to notice, imagined it wasn't there, and in so doing had made it all the harder for him to come clean.

The things she'd said. She groaned. Words could never be taken back. They were always there, always a reminder in the back of your mind. You could forgive, but not forget.

She didn't mean it. It'd been the shock of finding out who he really was.

You didn't throw the shield up in time. She gasped, remembering now. Just minutes before she and Michael were knocked to the ground, she'd noticed him. Cian standing behind her in the mirror.

Now she remembered the gorgeous man with great sadness in his eyes. That nagging feeling that she'd seen him once before had been right. Even then, married to Michael as she was, she'd been intrigued. Her heart instinctively reaching out to his.

He'd been there to take her that night, which could mean only one thing. He'd saved not just her but Michael as well. And the next day, the car accident…She'd been in such a pain-fogged haze she could remember very little of it. Yet for her to have survived the types of injuries she'd sustained, it had to have been him.

She'd hurt him, cut him to the bone. Bile rose in her throat. She was nothing but a judgmental coward.

Eve picked up the phone, staring at the numbers scrawled across the slip of paper Lise had given her. She ground her jaw and dialed.

It rang once.

Twice.

After the fifth ring, she finally admitted defeat. Either he wouldn't pick up, or he was gone, back to his home in faerie. Numb, she set the phone down, shame eating away at her. A huge lump formed in her throat. All of this was her fault. Every bit of it.

A hollow void swept through her. Lise had called her a fool, and she was. Hot tears gathered at the corners of her ears. She huffed at them, refusing to let them fall. She'd cried enough.

"You make your bed, you lie in it." Her voice cracked. These were the consequences of her actions, and she was woman enough to accept that.

Heaviness coiled around her heart, a tightening that left her breathless. The sadness of their parting left her bereft and in more pain than she'd ever known before. Anguish splintered her soul in two.

One fat tear fell and then another and then another. She threw her head into her hands and wept hot, bitter tears. Great choking sobs wracked her lungs and she cried until there was nothing left.

Like a pressure valve releasing its pent-up energy, she felt drained. No longer was there an overwhelming despair so much as a sickening throb of a broken heart.

Mouth tasting of cotton and head pounding like a rhino had

stomped on it, she reached out and snatched the only drink at hand. Not even aware of what she was grabbing, just knowing she needed to quench her parched throat.

She chugged down the entire drink, grimacing at the bitter, slightly astringent taste it left on her tongue.

Eve smacked her lips. They were beginning to go numb. What was this? She frowned and stared into the bottom of the cup. Tiny yellow flecks dotted the Styrofoam's rim. The numbness spread down her throat, and her stomach gave a violent heave.

Blinking in shock, she grabbed her gut and moaned.

Fiery claws shred her apart from the inside. Panic spread its wings. Poison. She'd been poisoned. How? When?

She gasped for breath, choking on the air itself. Fire filled her lungs as she fought desperately for breath. She opened her mouth in a soundless scream of agony.

Veins burst inside her eyes with the fighting need for breath. Her body trembled and her muscles spasmed, contracting as hard as a rock.

She shot to her feet. Whimpering. Moaning. Limbs refusing to work right. She tripped over her chair, landing face-first onto the cold floor. The flesh of her chin split open on contact. Warm blood oozed from the wound.

Then the convulsions started.

Absolute fear swept down her spine, as she was aware and conscious of it all.

Her body went rigid. There was no air in her lungs. Fire breathing down her skull. Heart beating out of control. Blackness sweeping in. Then a thought. In death she'd find solace from her despair.

With one last pitiful gasp, her heart stopped.

* * *

Cian passed his hand along the tree. The golden quickening surrounded him as he stepped through the entrance to the sithen.

The sylph's angelic voices greeted him. He inhaled the sharp, nature-infused winds of his lands. The inspiration he usually found from being on fae soil was now gone. He shoved his hands into his pockets, heart and soul shattered. Red madness creeping into his vision.

His nostrils flared. The oppressive pain began to fill him. It was tangible, choking the air from his lungs.

Find the queen. Plead her case. End this misery. That was his mantra, and he repeated it over and over, running faster and faster toward The Morrigan. Toward his death.

It no longer mattered what the queen chose to do to him. Strip him, flog him…none of it made a difference. Not anymore.

Pressure built inside his skull. He winced, trying to ignore it. He licked his lips and scrambled over the knoll.

He had time. Not much. But if he could reach the queen before a reaper could orchestrate Eve's death, then her fate could be averted. He had time. He ran faster.

The twisted spiraling steeple of the queen's castle stood just over the next hill. So close.

Suddenly, his fragile control was ripped asunder as a flash of volcanic heat exploded inside his head. He fell to his knees, clutching his stomach, pain licking at his flesh, heart threatening to punch a hole in his chest. Arcing back and throwing his arms out to his sides, he became engulfed by the inferno.

Shards of jagged ice tore down his spine. Limbs turned numb and heavy. Then a flash of darkness and he fell forward.

The scent of crushed grass wafted under his nose.

"Eve," he gasped, knowing her smell The awareness of her death ripped through every inch of his body.

A roar of anguish pulsed through the fabric of his soul and out his mouth. He shot to his feet. Nature went still. The sylphs went silent as the beast inside him came fully alive.

Misery encased him like a shroud, and he welcomed it, giving into the madness. She was dead…his beautiful witch.

Huge green eyes peeked at him from around the bend of an oak—a tree elf shaking like a sapling in the wind. Didn't matter what it was. Morality. Right or wrong. Innocent or no. He lost all ability to reason. He wanted death. Someone to hurt as badly as he did.

He ran, arms outstretched, ready to grab the elf by the neck and rip it in two.

The elf screamed, her long blond mane whipping behind her in her haste to run away.

A violent clap of thunder rocked in his ears and lightning consumed him, blinding his vision.

Next thing he heard was maniacal laughter, the sound prickling along his flesh. He twirled, disoriented and full of fighting fury.

Then he saw the queen, a lascivious smirk on her bloodred lips. She stood from her throne and sashayed toward him. The black strapless gown tapered to her body and glittered with the stars from the heavens. The shadowy fabric opened at the juncture between her breasts and formed a V all the way down to her navel.

To her side stood Dagda, his anger whipping through the room like thorny barbs, his dark face set into a grim mask. Remorse and pity shone in his hawklike eyes.

"What have you done?" Cian growled, taking a menacing step forward.

The Morrigan arched an obsidian brow, the ivory perfection of her face twisting into a sneer. "Me? Nothing that shouldn't have been done a long time ago. Ineptitude really disgusts me."

There was no remorse on her face, just a smile of victory. She didn't care. Eve had meant nothing to her.

With a roar, he rushed her, footsteps echoing like gunfire. The Morrigan flicked her wrist and invisible chains pulled him to the ground, forcing him prostrate. All breath left on impact with a loud oomph. He struggled, howling and clawing to reach her. She stood mere inches from him, her gown swishing in front of his eyes. If he could just stretch a little bit farther…

Fingers reached out and grabbed nothing but air. His futile attempt only brought on another bout of laughter from her.

"You know"—The Morrigan knelt in front of him, light blue of her eyes sparkling—"it would seem you've grown attached to this mortal. Of course, that's impossible, right?" She cocked her head, tapping her finger against her chin.

He snarled and snapped, wanting nothing more than to grab her by the neck and rip out the veins.

"Oh ho!" Her eyes widened with delight. "You fell in love. How deliciously ironic, touching, and strangely pathetic." She grabbed his chin, her nails pushing down into the flesh.

With one last wicked smirk, she threw his head aside and faced her king. "Well, what do you know, Dagda, I've won." The Morrigan sighed as if she were talking of a schoolgirl crush, rather than the death of a mortal. To her it was all the same. He wanted to strangle the goddess for her inhumanity.

No wonder Eve feared the fae. How could she not when the majority felt and acted like the queen? A bloodthirsty and self-involved race.

"Chaos," Dagda snapped, "gloating does not become you."

"You're wrong there. I think I want to savor this moment." With a satisfied smile, she nodded. "Frenzy, to me."

The same flash of lightning that had carted him to the queen's chamber flared through the room, bringing with it Frenzy.

Cian's eyes widened then narrowed, his hands fisting into balls by his sides.

This was a different Frenzy. He was in guise. His sea of red hair was replaced by tight white curls. His ivory skin now a dark brown.

"No. No. No," he groaned. He couldn't believe his eyes. The Morrigan had brought Frenzy to her, and here was Curtis standing in front of him and he wasn't getting any sense or vibe of death. There was nothing. No internal static or recognition of Frenzy. It was as if this man were mortal.

Frenzy turned to look at him, black eyes devoid of emotion, and grabbed on to a silver pendant hanging around his neck. "I did what I had to."

All feeling fled. Emptiness swooped down inside him, crowding his thoughts, his mind. But one incessant thought kept pounding through. *This was how she got through. This was it.*

The queen slipped her arm around Frenzy's back, never taking her gaze from Cian's. "And I am so proud of you."

She smiled and tipped the reaper's face toward hers. Frenzy closed his eyes, a bitter twist to his lips.

Cian could only stare, shattered and disgusted. His body trembled with the need to scream, to strip himself of his clothes, cut off his hair, sit in rags, and grieve for what he'd lost.

"There's just one last thing to do, then." She snapped her fingers and Eve's lifeless body appeared by her feet.

"No!" he wailed, heart jolting painfully. The blue mask of death upon her face. He couldn't breathe, couldn't take his gaze from Eve. That long black hair he loved so much lay limp and partially conceal-ing one corner of her face. Her golden eyes were open, the whites bloodshot. The light that had once shone so bright was now gone. Rosebud lips parted into a perfect O.

Heat crept into his eyes.

The Morrigan stepped over Eve with a tiny sniff.

Cian trembled. His beauty. His dark rose, broken and lifeless. But he wouldn't give the queen the pleasure of witnessing his pain.

"Cian," she snapped, and the force of her anger reverberated through the room, slamming against flesh like a physical blow. He shot his gaze to her face. The façade of calm was gone. The Morrigan was in full fury. Eyes a feral shade of red, brows lowered, and mouth set into a razor-thin line. "Now you will finish what I sent you to do in the first place."

She flicked her wrists, and her mental control over Cian snapped. He launched himself at Eve's prone body and cradled her to his chest, rocking them back and forth. She was nothing but dead weight in his arms.

The bluish mist of her soul seeped from her pores, ready to be harvested. A pulse of fire shot down his arm. He snatched his hand back seconds before it turned skeletal. "I won't do it," he growled, defying her, and flicked his wrist. The gloves once again covered his hands, keeping her safe. He would never hurt Eve again.

"Chaos! There is no need to torture him." Gold dust showered down from the walls and ceilings with the thunderous boom of Dagda's voice.

She hissed. "No. He's made a fool of me. A lesson must be taught, so that all will know never to try it again."

Then she stalked toward Cian. Her anger snapped into him with cutting force. The fury of her wrath glinted like fire in her red eyes.

"Do it, Cian, or I'll force you to." Hot spittle landed on the corner of his eye.

"Kill me if you must. I won't take her soul to the afterlife."

Her eyes widened and her arm moved in a blur of speed. She punched her hand through his chest, her fingers wrapping around his heart. She gave a gentle squeeze.

A shriek like the sound of a deranged animal fell from his lips. His body stiffened as the fires of hell filled his every crevice.

The Morrigan leaned in to whisper in his ear, "The defiance ends. One way or another, she will be harvested. And you, my dear Cian, will regret the day you ever thought to defy me." Each infinitesimal movement sent him into a spasm of vomit-inducing pain.

She narrowed her eyes, tightening her hold by a fraction. He stiffened, holding on to Eve's body like a lifeline. Sweat poured from his brows and down his neck.

"Frenzy, finish her now." The Morrigan's words had a sharp finality to them.

Frenzy walked forward, dropping to his knees before them. Eyes downcast, he reached forward.

"Don't touch her," Cian barked.

The queen clenched her fingers together. The pain was immediate, sharp spikes of lancing fire driving through him. His muscles spasmed, allowing Eve to slip from between his grasp.

"I'm sorry, Cian," Frenzy whispered, his silver gaze full of regret.

Warm blood trickled from the corner of his mouth. He glanced toward Dagda. The king refused to look at him.

The Morrigan threw her head back and laughed. She hissed, gritting her teeth. "He can't help you now, Cian. No one can."

Then Cian understood and the last shred of hope died out. They'd sworn a pact. The king was as helpless as he.

Frenzy reached out, skeletal hand twitching and mere inches from Eve's chest. He closed his eyes and waited for the end to come.

"Take her now, Frenzy!" With those words the queen squeezed Cian's heart in a viselike grip, and a white nova burst in his brain.

Frenzy shoved his skeletal hand through Eve's chest.

"NOOOO!" Cian screamed against the physical and mental anguish.

Eve jerked on the floor. A blue mist exploded from her chest, and a spiraling light of white opened before them.

Frenzy glanced at Cian, regret and sorrow expressed on his face. In his gaze.

Hot liquid trailed down the corners of his eyes, running a warm path down his cheek and landing finally on his lips. Without thought, he lapped at the wetness and tasted not the salt of tears but the metallic tang of blood. He was crying crimson.

Eve lay lifeless. The light-blue pallor of true death touched her flesh, and he welcomed the desolate darkness of eternal sleep.

Frenzy walked toward the portal, and the exceptionally small sliver of soul breezed through. Cian frowned, his thoughts disjointed, muddled. Agony speared him, cleaved his heart in two. He needed to think, to understand. Something hadn't seemed right.

He focused over the ache in his heart, blinked back the bloody tears, and fought to understand. Something wasn't right. Her soul. It'd been so small.

"It is done," Frenzy whispered and The Morrigan nodded, pulling her hand out of his chest with a loud suctioning pop.

Another angry explosion of fire filled his limbs. He looked down to see a gaping hole in his chest, his muscles strained and screamed. He gasped for breath. His lungs rattled with the effort and he coughed. A wet, spastic sound ripped through him. Each breath was torture. His body trembled, and his eyes began to roll to the back of his head.

"Badb. Nemain. Bring me the canes."

"Eve," he breathed.

The Morrigan stood tall over him, no longer gloating, her face expressionless and cold. Distant.

The birds dropped the one-inch rods at the queen's feet. When she stooped to pick them up, they gradually grew in size and thickness until they were as round as sturdy sapling and as long as a half-sized python.

There was no warning. No, get ready here it comes. A whistle and then black fire exploded across his back. He hissed, jerking automatically. One hit followed another. Then another. Gore splattered across the room.

And the queen never paused in the beating. One atop another, atop another. Faint, dizzy, he winced. Sheer agony, the likes of which he'd never felt before or thought to be possible, ate him alive. Like scalding oil caressing his back, stripping first the flesh, then the muscle.

White spots danced behind his eyes. He accepted the pain, welcomed the relief of the physical over the emotional. This wasn't enough to kill him. The Morrigan was toying with him. Drawing out the agony of the kill.

"I hate…you," he wheezed.

A spark of rage lit her eyes, and a wild scream escaped her blood-spattered lips. Drops of spit landed on his cheek with each huff she took, forcing the rod down harder and harder, ripping him to the bone.

The Morrigan lifted her hand, a deadly calm on her face, and he knew this next strike would send him into darkness.

The macabre scene slowed down. Every detail of the room, of The Morrigan, Dagda, and Frenzy was sharp and clearly defined, like his brain was shutting down. A coping mechanism, filtering every infinitesimal element into one sharp picture. Frenzy looking away. Dagda glaring and staring off at one corner of the room.

He watched her arms come down, so close he felt the whisper of air scant seconds before the metal would strike his back, when suddenly, the world around them rocked with incredible power, and a ripping gale threw The Morrigan and Frenzy aside. Foundations shifted and rocks crumbled. A fine mist of dust rained down around them.

"Enough!"

Cian groaned as the sharp bits of rock bit into his lacerated flesh. A blinding white light ripped through the room. The crawling flash of ivory seeped into his body, filling him with a healing warmth. Not nearly enough to close the jagged wounds, but just enough to get him to his feet and to Eve. Enough to hug her. To touch her.

He rocked with her and wept, burying his face in her neck, just wanting to hold her close to his shattered, bleeding heart.

"Your debt has been paid, Morrigan. Balance restored."

That's when the voice finally penetrated the fog of grief. Shocked, he glanced up to see Lise towering over the queen, her hunched-over body looking pathetically weak compared to The Morrigan's.

But there was no mistaking the infinite power crackling and radiating from the chosen one. An endless expanse of pulsating energy that singed the fine hairs on the back of his neck. A living entity hanging in the air. Lise was the very wellspring of magick itself.

"No," The Morrigan shrieked. "The deal was struck. I won. He is mine."

"You dare!" Lise lifted a hand, an eerie white glow covering her body. She became encased in iridescent flame so bright his eyes watered. He grimaced, only able to look upon her transformation through narrowed eyes.

There was an explosion, and Lise's body vanished, in its place a sphere of white-hot brilliance. "Have you forgotten us so soon? The works we entrusted you with?" The voice was Lise's, but deeper somehow, richer. The sphere glowed brighter with each question becoming as the burning sun. Blinding.

"You've lost your truth."

The Morrigan was staring at the ball of light, clenching her jaw, and trembling, fury evident in the lines of her back. Fear scrawling a path across her face. The red of her eyes slowly turning back to blue. "I never forgot who I was."

The sphere shot toward the queen, stopping inches from her. Tendrils of white flame shot out in all directions. The Morrigan flinched.

"You've grown self-righteous, believing yourself entitled to it all. Remember, oh queen..." Lise's words were trimmed in velvet.

Forged in fury. "We have the power to give and to take away. I've stood back and allowed you freedom to choose, much to the peril of humanity. That is your right but not in this."

The Morrigan said nothing.

The ball that was Lise turned and floated toward Cian. "My son."

He frowned, clutching Eve tighter to him.

"Such terrible sadness…"

A shaft of light reached out and engulfed him. He flinched, expecting…who knew what, only that touch had caused him much pain recently. Instead the sting of his wounds vanished. Gentle heat traveled through his limbs, banishing the monster inside, forcing it to return back to the shadowed depths. His heart sealed up with a small pop, the flesh of his chest knit together. Soothing heat, like the gentle waters of a natural spring, brushed against his back, healing him. The scent of a dewy spring day filled the antechamber.

He looked down at his bloody shirt. The gaping hole was gone.

Cian expected Lise to heal Eve. Bring her back from the dead. Something! Surely that couldn't be beyond her powers. She was one of the chosen. He'd seen her abilities firsthand.

"Please," he croaked, touching his witch's face. The plea ripped from his heart.

"She loved you." Lise's voice was everywhere and nowhere. In his mind, in the air, rippling through the room. And yet she hadn't uttered a word.

He closed his eyes and a shaky breath fell from his lips.

"Look inside yourself. Find the truth, and you'll find your Eve."

He frowned, turning to look down at the woman in his arms. The dark priestess of his fantasies and desires. The only thing that had ever meant anything to him.

The room was silent, nothing stirred. No one spoke. It was as if they weren't there at all.

Tracing the smoothness of her jaw with his finger, he searched, looking for whatever it was that Lise said he'd find. Memories flooded him.

Eve throwing him a baggie of blood, believing him to be a vamp. Her strength of character. That beautiful crooked smile of hers.

Something was happening. Something inside him, spreading throughout him. A coolness he'd never felt before. A strange entity coming to life.

More memories. That night at the tattoo parlor. The exotic woodpecker on her back. How she'd kissed his skull without disgust but with joy. The thought still wracked him with grief, and the rapid flutter of what felt like wings beat inside his chest.

His nostrils flared and he glanced at Lise. "What the hell is wrong with me?"

The ball glowed slightly brighter. He likened it to a gentle smile. "That is her. She is inside you."

"What?"

From the corner of his eye, he noticed all three figures lean slightly closer.

"When you made love, she shared her soul with you. The love was true. She is your mate. And only you can bring her back."

He blinked. Then blinked again. "H-How?" He felt tongue-tied, incapable of thought, or speech, for that matter. How was this possible?

"Did you notice a light that night? Dark and light?"

Mute, he nodded.

"You were sharing souls. Her light went into you, Cian. All you have to do…is reach inside yourself and pull her out."

He lifted his hand, staring at the rune-inscribed glove he'd always worn. His gaze flicked to Lise. "Won't my grabbing on to her soul kill it?"

"She shared her soul with you. That means your immortality, is now hers as well."

If there was even a chance…He tore off the glove and took a deep breath before he speared his hand through his chest. Ice and a raging inferno spread through his body, and he sucked in a breath through clenched teeth. Sweat poured from his brows and he reached inside, grabbing quickly on to the fluttering wings. and yanked it out.

The second his hand left his chest, the pain fled. Like the haunting memory of a fading dream. Within his palm rested the soul. It was not the typical blue of mortals but the bright golden wash of the immortals. It glittered, pulsed, and seemed to dance on his hand. The soul recognized him. Somehow he knew it, and a warm glow flowed down his spine.

"Lay her down, Cian. Place the soul upon her body and step back."

He looked to Lise. No way in hell was he letting her go. Not now. Not when he was so close.

"You did your part. Now it is my turn. Trust me."

It took every ounce of self-restraint he had to do as she bid. With great care he laid Eve's head upon the floor, briefly touching a curl before dropping the golden ball onto her chest. He clenched his jaw and slowly, agonizingly, stepped away.

The brilliant iridescence that was Lise floated down over Eve's body and then, like a gust of wind, flew into her. Magick, strong and potent, erupted inside the room. Fingers of wind riffled through his hair.

Eve was wrapped in ivory. White light shot from her pores, the tips of her fingers, until she glowed as Lise did and he could no longer see her through the brightness.

The white exploded and all went still, silent as the grave. He closed his eyes, turning aside until the flash died down. A quick inhalation of breath had his heart stuttering, and he snapped his eyes open.

Dazed but standing before him was the embodiment of all his desires. Beside her was the frail form of Lise, smiling down at him.

"Eve." Fear pierced his heart. His heart jackhammered in his chest.

She blinked. Twice. Three times. Her brows lowered, and she murmured a shaky "Cian."

That sultry voice had him shooting to his feet, pulling her into his embrace, and burying his nose in her hair. She wrapped her arms around his neck, and it was like coming home.

"My heart." His voice cracked, and he trembled. "I'm so sorry."

Eve shook her head. Reaching up on tiptoes, she planted a kiss against the corner of his mouth. "No. Don't apologize. It was all my fault. I should have been more understanding. I should have listened to you. I shouldn't have—"

He placed his finger against her mouth, stopping her. "We were both wrong. I'm so sorry I hurt you."

"Me too, Cian."

He gave a short bark of laughter. His gothic rose, back with him. Alive. Jubilant, he lifted Eve in his arms and twirled her around.

She laughed, that deep, throaty sound that shivered down his spine. "What are you doing?"

Her joy turned her eyes golden—not just lioness gold; this was the purest, glittering kind. If he'd had any doubts, then here was his proof. Eve was truly an immortal.

"Eve, you're immortal."

"What?" Doubt touched her brows. She touched a hand to her cheek.

Lise nodded. "Yes, that's right. An immortal, my dear. You are Cian's perfect mate and are destined to travel the long path with him. You need never fear death's touch again. As for you…" Lise glanced at the queen. "This is over," she sneered, turning the full might of her powers on the queen, her eyes raking The Morrigan's body like claws.

Dagda walked forward, grabbed Lise's hand, and dropped a kiss upon the knuckle. "Chosen. I'm only grateful that you arrived when you did."

The Morrigan hissed. Blue eyes going wide, she twirled on him. "You knew she'd come?"

"Of course, Chaos. Did you think me so foolish as to not plan ahead? I'm only sorry you got as far with Cian as you did."

Her nostrils flared, hands fisted by her side. But slowly the sparks of her anger subsided and she gave a jerky nod. A grudging smile tipped the corners of her mouth. "I guess that means I lost after all."

He grinned and grabbed her hand, pulling her into him. "It would seem so."

"Bastard."

Dagda shrugged and swatted her backside. "Let us leave, wench. These two have much to discuss."

"Tell me this: why did you two fight so hard to save them?" There was no disgust in her voice, merely curiosity.

"All in due time, Chaos. Now come. I believe it is time you tasted of your own punishment. The rack room. A good flogging perhaps."

A visible ripple traveled through The Morrigan. She bit her bottom lip.

"Lise. Cian. Eve." He nodded to the three and dragged his very willing queen out of the room.

Eve shook her head. "That woman scares the hell out of me. She's not right."

Cian ran his hand down her back. It was so good to have his witty, saucy witch back. "You *should* be scared of her, Eve. Dagda can control the queen, but barely. Always watch your back when at the court."

She looked at him, worry lines marring her forehead.

Lise clapped them on the shoulders. "Good advice, Cian. You might think about introducing your mate to the elders of the house. Garnering favor is never a bad thing. I'd start with the house of feathers. Wistafa maybe. I think she and Eve would get along admirably."

He nodded.

"One thing I don't understand, Lise." He hugged Eve tighter to him. "Why was Eve required to die in the first place, if I carried her soul within me?"

Lise gave a heavy sigh. Sorrow tipped the corners of her mouth. "Balance had to be restored. Her mortal self had to die. What you didn't know, Cian, was that you were saving her all along. You had to share souls. Once you did, she'd survive."

A physical tremble rushed through Eve, and Cian strummed his fingers down her back in a soothing, calming motion.

The noise of shifting feet alerted them to another presence. Cian looked up and Eve sucked in a breath.

"Oh my god, Curtis. You're a…"

Frenzy shook his head, pulling off the pendant and shifted to true form. Red hair and swirling silver eyes giving away his heritage. "I am called Frenzy, and yes, I am death." He opened his mouth as if to say more, but nothing came out.

Eve's jaw dropped open. "It was you, then. You bewitched me, caused me the headaches and blackouts. Why? What happened to the real Curtis?"

He crossed his hands behind his back, the reaper gesture of entreaty. A muscle ticked in his jaw. "He died several days past…"

She inhaled sharply. The sting of her friend's death washed through her. Cian rocked her, accepting her pain, becoming one with it, and giving his strength back to her. She sighed, calming almost instantly.

"I did what I had to do. It was my job."

Cian was wrapped in her anger and held her, let her know she wasn't alone.

"That night, when I helped you find Samhain…"

He nodded and glanced down.

"I reached out to touch you and you pulled away. I didn't get a headache or blackout." She paused. "You had to touch me to hurt me, didn't you?"

"Yes."

She paused. "Thank you."

There was still pain, and she was consumed by it. It would take some time for her to get over it, but this was definitely a start.

He released the breath he hadn't realized he'd been holding and dropped a kiss on her forehead. She was strong in so many ways. Even after all this, she'd thanked Frenzy.

Frenzy looked at Cian, confusion glittering in his eyes.

"I'll see you around, Frenzy," he said, knowing Eve could only take so much for one day.

With a final nod, the reaper turned and left.

"Hmm. I like happy endings, don't you?" Lise sighed and turned to them with a smile.

"I wouldn't call it happy." He glanced at Eve's upturned face. "But it's a fresh start."

She caressed his cheek and gave an almost-imperceptible nod.

"Touching as this all is, I really must go," Lise said.

"Wait"—Cian grabbed her arm—"how did you know there was a light?" Only now was he stopping to wonder about it. Eve turned in his arms, facing Lise brimming with confusion and curiosity.

"I felt the flow of power. We created your mates, after all. I'd recognize my own spell."

"What?" Eve asked on a breathless, half-nervous laugh.

He nodded. It all made sense now. "I'll tell you tonight, Eve, over dinner."

"You eat?" Her brows lowered, and she gave a tiny shake of her head. "I guess…there are some things I still have to learn about you."

"I guess you do." He brought her hand to his lips and dropped a kiss against the knuckle. "No more lies. Ever. My life is an open book to you."

She gave him her famous crooked smile and his heart soared.

"Come visit me at the club sometime. Gets a little boring and I must admit I've grown rather fond of my sisters three," Lise said.

Cian glanced down at Eve. She nodded. "It's a deal."

Lise waved good-bye, then faded.

"Well, what now?"

"I don't want to stay here, if you don't mind."

He kissed the tip of her nose and nodded. "Me either." She sighed in relief. "So where do you want to go?"

"I'd love to visit my sisters, they'll never believe this."

"Celeste least of all, I'd imagine."

She wrinkled her nose, giggling. "Snarky woman. No, I can't imagine that she would. I can't wait to see what she thinks."

He swiped his hand, opening the portal between the here and there. The swirling funnel spread out before them.

"Wow. What is that?"

"This, my love, will take us straight to your sisters."

Her eyes widened and she glanced at him beneath her lashes. "Do you have any idea how much money we'll save on taxis now?"

He chuckled. "I have a feeling life with you will never be boring." He guided her through the portal, gripping her elbow.

She stopped and turned to him, mischief glittering in her gold eyes. "So, a millennia, huh?"

He frowned. "What?"

"Your age."

"Who told you?"

"Lise, of course." She grinned and wagged her finger under his nose. "I told you I'd find out."

Cian threw his head back and laughed. "Yes, yes, you did."

Epilogue

Lise stood before her sisters—the chosen ones—and held out her hands in supplication. "It is done."

Clarion inclined her head. Ebony curls cascaded against the mother-of-pearl floor. "You've done well, Lise. Is this the match we hoped for?"

Beams of sunlight surrounded the sisters in a wash of rainbow. The heavenly setting of white clouds and blue sky was surreal to Lise now, used as she was to the smog and buildings of the mortal realm.

"The souls merged. This is a true joining and will bring the peace death has sought for so long."

Fatima scowled. Anger glittered in the dove gray of her eyes. "And what of the others? There must be balance. Order. Death grows weary, what if the rest decide to give up? What then?"

Lise narrowed her eyes and held her shoulders straight. "It won't happen. We will do what we must to maintain order. Even if that means meddling, which I know you love, sister dear."

Fatima turned a silver white, the air shivering with the snap of cold frost emanating from her every pore in a misty haze.

Naria stepped forward. Purple robes swirled around her ankles, golden bells tied to the sash of her belt jingled with each step. "Lise, the task *is* daunting. You know as well as I how violent and cold"—she glanced at Fatima—"death has become. Perhaps it is time we step back and allow this to happen. Allow it to end. We can rebuild, create a new species. One less prone to hostility."

Lise set her jaw. "No. I see them as you never will. I live amongst them. They are my children, good or bad. I cannot walk away from them now, not without knowing I've given them a hope of more than that god forsaken existence within the halls of the fae."

Clarion laid her hand on Lise's shoulder and gave it a gentle squeeze. "Then heed Fatima's vision, love. Aid the reapers to find their right mates and restore the balance of not only death, but life as well. Do not lose heart."

Her children would find their peace, and perhaps in the process Lise would also see that bloodthirsty queen heeled into submission.

Time ticked on…

Turn the page for a preview of the next book in the series,

Death's Redemption.

Chapter 1

They were coming.

Mila panted, sweat pouring down her brow, her back. Her lungs burned with fire as she raced around the corner of the brick stone building, trying to lose herself in the labyrinth of alleyways that bisected the city like a giant tic-tac-toe square.

A glass shard wedged itself into the sole of her foot, but she barely even felt it. Somewhere along the way she'd lost her slippers. She couldn't recall when or how.

She'd been in bed, dead to the world, and then the dreams had come—nightmares really, a vision of her future. She rarely had visions, but when she did, they always came true. There'd been four of them, shadows converging slowly on her house, their sharp, angular faces leering as they drew close. Mila had sensed their eager anticipation for her death; it'd clung in the air like oily tendrils, making her breathing hitch and her body shudder with an immediate wash of adrenaline.

She'd barely had time to grab a robe and slippers and slip out the bathroom window, running down the narrow pathway that separated her gingerbread-style home from her neighbors' before she'd have been caught. The only element of surprise she still had left was the knowledge that they didn't know she knew they were after her.

There was only one chance to escape them. If she could just reach Club X, Lise would give her sanctuary. Mila knew that, she didn't know how, but she knew that Lise had power, had always sensed the frail-looking woman was more than she seemed.

Footsteps echoed behind her. They were being loud on purpose. She knew what these monsters were; she'd lived in San Francisco long enough, been around the day the creatures had finally come out of hiding. They wanted her scared, wanted fear pumping through her veins; it was an aphrodisiac to them.

They could catch her, *would* catch her. Running was just prolonging the inevitable, but she couldn't stop, because stopping meant she'd given up, and Mila never gave up. Her grandmother and mother had raised her to fight, to be proud and to know that a woman's worth didn't come from being fearless but from being brave in the face of fear.

Her chest ached, her legs shook, she wouldn't last much longer. It was three in the morning. There were no cabs available right now, but even taking a cab wasn't safe. She'd put others in danger. They'd stop at nothing to get their hands on her, and she wouldn't put anyone else's life on the line—her conscious wouldn't allow it. The vampires wanted her, and she knew why: because of her powers. But they didn't know the truth. They'd kill her for something they could never hope to understand, could never hope to harness.

Somewhere an alley cat screeched.

The footsteps were getting louder. A whimper spilled from her lips. Her gaze frantically searching for any sign of escape, she spotted a dilapidated brownstone a few yards ahead. The windows were boarded up, and crime-scene tape was stretched across its doorless frame.

She'd seen that abandoned house before, in her dream. Below a metal grating was a secret entrance, a tunnel into the sewers dug out decades ago to help smuggle drugs. In the dream she'd crawled through it, finding a silver ladder affixed to the wall, which led up to the street. A sewer main had busted three days ago; city workers had been at the site, but the man responsible for replacing the manhole cover had gotten a call from his wife. She'd gone into early labor, he'd been careless, and the cover wasn't on all the way. Which meant she could maybe push it off. The tunnel was barely ten yards from the entrance of Club X. The chance of safety was slim, but it was her only hope.

The breeze stirred, carrying the stench of the streets with it along with the sound of a coat flapping, like the rustling movements of bat wings. Her heart lodged in her throat as she dove inside the door, landing hard on her knees. Pain exploded in her joints and she had to bite down on her lip to keep from whimpering.

They were toying with her, like a cat with a mouse seconds before the kill. A quiet sob tore through her chest as she scrabbled back to her feet. It was so dark in here, and the smells were terrible—the place was musty and squeaking with rat chatter. Trying not to think about any of that, she held her hands out in front of her and made her way toward the kitchen.

She didn't need to see to know where she was headed; the map of the house had imprinted itself in her mind the moment she'd dreamt of it. Ten steps down the hall, turn right at the first door, now she was in the kitchen.

Walk five steps forward and…Her fingers grazed the outline of an old fifties-style fridge. Planting her back against the side of it, she shoved off the balls of her feet, working it back away from the wall. From the metal grate hidden behind it, she was so close. A horrible metallic grinding sound reverberated like a gunshot through the nearly empty room as she pushed the fridge away from the wall. She was being too loud. They would find her, but she didn't have a choice to go more slowly. It was now or never.

Almost there, almost there, I'm almost—

"Did you really think you could run, little mortal?" The voice was like ice, heating her flesh in a frigid embrace, breaking her out in a wash of goose bumps.

Squealing, she didn't have time to think, because hard hands dug into her shoulders and flipped her around. Flailing wildly, she raked her nails down his face and then stomped down on his foot as hard as she could.

He hissed, then something connected with her jaw and all she could see was a halo of stars. Pain flared and throbbed through her skull as she sank to her knees.

"She's in here," the male called out, and Mila saw several shadows converge.

Reaching into her nightshirt, Mila yanked out her rosary. "Hail Mary full of grace, hail Mary full of grace—"

A woman laughed, then jerked her chin up. Nails bit into her skin, broke through it, and then something thick and warm slid slowly down Mila's jaw, bringing a wafting metallic scent with it.

"You think your God can save you now? We've been looking for you a very long time, little seer. The time for running has ended. We want what you have."

"I don't know what you're talking about." Her words came out short and choppy through clacking teeth.

This time the hands that touched her were gentle, gliding, and then they framed her face, forcing her to stare into the glowing blue-eyed gaze of her captor. The burn from his eyes highlighted his features, and she cringed. The man staring at her had half his face melted off; his lips were grotesque on the left side, looking almost like they were sliding slowly down. His skin was mottled and as pink a newborn rat's.

"We will get what we want, mortal." His voice shivered with raw power, and Mila knew there'd never been a chance of escape.

For the first time she'd seen a future that was not to be. But she didn't have time to question it. How she'd seen safety, felt deep in her bones that Lise would save her...only to now stare death straight in the face.

His thumb rubbed along her cheekbone; his one eye searched her face. The other was nothing but an empty socket. He smirked, the right side of his lips tilting up just slightly.

"This is what your kind has done to mine. You swore we were safe, and yet still you try to hunt us. But your powers..." His mouth parted and a sort of hungry gaze burned back at her, his breathing rose as if he were...sexually excited. It made her stomach turn. "Your powers will level the playing field."

"But you don't understand. It's not...It's not what you—"

His nostrils flared and he clamped her lips shut forcefully, his long nail nicking her flesh and making her hiss air between her teeth at the sharp burst of pain.

"Shut up. We played your game. Now it's time for you to play ours. Vanity"—he looked at the feminine shadow standing beside them—"hold her legs. This might get messy."

Her screams echoed through the night.

About the Author

Marie Hall has always had a dangerous fascination for creatures that go bump in the night. And mermaids. And, of course, fairies. Trolls. Unicorns. Shapeshifters. Vampires. Scottish brogues. Kilts. Beefy arms. Ummm...bad boys! Especially the sexy ones. Which is probably why she married one.

On top of that, she's a confirmed foodie; she nearly went to culinary school and then figured out she could save a ton of money if she just watched food shows religiously. She's a self-proclaimed master chef, certified deep-sea dolphin trainer, finder of leprechauns' gold at the end of the rainbow, and rumor has it she keeps the troll king locked away in her basement. All of which is untrue (except for the cooking part—she loves cooking); however, she does have an incredibly active imagination and loves to share her crazy thoughts with the world!

If you want to see what new creations she's got up her sleeve, check out her blog:

www.MarieHallWrites.blogspot.com

www.ingramcontent.com/pod-product-compliance
Ingram Content Group UK Ltd.
Pitfield, Milton Keynes, MK11 3LW, UK
UKHW022259280225
455674UK00001B/90